An Enemy in the Village

An Enemy in the Village

A BRUNO, CHIEF OF POLICE NOVEL

Martin Walker

Alfred A. Knopf   New York 2025

A BORZOI BOOK
FIRST HARDCOVER EDITION
PUBLISHED BY ALFRED A. KNOPF 2025

Published by Alfred A. Knopf, a division of Penguin Random House LLC,
1745 Broadway, New York, NY 10019.

Knopf, Borzoi Books, and the colophon are registered
trademarks of Penguin Random House LLC.

Library of Congress Cataloging-in-Publication Data
Names: Walker, Martin, [date] author.
Title: An enemy in the village / Martin Walker.
Description: First Hardcover Edition. | New York : Alfred A. Knopf, 2025. |
Series: A Bruno, Chief of Police Novel | "A Borzoi book"—Title page verso.
Identifiers: LCCN 2024061213 (print) | LCCN 2024061214 (ebook) |
ISBN 9780593536643 (hardcover) | ISBN 9780593536650 (ebook)
Subjects: LCSH: Police—France—Fiction. | Murder—Investigation—
Fiction. | LCGFT: Detective and mystery fiction. | Novels.
Classification: LCC PR6073.A413 E54 2025 (print) |
LCC PR6073.A413 (ebook) |
DDC 823/.914—dc23/eng/20241220
LC record available at https://lccn.loc.gov/2024061213
LC ebook record available at https://lccn.loc.gov/2024061214

penguinrandomhouse.com | aaknopf.com

Printed in the United States of America
2 4 6 8 9 7 5 3 1

The authorized representative in the EU for product safety
and compliance is Penguin Random House Ireland,
Morrison Chambers, 32 Nassau Street, Dublin D02 YH68,
Ireland, https://eu-contact.penguin.ie.

To Violette, in welcome—
A charming young basset who is the latest
inhabitant of our tiny hamlet.

*An Enemy
in the Village*

Chapter 1

Bruno Courrèges, chief of police of the small French town of St. Denis and of much of the valley of the Vézère River, liked to think of himself as *un homme moyen sensuel:* a man of conventional appetites, perhaps a little more sentimental than most. His feelings were easily stirred by children, puppies and damsels in distress, but also by good food and wine and the ever-beguiling landscape of the Périgord and its seasons. In this, he knew he was fortunate. The climate of his region was usually sensible, in that each of the four seasons had its moment and seldom overstayed its welcome.

He took pleasure in the changes, delighting in the usually reliable arrival of springtime in March and of summer in May and of autumn as September began to give way to October. He enjoyed a brisk chill in December and especially those rare years when sufficient snow fell for the children to go sledding down the slopes toward the river. But the recent extremes of the weather, with tempests and heat waves, forest fires and floods, together with the alarm among his friends in the vineyards at the bizarrely premature ripening of the Merlot grapes in August, had begun to alarm him. Bruno had been persuaded that climate change and global warming were now invading his home turf.

On this wintry morning, however, with the sun just peeking over the eastern hills to redden the layers of plump clouds and turn the frost-covered fields into a beguiling pink, Bruno slowed his police van to a crawl. He felt compelled to admire this unusual palette of wintry colors as he drove along the ridge that overlooked the Vézère Valley. His basset hound, Balzac, seemed equally impressed, sitting up in the passenger seat to stare into the glowing landscape below. As Bruno approached an overlook by the side of the road that he knew boasted a particularly spectacular view, his policeman's instinct nagged at him.

Unusually for the time of day, the scenic overview was already occupied by a Peugeot 508. Its license plate carried the digits 24, which identified it as a local car, registered in the *département* of the Dordogne. Bruno would not be able to check the owner's name until the registry opened at nine. His curiosity piqued, he pulled up behind the vehicle and turned off his engine. "Balzac, stay," he told the basset. "I'll be back in a second."

Approaching the Peugeot, Bruno saw a figure slumped over the steering wheel and knew he'd been right to stop. Trying the doors, glad to be wearing gloves on such a cold morning, he found three of them locked from the inside, but the front passenger door yielded to his grip. Bruno had never owned a car with separate locks for each door; indeed, he had never owned a car so expensive. He opened the door and leaned in, already suspecting from the smell of urine and voided bowels that this could be a suicide. He pulled off his left glove and with the back of his hand checked the cheek of the woman slumped over the wheel. It was ice cold. She had been dead for hours.

He lifted her arm by the sleeve and it scarcely budged, an

indicator that rigor mortis had already set in. Bruno pulled back into the open air and used his phone to report his find to the gendarmerie. He read out the number on the license plate to Jules, the desk sergeant, and asked for the presence of Dr. Gelletreau, the medical examiner, to certify what he knew to be—but could not legally confirm was—a death.

An almost empty bottle of water and a Chanel handbag lay on the passenger seat beside the dead woman. She was neatly dressed in a dark wool pantsuit and a gray turtleneck sweater. Her shoulder-length fair hair was remarkably tidy, and her mouth was hanging slackly open, revealing perfect, or perhaps expensive, teeth.

An empty plastic container of zolpidem, which Bruno knew to be a sleeping pill, was on the floor of the passenger side, bearing the label of a pharmacy in Sarlat. A cardboard folder lay on the passenger seat with three sealed envelopes inside. The first was addressed to Maître Rebecca Weil, whom Bruno knew to be a respected lawyer in Sarlat. Beneath the name was written a phone number and the words, "Please call her first." On a second envelope was the name Mademoiselle Laura Segret, with the words "Périgord concierge" below and a local phone number. The third was addressed to "My husband, Dominic," with a mobile phone number. On a sheet of expensive notepaper, headed "La Conciergerie du Périgord," with an address in Sarlat, was written, "My apologies to those who find my body and have to deal with the mess I leave here." It was signed "Monique Duhamel."

Bruno called the lawyer's number, but since it was not yet eight in the morning there was no reply. He then called the *conciergerie,* and the answering machine asked him to call back after the office opened at nine. A high-pitched male voice answered his third call. Bruno asked if he was speaking to Dominic. When the voice said yes, Bruno introduced himself and explained that he had bad news before asking if Dominic was alone.

"No, I'm having breakfast with family before going to a funeral," came the reply, in perfect French but with an Alsatian accent, which Bruno recognized from the annual visits by people from Alsace to commemorate their wartime evacuation to the Périgord. He was taken aback, however, by the reply. The body in front of him was in no way ready for burial, so Bruno resigned himself to the bearing of additional bad news on what he presumed was an already challenging morning.

"Is Monique Duhamel your wife, monsieur?" Bruno asked, feeling he was making a mess of this conversation.

"Yes, but she's at home while I'm in Strasbourg at this funeral. You say you're a policeman? What's this bad news?"

"I'm at the scene of what seems to be a suicide of a woman in her forties who I think is your wife. She was found in a Peugeot 508, and in the car there's an envelope addressed to you with your mobile number." He paused before adding, "I'm sorry to be the bearer of this news."

The phone seemed to be dropped, and after some confusion a woman's voice came on the line, asking who he was. Bruno explained and asked whom he was speaking with.

"I'm Sabine, Dominic's sister, actually his foster sister. We're here in Strasbourg for the funeral of our foster father. Are you sure the dead woman is Monique?"

"We can't be sure until we get a positive identification from a close friend or family member, but I have checked the handbag in the car and found her ID and credit cards. I'm sorry, but from the photo on the ID it looks to be her. The car was parked in a remote place, and there was an empty box of pills beside the body, envelopes for her husband, her lawyer and another woman, and a note of apology for causing trouble. It looks very much like a suicide."

"Understood. What happens now?"

"There will have to be an autopsy to be sure of the cause of death, and then we can have the body taken to a funeral parlor of your brother's choice. But we really need a visual identification today if at all possible. Does your brother know of any close friends or colleagues who could do it?"

"I'll ask," the woman said. Bruno heard murmuring before she came back to say that Dominic was writing down the names and contact numbers of Monique's best friend and her doctor.

"Dominic will drive down as soon as he can after the funeral, but it will take some time," Sabine said. "Our father was the stonemason at the cathedral here, and that's where the service is being held."

Bruno gave her his phone number and email address, adding that Monique's body would be taken to the morgue in Sarlat, and he would have her Peugeot moved to the local gendarmerie in St. Denis.

"Okay," the sister said. "The gendarmerie is fine. But Dominic is in shock, as I'm sure you can imagine." There was a sharp intake of breath down the line. "Losing your wife on the day of your dad's funeral, you can hardly imagine." A pause. "And only a week after she lost her baby."

"*Mon Dieu.* That's terrible, and I'm deeply sorry to be the bearer of yet more bad news," said Bruno. "Maybe your brother need not drive down tonight. Tomorrow should be fine. He has my number. You and I should stay in touch, so please text me your phone number and email address. And ask your brother if there is any special friend in Sarlat I should contact."

"Wait a minute." Bruno heard muttering before she came back to say that Monique was good friends with a local magistrate named Annette Meraillon.

"I know Annette well," Bruno replied. "I'll call her as soon as we're done."

He took down Sabine's details and the name of Monique's gynecologist, but was surprised when Sabine said that the dead woman's usual doctor was Fabiola Stern, of the medical center in Bruno's hometown of St. Denis.

"I know Fabiola," Bruno said, wondering why the dead woman had chosen a general practitioner who lived at least thirty minutes from her home. "I'll call her now."

He called the gendarmerie to inform them that Dr. Gelletreau's services would no longer be required, and as soon as that was done he found Fabiola's number in his list of recent calls. Bruno reached Fabiola as she was arriving at the clinic and asked her to delay her first appointment, as he needed her to confirm a death.

"It's about one of your patients, Monique Duhamel. There hasn't been a formal identification yet, nor a death certificate, but I think she's the suicide I just found. I was going to summon Gelletreau, since he's on the duty roster, but given that she's a patient of yours it would be best if you come here."

"*Merde*, just after her miscarriage," Fabiola said. "Okay, I'm on my way."

A little under twenty minutes later Bruno was gratefully accepting from Fabiola a cup of take-out coffee from a gas station along her route. Handing both cups to Bruno, she slipped on a pair of disposable gloves before sliding into the passenger seat of the Peugeot. "It's Monique, that I can confirm."

Fabiola applied a stethoscope to her friend's chest and put a thermometer into her mouth, and Bruno noticed the care she took to be gentle, treating Monique's body with the same respect she would have done were Monique still living. Fabiola listened to the stethoscope and glanced at the thermometer, then pulled a pad from her bag and wrote out the death certificate.

"Dead for six hours and more, no obvious signs of injury. I've authorized a postmortem to confirm those sleeping pills were the cause of death," she said with a sigh as she climbed out of the car. "Monique has been depressed and not sleeping well since the miscarriage, but I never thought she might be suicidal. Mind you, I only saw her once after she lost the baby, since she was still under the gynecologist's care."

Bruno showed Fabiola the empty bottle of pills. Fabiola grunted that it was zolpidem to help people sleep through the night but not what she would have prescribed. She looked carefully at the label.

"Twelve point five milligrams, that's strong," she said. "And thirty-six pills, that's too many for depression after a miscarriage." She shook her head. "She was old for a first pregnancy, forty-five, I think. I'd advised her against it, but she was childless and determined for one last try. There's only so much you can do for some patients. *Merde, merde, merde.*"

Bruno watched as Fabiola ran her thumb around the rim of her paper cup, so hard that some of the coffee spilled onto the ground.

"She was on her own," Bruno said. "Her husband had to go up to Strasbourg for his father's funeral. He's still there, back tomorrow."

"So she was alone as well, poor woman."

"She lived in Sarlat," Bruno said. "How did she come to know of you?"

"Our Pilates group, after we got the new gym," Fabiola said. "She joined last year with Annette, delighted that we had an all-female thing. She wasn't happy with the male doctors in Sarlat, and when we became friends, she badgered me to become her doctor until I agreed. She was quite a persuasive woman. I suppose she had to be in her business."

"What did she do?" Bruno asked.

"She was a *notaire,* third or fourth generation in the family business," Fabiola replied. "But then she reinvented herself when she saw that there was a new market opportunity opening up. She'd been dealing with all these wealthy British, Dutch, Swiss and German couples buying charming little châteaus and manor houses for their retirement but using them only for a few weeks in summer. They've already bought up Minorca, Tuscany, Corfu, the Algarve, and now they are settling here in the Périgord. So Monique decided to set herself up as a super-concierge, taking care of their châteaus and the pools and gardens for a fee, and then renting them out when the owners weren't there and taking a fat commission along the way." Fabiola gave a short laugh. "Maybe you and I should have thought of that, Bruno."

After Fabiola had left for the clinic, Bruno got out his phone for the first of what he knew would be many calls. He reached Annette at home, gave her the news and told her that he would be reachable on his *portable* when she had a moment to talk.

An ambulance soon arrived to take the dead woman to the hospital in Sarlat. As the ambulance pulled away, Sergeant Jules drove his police van into the space it left. Another gendarme was with him to drive the Peugeot to the police pound, a young recruit in his twenties whom Bruno recognized by sight. He seemed to be wearing a tailor-made uniform that almost disguised his plumpness. The three new recruits at the gendarmerie were all young men who had opted to take a weekly seminar with a lawyer in Périgueux on legal issues and practice. Bruno thought this was unusual, but maybe they thought it would help their careers.

The young gendarme had brought with him a flattened cardboard box, which he placed on the driver's seat to protect his trousers. He climbed behind the steering wheel, lit a cigarette and, with an arrogant glance at Bruno, gunned the motor and drove off fast. He was followed more sedately by Jules in the gendarmes' van.

Bruno had just waved them off when his mobile vibrated. It was Annette. Bruno explained about the postmortem and the husband's presence at a family funeral in Strasbourg, then related what Fabiola had said.

"I know you and the dead woman were friends," Bruno said, gently. "When did you last meet?"

"Over the weekend; we had brunch at my place on Sunday morning, just the two of us, catching up, after she'd gone to Paris with Dominic for a break," Annette said. "I was rocked when she told me about the miscarriage. She seemed more quiet than depressed, like she was still working out how to come to terms with it."

"She was certainly well organized," said Bruno. "On the seat beside her body she left envelopes for her husband, a colleague at the concierge named Laura and a third for Maître Weil. I presume that's her lawyer. There's also a letter apologizing to the people who have to clean up after the mess she left, which was thoughtful of her. I never saw one of those before at a suicide."

"Yes, I see. But until we can be reasonably sure it was suicide, Bruno, you'd better bring all those envelopes to me, along with that empty pill bottle, the death certificate, an inventory of what's in the car and anything else you think might be relevant."

Chapter 2

The traffic was busy going through Les Eyzies and was heavier still once Bruno reached Sarlat. He took the bypass around the heart of the old town to reach the subprefecture, the building that housed the representatives of the French state, where he could leave his van in the parking lot. Once parked, he took a folder with official notepaper and wrote a brief statement of where, when and how Monique Duhamel's death had occurred, adding that her car was now at the gendarmerie in St. Denis and the body in the Sarlat morgue. He signed it and attached Fabiola's death certificate. Then he set off on foot with Balzac to the place de la Grande Rigaudie, heading for the region's legal office, the *tribunal de proximité,* and the office of his friend Annette, the magistrate who was also one of the best rally drivers in the region. Once in her office he kissed her on both cheeks, accepted a coffee from her private espresso machine and handed her the declaration of death, Monique's three sealed envelopes, her handbag and the pillbox wrapped in an evidence bag. He was given a signed receipt before Annette bent down to give Balzac his own special welcome.

"I can take over at this point, check with the hospital on the postmortem and with the prescribing doctor," she said, once

Balzac had been given his treat. "It looks to be a straightforward suicide of a depressed woman after a miscarriage when her husband had to be out of town. It's not the first time I've seen one death in a family swiftly followed by another and I don't think it will be the last."

Annette paused. "*Mon Dieu,* there are times I hate being a magistrate. The formal, wooden words come almost automatically from my tongue and yet say nothing of what I feel. She was Monique, not just a corpse, but a woman I could be indiscreet and laugh with, go shopping and have lunch and drink a glass too much with . . ."

"I know you were friendly with her," Bruno said, gently. "Did you know her husband?"

"A bit, from the book club at the library and a dinner every now and then," Annette replied. "But he's a quiet type, amiable enough, very polite, obviously intelligent and a good ten years younger than Monique. She told me once he was a perfect listener, always paid attention and never interrupted. From what I saw he invariably left most of the talking to Monique, and she was never at a loss for words! But when he did speak, or answered her, it was usually worth paying attention."

"He's from Strasbourg," said Bruno. "The funeral was for his foster father. I spoke on the phone with his sister, or foster sister. I'm told the father had something to do with the cathedral, a stonemason."

"A very senior stonemason," said Annette, a sudden enthusiasm in her voice, "responsible for the cathedral that was for hundreds of years the tallest building in Europe. One night after dinner Monique put on some new documentary about the cathedral history and the way the medieval architects invented things like drilling holes for huge iron staples to hold the great stones together and then pouring molten lead into the grooves to hold the staples in place. You know how it is when you come across something new that catches your imagination. And then they designed this amazing steeple made of eight delicate spiral staircases, each interlocking so that it was light and airy; the winds could pass through and yet it was extremely strong. It sounds boring, but I was fascinated. The fifteenth-century architect d'Ensingen had the same name as the foster father, and that was the name Dominic and his sister took."

"Was it the same family, through all those centuries?" Bruno asked, intrigued by this unusual inheritance.

She answered with a shrug and then explained that the foster father's family had played no part in Dominic's ancestry. But his background was strange enough.

"Monique told me the story," she said. "Dominic was abandoned under a pew in the cathedral at just a few days old. There was a note left with the baby. It was the summer of 1990, and the note said the baby had been conceived in Berlin on the night the Berlin Wall came down, to a German father and a French mother. So Monique's take was that this child was the first of the new Europeans, born in Strasbourg, pivot of the new Europe where France and Germany meet."

"That's really bizarre," said Bruno, almost laughing in surprise. "Did Dominic take it seriously?"

"I'm not sure," Annette replied. "Dominic was there at the table when Monique told the story, quietly nodding and then looking at me and the other guests in the eye for a moment before shrugging and laughing it off. But one thing I'm sure of is that Monique took it seriously. She thought it was really something to have that history. Another time, when Dominic was not present, she told me that he'd been seriously ill with asthma as a child and was scrawny and frail, which was why nobody ever wanted to adopt him. That's rare—white boys are usually the first to be snapped up in the orphanages. He was ten when he was taken into the stonemason's foster family, so he'd been through a grim childhood, a rotten school and bullied by the other kids."

"I gather he's in his midthirties," said Bruno.

"He looks even younger, almost boyish," she replied. "You wouldn't think he's thirty. I teased Monique about it once, called him her boy toy. She laughed it off, but I could see she didn't like it, that it stung her somehow." A pause. "She was a good friend to me, I'll miss her."

"One thing that's unusual," he said, and showed her the three sealed envelopes. "Why do you think she wanted her lawyer to be informed first, before her husband?"

"Because of the inheritance, I imagine," Annette replied, using a paper knife to unseal each of the envelopes. She quickly glanced through the letters before she spoke.

"It was suicide, sure enough," she said. "And Monique wanted the lawyer informed first because she wants to ensure that Laura and her business partners get the company, not her husband."

"Is there big money involved?" Bruno asked.

"Monique was well off," Annette replied. "She owned the Sarlat property, the family's notary business, then the concierge operation she started, plus the country house near the river at Castel-Merle. She was an only child. Normally everything would go to her husband, but I think she made special arrangements with her lawyer, Rebecca Weil. And Monique was very close to Laura, who is also in our Pilates group. Laura was her first hire as a translator and later became her partner in the concierge business. With Laura's help Monique built it up from nothing and it's a real gold mine. She told me it pulls in more than two million a year."

"*Mon Dieu,* I'm in the wrong business," said Bruno, not really meaning it. But he knew this meant that the death would probably be treated with more official attention than a usual suicide. There were not many people in the *département* who earned that kind of money, and it explained why Annette was now putting the three letters through the copier and making sure of the paper trail before returning to her chair with the copies and the originals, which she returned to Bruno within the three envelopes.

"What did Fabiola say?" Annette asked.

"That Monique was very depressed after the miscarriage, and she had been alone since her husband left to attend his father's funeral in Strasbourg. So Monique had the means, motive and opportunity," Bruno said. "That doesn't explain why she chose that spot, much closer to St. Denis than to Sarlat, as the place to take her life."

"Maybe it meant something to her? You'll probably need someone who knew her for much longer than I did to get to the bottom of it. It could be the scene of some youthful romance, a first kiss or lost love, but I'm just guessing," Annette said, and then paused, a faraway look in her eyes. "I'll really miss Monique, and I'll also miss her Christmas parties, although I suppose Laura and her team will organize them instead, so long as Dominic lets them use the country house. That's where Monique held her events. All her foreign clients were invited along with her team. It's a charming *chartreuse* on that long hill above Castel-Merle with a view over the valley and toward St. Léon. There's one long wing with an enormous room and a great view."

"I think I might have seen the house from the turnoff to Sergeac," said Bruno. "Castel-Merle is one of my favorite prehistoric sites with all its separate caves. You probably know it for the huge collection of shells from the Mediterranean and the Atlantic coasts, evidence of early trade routes. But I like the engraving of the special vulva in the Grotte de Castanet."

"What's so special about it?" she asked, turning back to

the second letter. "The vulva was the favorite image of prehistoric people; you find those graffiti everywhere in the caves. A big improvement on the modern craze for drawing penises on every available surface, if you ask me."

"The one at Castel-Merle is sometimes called the new life vulva," he replied. "It's the only one known that depicts a placenta emerging after birth."

She glanced up at him, a little startled but also amused. "You do have an original style in conversational gambits, Bruno. That line would certainly enliven the *conciergerie*'s Christmas party." She took a sip of her coffee. "Do we have any reason to doubt that this is anything more than a conventional suicide?"

"Not that I can see," he replied. "Fabiola said that she should have seen it as a real possibility after Monique's miscarriage. Had it crossed your mind that she might have been more depressed than she was letting on?"

"I suppose all her friends will feel guilty, wondering if there was something we might have done to help her," Annette said, and picked up the third letter.

"If this becomes a legal issue with the will, would you have to recuse yourself?"

"That's unlikely, since Rebecca Weil is a very good lawyer and she drafted the will. But if there were to be a problem my role would depend on the *procureur;* he's my boss. But this is a small town and Monique knew him, too. She went to school here, Bruno, and she employs a lot of people, so she's well known locally. The mayor was hoping to get her onto his team for the council elections, but she deliberately steered clear of party politics."

"Everybody knows everybody else," said Bruno. "Sounds just like St. Denis."

"You tend to trust people you've known since childhood, but don't forget I'm new here," Annette said, "so I have to earn that trust, which is fair enough. And that's also true for Dominic."

"Is he trusted locally?" Bruno asked, thinking that in his experience the instincts of a small community about some new arrival, whether the townspeople or a squad of troops, tended to be sound.

"He's not distrusted," Annette said thoughtfully. "And if he isn't much liked, he's accepted, but that's mainly because of Monique. No problems or scandals so far in his work and he's been here three years so he's evidently competent. He's clean, well mannered, polite . . ." Her voice trailed off.

"But . . . ," said Bruno. "It sounds very much like you want to say 'but.'"

"Yes, I do. He has no particular friends, never seems to share a drink after work, never goes to watch the rugby team or take a *p'tit apéro* while watching the matches at the tennis club, doesn't volunteer to dress up as Père Noël."

"You mean he doesn't make an effort to fit in?" suggested Bruno.

"That's exactly it!" she said. "You weren't born and raised in St. Denis, but now you know everybody, volunteer for everything, teach the kids to play tennis and rugby, go to all the town dances and waltz with all the old ladies."

"But I enjoy all that," he protested.

"And it shows," she said. "That's the point. You make it clear you like your neighbors in St. Denis and you're always there for them. You're at the funerals, the weddings and christenings, the school sports days, you built the women's rugby team. You help pick the grapes at the *vendange*."

"That's what life is all about."

"Well, that's you, Bruno. But Dominic's problem, and it was becoming Monique's problem as well, was that he did none of that. He didn't seem to know or care that it mattered. He was polite to her friends but didn't even try to fit in."

"So how did he spend his spare time?" Bruno asked.

Annette rolled her eyes. "Monique said he read a lot, listened to music and juggled his investments." She shrugged.

"Before I go," Bruno asked, "would you please put your official stamp on those envelopes and sign them, so the recipients will know they were opened legally?"

"Of course, no problem," she said, pulling her stamp from her drawer. "In return you could leave Balzac with me while you visit Becca Weil and Laura—you know how I enjoy having him around. I can hardly wait until he has more puppies, and remember, I'm at the top of the waiting list."

"Before Maître Weil asks, perhaps you could tell me if there is anything in any of the letters that might make me question the suicide verdict?"

"That's what I was looking for. Quite the reverse, in fact— she says in each of them that she had decided to take her own life because she couldn't bear the idea of growing old without having had children." Annette glanced again at the letter and looked up thoughtfully at Bruno.

"I may be reading too much into it, but the tone of this letter to her husband is different—full of despair yet more formal than her notes to Laura and the lawyer. Maybe it's because she was writing to two women friends from whom she had few secrets?" Annette handed Bruno the letter. "See what you think."

Slightly surprised and more than a little gratified that Annette would think him at all qualified in the nuances of female phrasing, Bruno took the letter. Like those to her lawyer and business partner, it was typewritten.

"I believe you are aware of my very deep sadness at the loss of the baby, made all the deeper by the knowledge that this was my last chance to become a mother," Bruno read.

"Perhaps inevitably, given the differences in age, sex and backgrounds between us, you may not be aware of the utter despair that now grips me. Why put off the moment to acknowledge that without the prospect of a child my life in any profound sense is already terminated? It is therefore pointless to go on. But I want to reassure you that my decision to bequeath the *conciergerie* to my female colleagues is neither a snub nor reproach to you, but a reflection of my deep love for them, the nearest to a family that I have. They built the business with me, while you entered my life only when it was already flourishing, so you must agree that you played no role in it. I am sorry that our marriage was not a success, resulting in neither children nor contentment, but I thank you for your efforts to make it work, even if only in ways that suited you. I can thank you for the mood of calm that usually surrounds you. I had always hoped that I might someday come to share it, might even believe in it. Alas not. Regards, Monique."

Mon Dieu, thought Bruno. If a woman I lived with ever sent me a letter like this, I'd shoot myself. At least, I'd want to. How could a man live with a woman and yet not know the depth of her despair?

"You'll find Maître Weil at home, just around the corner," said Annette. "She's great and the best lawyer in town. She said she would rather see you there than at her office. I can't see any likely problems emerging over Monique's cause of death, but I'll keep you informed."

Chapter 3

Maître Rebecca Weil had red eyes and a crumpled tissue in her hand when she greeted Bruno at the door to her apartment in a fine old building on the rue Fénelon. An evidently busy woman in her fifties, she welcomed him and hit him with a tsunami of small talk before the door was closed behind him.

"You're lucky to catch me at home," she said, "I'm usually in court on weekdays. But I'd much rather welcome you to my home than meet you formally in my office. I understand we have a mutual friend in Annette?" Bruno made to answer, but the wave surged on. "She just called to let me know you were on your way. I remember you, of course—I saw you playing against my son in a doubles match not long ago. You beat him.

"That means I'll never forgive you, but I must confess to being slightly grateful that you spared me having to suffer his disappointments in never becoming a tennis star," she went on, steering Bruno into her kitchen where an old-fashioned Italian coffeepot was bubbling on the stove. She turned off the heat just in time, opened the oven door to bring out two croissants, then sat him down facing her at the kitchen table and said, "I presume Monique's suicide meant you missed breakfast. And where's that photogenic dog of yours who's always in the newspaper?"

Bruno laughed, the first time he'd broken his silence since crossing the threshold. "I did miss breakfast, so thank you, and Annette wanted to look after my basset for a while. She's known Balzac since he was a puppy." He handed her the letter with her name on it while trying to keep his face looking suitably solemn. "You'll see Annette's stamp to show that she opened and read it to be sure that her boss could formally announce it as a suicide. And I'm here because Monique left written instructions that I should contact you first, before either her husband or her colleagues at work. Why do you think she did that?"

"To ensure that the process of inheritance goes swiftly and precisely according to her wishes," she said. "That's the least I can do. I suppose we all feel guilty when a good friend commits suicide. I hadn't realized that Monique was so seriously depressed, and I should have. I knew how very much she wanted that baby."

Bruno nodded but kept silent, having no idea what he could possibly say that would make any difference.

She carried on, "Please call me Becca, short for Rebecca. May I call you Bruno?"

"Please do, Becca. Why might the inheritance not go according to Monique's wishes?"

"Because some of my esteemed colleagues in the law are ruthless scumbags who will try to extract large sums from Monique's estate by challenging her will in the name of her husband, her extended family and anyone else who can concoct some kind of claim," she said, and then groaned with pleasure as she took a large bite from her croissant. Bruno smiled and nodded as he enjoyed his own.

She swallowed, took a sip of coffee and then went on: "I took the precaution of having her signing of the will witnessed by the second- and third-best lawyers in the *département*." Bruno suppressed a small smile at the modest implication that she herself was the best. "One of them is a past chairman of the tribunal, and I have an appointment with him this afternoon to begin the process, so I think all should proceed according to her wishes."

"Monique's husband is in Strasbourg for the funeral of his foster father," said Bruno. "He's expected back tomorrow." He paused. "Given what you say about possible challenges to the will, might the timing of her suicide be significant?"

"Aha! A suspicious mind. Very good," said the lawyer, her face breaking into a beaming smile. "I have no idea whether it is significant or not, but I imagine Monique's husband will find his grief eased by his good fortune in inheriting a lifetime lease on the convenient penthouse apartment in that fine old house on rue de la Libération."

"But not the concierge business? And what of the country house near Sergeac?"

"The country house is locked into a family trust, and since she had no children it goes to a cousin. All Monique's shares in the *conciergerie* go to her partners and staff in the business, to help assure its continuing success."

"Annette suggested it was making close to two million a year."

"Maybe more this year. They have some new clients and a more efficient tax structure. Of course, that's not all profit. Monique and Laura and the other managers had to pay their own salaries out of that.

"They have become quite a significant local employer, since they now manage more than thirty properties and offer auxiliary services," she went on. "So there are a dozen full-time gardeners, maybe more by now, each with an apprentice, and the full-time cleaners, plus part-timers brought in for the usual changeover on Saturdays. They have a swimming pool service which also has other clients, and an agency to install solar panels. They have a deal with a local car rental business and act as an insurance brokerage for health care, accidents and any property damage. They also organize weddings, cater parties and dinners and supply chefs and waitresses as required."

The properties it managed were all upmarket, she went on. Typically they had at least six bedrooms, and several of the châteaus had a dozen or even more full-size bedrooms with baths, plus some of the former maids' rooms turned into single bedrooms, so there could be as many as thirty people in residence. That meant they could charge up to thirty thousand euros a week in season. Usually the owners wanted the place to themselves for Christmas, July and August. The *conciergerie* had it the rest of the year, and May, June and September were always fully booked.

"That means twelve weeks at a rough average of ten thousand a week for thirty properties; add in the cheaper rentals for the rest of the year, and you're looking at a total income of more than seven million," she said. "Staff costs, property and other taxes take around two million each, and the *conciergerie* costs are nearly a million.

"That leaves around two million, which of course is shared in a tax-efficient way with the owners, with the *conciergerie* taking thirty percent. Depending on the size of the property, the owners live there for free, know that their property is being constantly maintained and collect up to fifty thousand a year. And almost all that remains after taxes are paid is spent locally by the owners. Seven million a year brought in, and almost every centime stays here in the Périgord."

"And Monique planned and managed the whole thing?" Bruno asked, shaking his head in admiration.

"Yes, starting nearly twenty years ago. I was her lawyer from the beginning. She saw the potential long before I did, not just in the money but the local jobs, all of them above minimum wage, including the cleaners. She even has a special dental service for the Americans, who can get crowns and cosmetic care for a fraction of what they pay back home. So that's a growth market for January and February."

Bruno shook his head with a chuckle. "She deserved a better fate," he said.

"Yes, she did," said Becca. "At least we can make sure her will gets carried out, just as she wanted."

"I'll do my best," he said.

He watched the lawyer take Monique's letter from the envelope and read through the contents before pursing her lips and taking a deep breath. She then folded the letter and returned it to the envelope.

"Do you have any idea why she chose that spot by St. Cirq to die?" he asked. "It's a bit off the beaten track for someone from Sarlat. Did she have some connection to the area?"

"Not that I know of. It's certainly intriguing."

"Do you know of any close friends Monique had known since girlhood, someone who might know youthful secrets, perhaps a schoolmate?"

"Not offhand," Becca replied, shaking her head thoughtfully before raising a finger. "Wait, maybe there's someone, a school friend who was the sister of her first love. The family lived somewhere beyond Les Eyzies. The school friend went to Sciences Po, and then spent some time at the World Bank in America and then came back to Paris and went into some big international consultancy. Monique would stay with her whenever she went to Paris. So look at Monique's phone, check for a frequently dialed Paris number and that will probably be her."

Bruno scribbled a note to himself and then asked, "Will the *conciergerie* continue to be so well run without her?"

"I hope so," she said. "Monique set it up with great care, and she had a lot of confidence in Laura and the rest of the team. You'll like Laura, who was the first staffer Monique hired, and then as the business began to take off, Laura became her first partner in the business. Her mother is English, but Laura was born and raised here. I like her a lot—a cheerful woman and quite an athlete, played basketball for her university and coached the girls' team when she was teaching languages at the lycée here. There's also a separate management board, which includes a friend of yours, Romain, the deputy mayor of Sarlat."

"He's a good man," said Bruno, nodding. "Before I go, do you see any threats to this system Monique set up? Are any of the owners looking to get a larger share of the pie?"

"I don't think so, and I know most of them from the Christmas party Monique hosted every year. If there is a threat, I suppose it could come from the husband over the will, but I think I've taken care of that. Monique wanted me to sit on the board, but I said no, thinking that could create a potential conflict of interest."

"That makes sense."

"All along, she told me she was praying that she'd get pregnant and have the child to inherit what she'd built. She'd known my Adam since he was born, and she'd look at him sometimes with a kind of yearning that nearly broke my heart."

"Where's Adam now?" Bruno asked, trying to remember a young opponent across the net at a match against Sarlat.

"Warsaw, where his father's family originally came from. He's doing an exchange year at a business school there, on a

European scholarship. The teaching is in English as well as Polish." There was a touch of pride in her voice. "When Adam was in the lycée he spent a summer with the concierge team servicing the swimming pools and made enough money to go to London for three weeks, staying with my cousins."

"You must miss him."

She shrugged. "That's why you have them, so they can grow up and leave to have lives of their own. If you're lucky, you get to know your grandchildren." She rose to see him out. "I'll let you know if any problems arise with the will. And thanks to you for coming by, doing more than your duty. I'd heard good things about you from Annette, so it's nice to finally meet in person."

"It's my job and I'm glad to help. And it's always good to meet one of Annette's friends. Thanks again for breakfast," he said, giving a half wave, half salute, as he left.

Chapter 4

Bruno strolled down to Sarlat's main square, where *mairie* employees were already erecting Christmas lights and a giant tree. He took the shortcut through the rue des Consuls to the rue de la Libération where the notary, founded by Monique's ancestors almost a hundred and fifty years ago, was based. The *notaires* had the first floor, while the real estate agency had the ground floor with big windows to display the properties available for sale. They were all imposing, even grandiose. To one side was a separate entrance with the choice of stairs or a small elevator for the notary and the *conciergerie*. Bruno took the stairs to the office on the third floor, where he found a woman in the open doorway with her back toward him. She was talking to someone else inside while kneeling to tape a large sign on the door that said the office was closed in mourning.

"Sorry to disturb you, but I'm looking for Laura."

"That's me," said the woman with the sign, not turning around as she used her teeth to tear a strip from the roll of adhesive tape. She was wearing jeans and a black turtleneck sweater. Her voice was blurred by her efforts to tear the tape. "But we're closing today for the death of a colleague."

"I know, I'm a policeman, dealing with Monique's death,"

he said. "And I have an envelope with a copy of the letter for you from her that was left beside her body. With the magistrate at the tribunal we opened it to see if there was anything relevant to the inquiry into her death, but it looks very much as though it was a suicide, so I brought it along for you."

"Ah, sorry." She almost grunted as the piece of tape came free and she stuck the sign on the door. She turned around, gave him a polite smile and guided him into the reception room. "This is Geraldine," she said, gesturing to a young woman who sat behind a reception desk. "And I'm Laura Segret. I help run this place and it's going to be ten times tougher without Monique. Are you the policeman who found her?"

"I am." Bruno then handed her the envelope and drew her attention to Annette's official stamp. He took the opportunity to study her as she pulled out the accompanying letter, skimmed it quickly and then seemed to return to the beginning and read it carefully. Laura was around thirty, Bruno guessed, maybe a little older, with a generous mouth and a high brow. She had curly fair hair cut short, fine eyes and that clear complexion that came from generations of ancestors growing up in British mists and fog. Her skin had the healthy glow of someone who exercised frequently.

Bruno glanced around the room, nodding politely to the young woman at the reception desk. She looked young enough to be a schoolgirl, and despite the grown-up working clothes she looked familiar as she smiled. Suddenly remembering that Laura had called her Geraldine, the penny dropped.

"You're Geraldine from the Sarlat tennis tournament," he said, and stepped to the desk to shake her hand. "You and your big brother took the first set from us in the semifinals of the mixed doubles, and now you've finished school and have a job. Enjoying it?"

"Very much, Bruno, and thanks for asking. How's that

Englishwoman who runs a riding stable, the one who was your partner?"

"Pamela? She's fine, thanks, and I'll tell her you asked after her, but she'd want me to remind you that she's from Scotland."

"I'm sorry, you must think me very rude," Laura interrupted. "Can we offer you some coffee?"

"I already had coffee with the magistrate, thanks, and then another a few minutes ago with Maître Weil."

"A sad occasion, but it's good to meet you, since we have a lot of friends in common," she said, giving him a practiced smile that Bruno felt was out of place in the circumstances. "Annette and Romain, and of course you know Philippe Delaron of *Sud Ouest,* plus Clothilde from the museum, and I think you also knew René, the head of the Castanet family from Sergeac."

"He was probably the last of the great amateur archaeologists, God rest his soul," Bruno said, smiling at the memory. "He was the one who showed me the power of the spear-thrower, the technology that he claimed gave humans the edge over all the animals. He defied me to throw a spear through one of those thick straw targets he had, and of course I couldn't. Then he showed me how to do it with a spear-thrower, even at his age. He was already over eighty."

Laura made a point of encouraging his account, widening her eyes and nodding with enthusiasm as Bruno spoke, although she must have heard such stories before. She was working hard at establishing a connection with him, which was probably a requisite of a job that required dealing with clients. She nodded as he finished, then told Geraldine to take the rest of the day off and steered Bruno down a corridor, pausing at a closed door.

"As the policeman from St. Denis, you must be the one with the basset hound, aren't you?" she asked, and as he nodded agreement she went on, "Was that where Monique died? It seems far from her usual haunts."

"Yes, I found her on a very quiet road near St. Cirq with a fine view of the Vézère River and across the valley to Campagne. I've been hoping that you might be able to tell me if the place had any special significance for her."

"We have a couple of clients around there, but I honestly have no idea," she said, shaking her head. "Maybe you should ask her old school friends. But the reason I asked about your dog is that you'll find a pleasant surprise in this room." She opened the door with a flourish and steered him in.

Curled up on the floor on the spot where wintry sunlight fell through the window was a very attractive and young female basset, white except for some light brown patches on her sides and rump. The brown of her ears rose to cover each of her eyes, but a white stripe ran from her muzzle to separate the eyes and continued to the top of her skull and down to her back.

"Aren't you lovely?" Bruno asked softly as he sank to his knees and let the dog come to him.

She must at once have recognized the scent of Balzac on Bruno's hands and clothes, and having let her nose control the inspection for a good ten seconds, she finally raised two magnificent eyes to study him with care before rubbing the side of her face along his leg.

"She's what, about two, maybe a little more?" he asked Laura, gently scratching at that spot just behind the ear that would send Balzac into an ecstatic trance, and not taking his eyes from the dog.

"Two years and six months, and her formal name is Amantine-Lucile-Aurore Dupin de Francueil . . ."

"Better known as George Sand," said Bruno, glancing up at Laura and smiling at her look of surprise. "So your dog is named for the outstanding woman writer of her century, the lover of Chopin, of Mérimée and of the socialist leader Louis Blanc and many others, including women."

"Chapeau," she said, raising her hand to her brow as if doffing her hat. "Good for you. Do you have a favorite book of hers?"

"I read *Indiana,* which I found heavy going, but enjoyed her *Winter in Majorca,* about the time she spent on the island with Chopin," he said. "I came across her work by chance. You remember that fuss a few years ago about whether her remains should be placed in the Panthéon? That was when I took one of her books out of the library, simple curiosity."

"I became intrigued by Sand when we had to read her novel *Mauprat* at my lycée and was captivated by the sexual politics," she said, giving him a look that was half challenging, half teasing. "The brutish man civilized by the beautiful, intelligent woman."

"Did you choose the name for this glorious princess among hounds? I can't think when I last saw a lovelier basset. Do you think your George Sand might civilize my Balzac?" he inquired innocently.

She gave a hoot of laughter that was so genuine he had to join in, and when their chuckles finally died away he said, "It was meant to be a serious question."

"You'd have to convince my mother. She runs the kennels, so she controls the genetics. It will depend on his breeding."

"You can tell her Balzac comes from the kennels of the renowned Léon Verrier," Bruno said, adopting a serious tone. "And his grandmother was crossed with the Stonewall Jackson breed from America, which comes from the basset hounds that the Marquis of Lafayette presented to George Washington when he went over to help liberate the Americans from the English."

"That sounds promising. And the American Revolution is

part of the backdrop to the novel of Sand's that I mentioned, *Mauprat.*"

"I'll make a point of reading it," he replied, and for the first time took his attention from the hound and looked around. It was a pleasant room with a desk, bookshelves and filing cabinets that seemed to be her own office and perhaps also a conference room. It was large enough for six hardback chairs around what might have been a dining table but was probably used for meetings. The wall between the windows displayed a portrait of a pretty but rather solemn schoolgirl, and the longest wall was covered with row upon row of framed photographs of châteaus and *gentilhommières.*

"Are those the places you rent out for their owners?" he asked, gesturing at the photos. "Maître Weil told me a bit about the business."

"Yes, they are, although there are a couple of new ones not yet up there. And that's a portrait of Monique as a girl," she said, pointing at the wall. "Would you like a chair?" Laura pulled out one for herself and took a seat at the long table.

"I'm happy down here with the enchanting George Sand." Bruno lifted a velvety ear in emphasis. "When Annette opened the letters they made it clear that she had planned to take her own life. Does that surprise you?"

"I couldn't say, I'm still trying to absorb it. She was a remarkable woman and I'll miss her a lot, and not just because she was central to this whole business that we've built up. She was a very dear friend to me, a mentor . . ." Laura's voice broke off and she paused before going on, "I'm not the only one who'll miss her. She loomed large in the lives of all the women here and of the staff in the field, an inspiration to everyone. And it must be a very grim time for Dominic, losing his wife and his father, two deaths in the same week," she said. She paused again before asking how Monique had killed herself.

Bruno explained, adding that he thought she had not suffered, and then asked if Laura was surprised by the farewell letter.

"No, the future of the firm was something we had talked about. Monique had discussed it several times with me and the rest of the team, and with Becca Weil. She thought it would be unfair for Dominic to inherit any of the success of the *conciergerie* business in which he'd played no part and showed no interest. He even begrudged Monique the time she spent with us rather than with him. So I certainly agreed with Monique's plan, and so did the whole team. Not that it will be easy to continue without her vision and her leadership style. She made everybody feel really involved."

"Was there anyone Monique might have confided in?" he asked. "I hear she was close to an old school friend who now lives in Paris."

"Yes, Ghislaine. She's a finance expert who works in consulting. She comes down once a year to hold conferences in one of our biggest châteaus, and because it's out of season she gets the team from the Vieux Logis to do the catering. Monique would always stay with her when she went to Paris, a very fancy apartment on the rue du Bac." As she spoke, Laura pulled out her phone, checked the list of contacts and then read out to him a Paris number for Ghislaine Cardaillac.

"Will you keep your base here in Sarlat?" Bruno asked, scribbling down the number. "It may be a problem, if Monique's husband is not happy at being excluded."

"Monique was very clear about the marriage being based on separation of his and her estates, so Dominic has no involvement in our business," she said briskly. "It could even be argued that it predated Monique. Her grandfather, Louis, was a notary who began the expansion back in the 1950s when he helped his sister to start a real estate agency as a separate business," Laura explained. "The sister brought in an old school friend who then married Louis and became Monique's grandmother."

"How did you get involved?" Bruno asked.

"I was teaching languages at the lycée here and Monique would ask me to translate for German or English clients. We became friends, and when she started the *conciergerie* I was the first to be hired, years before Dominic turned up. It was already a thriving business with four other employees and Becca Weil, our lawyer, long before Monique met and married Dominic," Laura said firmly.

"What happens now?" Bruno asked.

"It was Monique who wanted to stay here. The rest of us all want to move out of Sarlat, lovely old town though it is. This place is so packed in high season that parking is impossible, and our clients have trouble coming to us. I've been saying for ages that we should be near the airport at Bergerac, or at least somewhere with rail access to Paris and Bordeaux. Monique was a Sarlat girl, born and bred, but that doesn't apply to the rest of us, and I think we'll be moving."

Laura explained that the team now comprised four women in Sarlat, two in an office in Bergerac and two more in Périgueux to deal with the growing number of clients in the rest of the *département* for whom they provided concierge services. They had used the government's green subsidies to install solar panels and heat pumps in all the properties they ran.

"Monique's breakthrough was to realize that one of the most attractive selling points we had was insurance," Laura said, leaning forward and speaking earnestly. "Without our service, which ensures that these valuable châteaus and estates are inhabited almost year-round, most of our clients would be looking at one hundred thousand euros annually in insurance costs alone, more even. With our system of almost permanent occupation, along with permanent gardeners and housekeepers and swimming pool maintenance, insurance comes down dramatically to around ten thousand a year. It also helps that there's no oil or gas needed for heating."

"What's in it for the ordinary folk, the French people who have to get up early in the morning?" Bruno asked.

"I'm glad you asked," said Laura, with a sigh of what sounded like relief followed by a very genuine grin. "This is the bit I really like."

She began to count the benefits on her fingers. Fourteen full-time jobs for gardeners, and each gardener had two apprentices who were learning their trade while spending one or two days a week at trade school to earn the *brevet,* the professional qualification that was the equivalent of a degree. Thirty full-time jobs for housekeepers, each one responsible for a specific building, plus part-time cleaning jobs for women who preferred shorter hours.

"And we've opened a free crèche and nursery school where young mothers can leave their kids in safety while earning fifteen euros an hour cleaning—they won't earn that as part-timers anywhere else," Laura said. "And we pay their social insurance. Above all, we've helped all of these people, gardeners and cleaners and the plumbers and electricians that we have on call, to take advantage of the new rules for *autoentrepreneurs,* with simplified tax and social insurance systems, and tax relief on their cars," she said. "Working with us, a gardener makes twenty-five euros an hour for a thirty-five-hour week, with six weeks' holiday a year. That gives them a guaranteed income of forty-five thousand a year, when the average French salary is just over thirty thousand. The housekeepers get twenty euros an hour, which is more than thirty grand a year, more than many office workers. Plus they have free accommodations. And we're pumping over seven million euros a year into the local economy."

"Well, I'm very happy about that," said Bruno. "But I was startled when your lawyer told me that you were making as much as two million a year."

"That's before we pay ourselves," Laura said, bridling. "That is, the eight of us who run the business," she said. "We pay ourselves forty grand a year each, which is less than we pay the gardeners, and any money left over goes into a retirement fund. And don't forget that we are paying the trainee gardeners, hiring caterers and rental cars, travel guides and so on. We have painters and decorators and handymen on retainers, along with a tree surgeon, and a couple of families that deliver fresh eggs from their own free-range chickens. We've set up a deal with a local builder and an architect to convert disused tobacco barns into housing. I think you know one of the barns, the home of Flavie, the singer with Les Troubadours. We also organize various events, particularly weddings but also truffle hunts, wine tours and tastings, cooking classes—whatever the customers want."

"Okay, I'm sold, and I think Flavie's house is terrific," Bruno said, grinning, and held up his hands, palms open in surrender. "It all sounded a little too good to be true the way Becca described it, and I'm surprised I haven't read or heard about your operation before."

"We don't advertise here in France, and mainly work with travel agents in the UK, Holland, Germany, North America and now China," she said. "It was all Monique's idea. She thought it was tragic that so many of the small châteaus were falling into ruin since nobody wanted to buy them and the owners could hardly afford to run them. So she dreamed up this brilliant way of keeping the places alive and lived in. And now it's not just vacationers or weddings, which is how we started. But we've got film companies hiring us, and companies holding special conferences or planning sessions. We have a Japanese corporation that brings its senior European staff here for a week each May, and a German think tank that holds weeklong sessions on global affairs. They'd much rather be in a real château with its own grounds than in some hotel. And we don't need to advertise. It tends to be people who have been here as guests who contact us if they start thinking about buying a château for themselves, knowing they can use us to defray the running costs."

"With more than a thousand châteaus in the Périgord it sounds like the sky's the limit," said Bruno. "How big do you plan to get?"

"I'm not sure we could manage any more," said Laura. "There are only eight of us to manage all these places, so each one of us is juggling four properties. Frankly, it's a relief when the real owners take over in July and August."

"I can understand that," Bruno laughed. "But it must be really satisfying, not just for you but for all your team, putting these great old buildings to new use, creating all these jobs."

"Yes, of course it makes us feel good—except when we're too tired, or when we get sick of dealing with the bureaucrats in the *département* or in Bâtiments de France. Still, we have some good allies who can help, which reminds me of our mutual friend Romain. He was a huge help when he was deputy mayor here, and it was partly through him that I first met you, although I bet you've forgotten." She said it with a cheerful smile.

"That's hard to believe," said Bruno, embarrassed. "I really don't recall . . ."

"I was a whore at the time, if that helps trigger your memory."

Her smile was even wider and she began to laugh openly as Bruno simply gaped at her, speechless.

"I'm teasing you," she said, smiling. "I was a tavern wench when you were at the reenactment of the liberation of Sarlat, playing the role of one of the women of easy virtue on the arm of a drunken English soldier."

He began to laugh and confessed that he remembered the scene, adding, "You must have been disguised in very heavy makeup."

"I wanted to be sure that even my mother wouldn't recognize me."

"I can imagine," Bruno said with a smile. "Much as I'd like to stay here with the wonderful George Sand, I'd better go back to collect my dog from the magistrate's office," Bruno said, rising, and privately wondering what gambit he might use to arrange to see her again.

"May we come with you?" Laura asked, as though she'd read his mind. "I'd like to meet Balzac and so would George Sand, then I'd better go home and catch up on the housekeeping."

The meeting of the two basset hounds went well, with a lot of polite and amiable sniffing at each other, and Laura welcomed Bruno's suggestion that she and George Sand might want to join him and Balzac for a favorite walk on Sunday, to be followed by brunch. Laura then took some photos of Balzac on her phone to send to her mother, which Bruno read as a hopeful sign, and he promised to forward her the details of Balzac's imposing pedigree.

"It sounds as though our dogs are more grandly born than either one of us peasants," she said, and leaned forward for the exchange of an affectionate *bise* on each cheek. Not for the first time, Bruno was grateful for this delightful French custom, with its hint of flirtation.

He drove back to St. Denis, smiling cheerfully to himself and wondering already what would be a perfect second date if the walk and brunch on Sunday went as well as he hoped. He began thinking of menus, which always put him in a good mood, despite the unpleasant physiotherapy session that now loomed ahead.

Chapter 5

Bruno pulled into the parking lot in front of the St. Denis medical center with five minutes to spare before his appointment with the physiotherapist. Her office on the lowest floor, reached by a separate entrance, had only recently been reopened after being inundated by the autumn's dramatic floods. And Bruno was in sore need of her skills. Two men had died when their car had been swept away by the raging Vézère River, but a woman and her child had been saved by Bruno and several volunteers. That rescue had badly wrenched his shoulder, which had undone much of the healing achieved since Bruno had been shot the previous summer. That first injury had required three weeks in the hospital followed by six weeks in a convalescent home for French police officers wounded while on duty. This second injury had required four days in the hospital, three weeks in a convalescent home and three physiotherapy sessions each week now that he was back at work. He had been told that his shoulder would never recover fully. He was barred from playing any more rugby and for the foreseeable future was resigned to a feeble form of tennis imposed by serving underarm.

"You're coming along nicely," said Nicole, as Bruno lay on

his back on a floor mat, his arms outstretched behind his head as he tried to lower them to touch the ground with the back of his hands.

"Now sit up slowly and bend forward at the waist to try and touch your toes, and again, and again," came that voice, which seemed all the more heartless for its soothing tones of goodwill. "And now lie back again, arms stretched straight up, and now lower them behind your head again to touch the floor. A bit more effort and reach for that floor. And again, Bruno, you're almost there. Come on, we both know you can do better than that."

There were few things in life more infuriating than being told he could do better by a young girl whom he'd taught to play tennis. And now, on the basis of a couple of diplomas and the white coat she wore, Nicole had the authority to humiliate him, to push his reluctant limbs an inch or two farther than they were able to go. Worst of all, she had the effrontery to tell him that he wasn't trying hard enough and could easily do better. He had suffered similar humiliating critiques hiding behind insincere phrases of encouragement at the convalescent home.

"Almost there," she said, with less-than-convincing encouragement. Then she returned mercilessly to the torment, making him sit up only to be ordered to lean forward once more, bending at the waist and stretching out his arms so he could touch his toes. He almost succeeded.

"There, that wasn't too hard, was it?" Nicole asked brightly. "You're coming along very well, and I can tell you're keeping up your morning runs. Another three or four sessions and we'll have you touching your toes again. And before you ask, no, you're not ready to start weight training again. We want your tendons and your skeletal structure pulling their full weight, and not letting your pumped-up muscles do the work.

That's the mistake men always make. Now, off you go to the swimming pool, twenty laps and a shower and you'll feel like a new man."

Resisting the urge to say that he preferred the old one, Bruno thanked Nicole politely and drove to the town pool. The old open-air pool that was open only from the first of May through September had been enhanced with a covered all-weather pool. This new addition opened at six each morning and was very popular with the early birds until nine, when it was reserved for the next four hours for the aquarobics classes, which seemed to consist of women of a certain age performing stately dances in the shallow end to vintage disco music. Three lanes were roped off for those instructed to swim laps, like Bruno. He did his duty, and at three minutes before one, feeling like a new man, he entered the *mairie.* He was greeted with a cheery wave from the receptionist, who was engrossed in a conversation on her phone but gestured him toward the mayor's door—he was expected to go straight in.

"Ah, Bruno, I gather this suicide you found this morning is not one of ours," the mayor said.

"No, Monsieur le Maire. Monique Duhamel worked in Sarlat as a *notaire* and inherited a grand family home in Sergeac, but also founded a very upscale rental agency that represents two properties that are near us. She had about thirty places all across the *département,* and employed at least a dozen around here: gardeners, builders, housekeepers."

"Why haven't we heard of her before, and why would such an enterprising woman want to kill herself?"

Bruno explained about the miscarriage and her husband's absence at a funeral and described the team of women that had been recruited to run the company. He saved the best for last.

"They are thinking of moving out of Sarlat, since it's so crowded, hard to reach and impossible for their clients to park.

They're thinking of somewhere nearer to Bergerac airport—but we may have an outside shot at enticing them here," Bruno explained. "I don't know whether there may be difficulties with the will, which leaves the company to Monique's all-female staff rather than to her husband. But I'm told the marriage took place under the separation of properties."

"Who will make the decision where to move?" The mayor got to his feet, and Bruno moved to follow.

"The woman who seems likely to take the helm is Mademoiselle Laura Segret, who worked with Monique from the start and became the first of what are now seven partners," Bruno replied. "She was born here to a French father. Her English mother runs a kennel and raises basset hounds. Laura has a young lady basset, and I say 'lady' deliberately because she is a true princess. I've never seen a more beautiful basset."

"Does Balzac share your admiration?" the mayor asked, leading the way down the ancient spiral staircase with its deep grooves worn by generations of feet.

"I'm sure he will," Bruno replied, falling in step beside the mayor once they emerged onto the square. "Laura and I are going to walk the dogs together Sunday to see how relations progress."

"And are the attractions of Mademoiselle Segret as impressive as those of her basset hound?" the mayor asked as they paused before crossing the road to enter the rue de Paris.

"She's a very interesting woman," said Bruno as they strolled toward Ivan's restaurant, pausing every few steps to shake hands with some acquaintance. "She's obviously intelligent, business-like, and I heard from a mutual acquaintance that she was also a terrific basketball player."

"Well, then," said the mayor, pausing before Ivan's door. "It sounds, my dear Bruno, as though you're very interested."

"We'll see," Bruno replied, opening the restaurant door

and enjoying the smells of cooking that emerged. Ivan came to greet and lead them to a corner between the bar and the corridor that led to the outside yard that Ivan called his beer garden, which was open only in summer. It was the closest to privacy that Ivan could offer, and the table was set for two.

"A small carafe of the new house white, the one with Floréal. Bruno hasn't tried it yet," the mayor said to Ivan as he and Bruno took their seats.

"We only planted it this spring," said Bruno. "It can't be ready this soon."

"It could be if we wanted to copy the Beaujolais and make a Périgord nouveau, and come to think of it, that's not a bad idea. Still, this isn't ours," the mayor replied. "We got this from that friend of yours, Patrick Barde at Château le Raz in Montravel. Like you, he says the *appellation contrôlée* system has become too restricted now that we need to explore new varieties to cope with climate change. He was an early adopter, and he's using it in a blend with sauvignon. He let us have enough to try it ourselves at the town vineyard. Hubert and I agree with you that Patrick makes some of the best new wines in the region, so I thought we'd try it his way."

"This is pretty good, lots of fruit and fresh on the palate," said Bruno after sipping. "A bit of grapefruit in the nose with maybe a hint of something more woody, maybe a bit like boxwood, but it's pleasantly fresh and dry. I think I prefer it to that Viognier we were trying."

"Good, not just because I agree with you, but it also gives us about ten to fifteen percent more yield per hectare than the Viognier," the mayor said. "And there's less alcohol in the Floréal—around eleven point five percent rather than the twelve point five or thirteen percent of Viognier."

Bruno nodded. Too many French drivers still believed in the old rule that they could drink two glasses of wine and still pass a Breathalyzer test. That had been true when most French wines were thirteen percent or less, but with climate change boosting the alcohol level of Merlot as high as fifteen percent, two glasses could be breaking the law.

"I hope you don't mind," the mayor said. "I ordered the light lunch—Jacqueline's orders. She says I put on weight while she was teaching in Paris, and with Christmas coming . . ." The mayor broke off, looking disconsolate.

"Fine by me, but this idea of Ivan's light lunch is new to me," said Bruno.

"Ivan began with what he called his summer menu," the mayor said. "And now there's this version for winter. You can have soup, salad and dessert, or soup and main course, or main course and dessert."

"A real Périgord soup can contain as many calories as a Parisian banquet," Bruno said. "What's the plat du jour?"

"Poached chicken with *cèpes* and lentils braised in the poaching liquid, so full of nutrients and free from butter." The mayor sighed. "And I don't dare have it, just in case you want to demand a pay raise and threaten to tell Jacqueline."

"Heaven forbid I'd do such a thing, but what's on your mind?"

"You may not have heard, but Pascal is shutting his shop after Christmas, even though he has no buyer in sight. He'll probably sell the whole building after turning it into separate apartments. The shops on the rue de Paris are closing down faster than I can find any kind of replacements."

"Are you surprised? We've got a big Intermarché, a Lidl and an Aldi and a *bio* supermarket, all on the outskirts of town. We're lucky to still have a real butcher and three boulangeries on the rue de Paris, plus a florist, a hairdresser, a pharmacy, a cheese shop, two cafés, a wine bar, two pizza joints, a beautician, fancy furnishings, a bicycle store and a carpenter's craft shop. It's a real shame to lose the hunters' shop, but we're doing better than all the other small towns around here."

"We're not doing better than St. Cyprien," the mayor grumbled. "They've got two antiques shops, a bookstore, that fashionable *traiteur* who's a friend of yours, the yogurt factory and that very fancy new hotel. Worst of all, their Sunday market is becoming a serious rival."

"How can they be a rival when their market is Sunday and we are on Tuesday?" Bruno countered. "And Sylvain, the *traiteur,* is a cousin of our cheese maker Stéphane, so of course they coordinate. And they have the weekend customers, so their Vietnamese woman making small *nem* charges more than our own Madame Duong charges for her big ones. We aren't rivals here. And if they have their new hotel, we have the new Domaine de la Barde and the new gymnasium at the *collège* and the new indoor pool. But I agree that it would be good to have a decent antiques shop here." He paused. "What I'd most like to see is a secondhand bookstore, the kind of place where you can just browse for hours."

"We have the bookstore in the entrance to the big supermarket," the mayor said.

"You're a booklover," Bruno said. "I've heard you get all lyrical about browsing in those book carts in Paris along the banks of the Seine. And who's first in the doors every year at the retirement-home book sale here in town?"

"I am, unless you beat me to it," the mayor replied with an affectionate smile. "Maybe that's something we could do with an empty shop front. I think we might get some volunteers to run it, retired people. It could be a way for them to keep active, meet people."

"It's the kind of activity Fabiola would happily recommend to her retired patients," said Bruno.

"We'd need to look at the books that are donated or handed

on by the heirs," the mayor said. "Some might be valuable, or rare, or of special local interest. I'd happily volunteer to help look through new donations, and so would several others, you included, I presume."

"You're right, and don't forget this new option for school students, extra credit for voluntary work. There's always a bookworm or two in every new class, and that would be perfect for them," said Bruno as Ivan presented the mayor with a bowl of chicken soup, a clear broth, enlivened with small cubes of carrot and shreds of cabbage.

Bruno, by contrast, was handed a plate of poached chicken and lentils in a thick broth that was glossy with a rich and fatty stock. Ivan then returned to place a bowl with roast potatoes, carrots and parsnips beside Bruno along with a basket of bread.

"It's perfect," Bruno assured Ivan as the mayor stared hungrily at the bounty on Bruno's plates. He took a deep breath and addressed himself to his own bowl, until there was just an inch of liquid left. He then poured in half a glass of wine, allowed it to blend with the thin broth and then raised the bowl to his lips and drank.

"*Vive le chabrol,*" said Bruno as the mayor set down the empty bowl, smacked his lips and looked a great deal more cheerful, having enjoyed once again a much loved tradition.

"You realize we can only do this bookstore plan if the vacant shop belongs to the town," he said. "A private owner would happily sell the place to any buyer who comes along."

"Wasn't it you who once assured me that there are few rights so absolute as those of a French mayor in possession of a solid majority in council?" Bruno asked calmly.

"Except for the rights of private property," the mayor added.

"So if the owner of the property whose business is not doing well decides he should sell the place or convert it into apartments, there is not much the council can do. But it can impose delays to investigate other possibilities, or demand a survey to prove that the building is structurally sound or perhaps to revalue the property for tax purposes. Best of all, you could declare it to be so historic that it merits an opinion from Bâtiments de France, which can take forever to arrange."

"Exactly, Bruno. I've trained you well." He refilled his glass and raised it in a mock toast. "We can make sure that no hasty decisions will be made that we might later come to regret," said the mayor, sitting back and taking a sip of his wine. Then he firmly replaced his glass and crossed his hands on the table before leaning intimately forward to demand, "What do you know about Xavier's problem?"

"I wasn't aware that he had one, except that the big car firms think the family garage is too small and remote to continue as an official showroom, which will probably dent his income," Bruno said. "But he'll still be part of one of the wealthiest families in St. Denis. And his wife comes from a flourishing sawmill and timber business, so they're unlikely to starve."

"So you don't know that the marriage is in trouble and my deputy mayor seems to have moved out of the family home?"

"No, it's news to me. Is this recent?" Bruno asked. He had been away over the weekend with the town's junior rugby team at a regional tournament.

"Xavier was in Bordeaux last week for a three-day course on how the local *mairies* should adapt to the new recycling legislation. He came home, and two days later his wife threw him out. What do you make of that?"

"I'd hate to speculate," said Bruno, frowning. "But if a husband has a romantic dalliance while out of town, it is always possible that some busybody happens to see it and spreads the news."

"My thoughts exactly," said the mayor.

"Mirabelle has always been pretty spirited, in a good sense, not just in wanting to get her own way," Bruno went on thoughtfully, recalling the cheerful, enthusiastic girl she had been when first joining his tennis class. "She can be ruthless on the tennis court, and she still keeps a watchful eye on the family business even while she's devoted to her two children. And I never heard of the marriage being in trouble before."

"Nor me," the mayor replied. "But this has obvious implications for two of our town's important employers, so find out what you can."

"Where is Xavier staying?" Bruno asked.

"I don't know; I didn't want to make a big thing of it. I assume his dad would know."

"If our suspicions are correct, his dad would be even more furious with Xavier than Mirabelle," said Bruno. "And if the old man doesn't know that Xavier has moved out of the family home, he'll be in a real rage. I can see why you'd rather have me find out than do it yourself." He rolled his eyes and gave a wry smile.

"Ah, Bruno, after all these years working closely together, you can read me like a book. It's very reassuring to know that my subtle hints will not be misunderstood. I'm having the compote for dessert. What about you?"

Chapter 6

After lunch, Bruno was about to call the Paris number for
Ghislaine Cardaillac, Monique's old school friend, when he
paused. The surname nagged at him. It was almost familiar
but elusive. The image of a château came into his head, and
he muttered to himself, "Milandes," and thought of the fashionable young wife of the old warrior of the great fortress of
Castelnaud. Bruno had always wondered at the skill of Claude
de Cardaillac, a young bride at the end of the fifteenth century
who persuaded her elderly husband to build something less
warlike and more comfortable for her, in the modern style just
spreading to France from Italy's Renaissance. The result was
the charming Château des Milandes, and he had heard that her
family of Cardaillac had prospered or at least survived down
the centuries.

He called the mayor and asked if there were any branches
of the Cardaillac family still around St. Denis. Indeed, he was
told, there was a small château up in the hills around La Peyrière, on the way to Les Eyzies, that had belonged to a branch
of the family. The mayor thought it had changed hands a
decade or more ago. Why was Bruno asking?

"I'm trying to track down a childhood friend of this morning's suicide," Bruno said. "I was wondering why she chose to take her life up there around La Peyrière, and I think you've given me the answer. I'll keep you informed."

Bruno ended the call and then dialed Ghislaine Cardaillac's number, reaching a recorded message, a woman's voice asking him to state his business. He gave his name, rank and number, suggesting she call the *mairie* of St. Denis to verify his identity, and explained that he wanted to talk with Ghislaine Cardaillac on police business. Wondering how long it would take for his call to be returned, Bruno set off for the scenic overlook where Monique had taken her own life to look for a small château. He was curious, since he recalled no such building in a district he thought he knew well.

He had barely reached the outskirts of town when his call was returned, and a voice that spoke a classic, educated French without the brisk condescension of a true Parisian said, "Monsieur le Chef de Police, you have a very handsome basset hound."

"Bonjour, madame, and how do you know that?"

"From Google, which offers several photos of you in past issues of *Sud Ouest,* along with one of you doing something apparently heroic in a rugby game and another of you with an equally handsome horse."

Bruno felt confused by the woman's approach. He took refuge in the conventions of procedure.

"Am I right in thinking that you're Ghislaine Cardaillac, a friend of Monique Duhamel from school days?" he asked. "And that you lived outside St. Denis near La Peyrière?"

"Correct on all counts."

"I have to convey the sad news that Monique is dead by her own hand, in a car that was found this morning parked in a scenic overlook near La Peyrière. And I need to ask you why she might have chosen such a place."

"What terrible news." There was a long silence. Then she spoke again. "I have to say I'm not as surprised as I might have been, after the miscarriage. It devastated her." There followed another silence. "Did she leave any message for me?"

"Not that I found, madame."

"I am mademoiselle, but no matter. Please call me Ghislaine. She probably wrote me a letter; she usually did when she was deciding something. Did she leave any letters?"

"Yes, three: to her business associate, her lawyer and her husband."

"So if there was no letter to me, why did you call?"

"I was told you and she were very close for many years and she always stayed with you in Paris."

"That's true enough. Did anyone mention my brother and what happened to him?"

"No, only that Monique was thought to have known him when they were young, a time when you must have known her well."

"I suppose someone who didn't know the real story could put it that way," she replied. "And it wasn't the kind of story we wanted to spread around. It was just too overwhelming. It would have blocked out everything else about the two of them, our family, everything. But it may as well come out now, when none of the participants is still with us. So, yes, Monique and I became close friends at the lycée in Sarlat, and she and I would spend weekends together, either with her at Sergeac or at our place near Les Eyzies. And one day at the end of our second year at Sciences Po in Paris, she was staying with us when my big brother came down for the summer after getting his master's at the London School of Economics. Monique and my brother had not met since she and I had been in our first year at the lycée."

Her voice seemed to change as she said this. She spoke

more slowly, and a softness had crept into her voice, perhaps the effect of memories being triggered.

"I remember it so well," she went on. "Raoul was four years older, handsome and charming, and I think it was the first time that I, her closest friend, realized that Monique had become a lovely young woman, glowing with health and energy, just coming into bloom. We had a grass court, and she and I were playing tennis when Raoul came by on horseback. He stopped to watch, but Monique was so intent on her service she had not noticed. She served and then came in to volley my return into the corner, and Raoul called out, quite spontaneously, 'Bravo.' And you could hear the admiration in his voice. She turned to see who was shouting and that was it. Whoof! The magical moment, the ball bouncing away unnoticed into the back of the court, the horse suddenly rearing up its head, Monique magnificent in the triumph of her volley. For each of them it hit at once. Like a missile landing perfectly on target."

"Love at first sight," exclaimed Bruno, the romantic in him enchanted by the tale.

"You can imagine the rest," said Ghislaine, her voice sounding suddenly tired. "Young love. Two families of excellent standing with two châteaus. Delighted that their young had shown such good taste to choose a mate from within their own wellborn ranks. Parental approval, but of course young Monique had to first finish her studies, and young Raoul had to get launched on what was bound to be a brilliant career. A suitable post was found in a New York investment firm. He flew to JFK on the last day of August 2001, started work on September the first. He was on the eightieth floor of one of the Twin Towers at the World Trade Center. You know what happened next.

"That airliner crashing into the building was an image

Monique could never escape, the death of her lover constantly replayed."

"*Mon Dieu!*" Bruno exclaimed, appalled. "They had, what, only two months together?"

"Fifty-five days. In some ways, Monique never got over it. The worst of it was the waiting; it took weeks to confirm his death. We could only hope that his death was instant, not that any of us could ever be sure of that." Ghislaine paused, and then her voice became matter of fact. "Do you know when or where the funeral will be held?"

Captivated by her tale of young love blighted by a tragedy, Bruno struggled to change focus and answer her question.

"Not yet. I presume her husband will decide, but he won't arrive until late tomorrow," Bruno replied, and explained about the funeral in Strasbourg.

"I know she hated cremations . . ." Her voice broke off. "My parents died in a car crash, and they were buried in the family plot in the cemetery of St. Denis, where I presume I'll be laid to rest myself. There were no remains of my brother, but my parents had the usual mementos of his childhood, locks of hair and milk teeth, so I put them in a casket and had it buried with them. Monique said to me at the time that the casket was the nearest she'd ever get to him again and perhaps she, too, could be buried there."

"I'll let her husband know that, and perhaps see if our Father Sentout might officiate."

"Let me know when you find out the date and where. I want to come down," she said. "And I look forward to meeting your basset."

"Before you go, your family's château—do you still have it?" Bruno asked.

"Not anymore," she said. "When my parents died, I got

rid of it. It was too much trouble and upkeep while I was in Washington at the World Bank and after that in Paris almost all the year. So I put it in Monique's hands, the tiny château that launched what became her successful business."

"I'm amazed that the story of Monique and your brother never became public," Bruno said. "How do you keep secret the tragedy of a young Frenchman dying in the most televised mass execution in history?"

"He was a young stranger in a brand-new job, and there was no body. You can imagine what happened to the people on those floors when the airliner flew into them at some horrendous speed. Our parents had no idea that was the building where he was working. He'd sent them a postcard when he arrived in the city and said he'd write when he got a proper address, but never did. I got an email, sent the day before the attack. Monique got emails every day, and then nothing. But somehow, she knew he was dead. She told me she had a sudden sense of utter despair on the very day it happened, but in the morning, before the news came. We were in Paris, looking for an apartment to share. And of course there was the six-hour time difference. Maybe it was a premonition that she had. Who knows?"

"So she and you and your family never got caught up in the media circus?"

"No, but Monique was sure. She knew the name of the investment group where he had started work, found that they had offices in the World Trade Center, then began checking with the firm's other offices in Houston and Toronto and Zurich that Raoul had started work, had been given a security pass and an email address. His security pass had been registered with the building, and Raoul had used it that morning, although it took some weeks for all the data to be assembled. I had a cousin living in New York, a diplomat with the French delegation to the UN, and he kept pestering the authorities until he finally got confirmation that Raoul would be listed among the victims some weeks later. By then, Monique had built around herself the carapace that became her protective cover for the rest of her life. I think I was the only one to be allowed inside, to know just what she had lost."

"Your brother's death must have had a powerful effect on you as well," Bruno said.

"Yes, a cautionary tale on the dangers of a *grande passion.* It cured me for life of any such romantic dream." She said it almost lightly, as if it were a phrase she had used before, the kind of light remark that can pass for sophistication or even wit at a cocktail party.

"I thought it might have brought you and Monique closer together," Bruno suggested.

"Perhaps it did, a shared grief prolonging the friendship of schoolgirls into something more lasting," she said. "Not that I would ever suggest that my loss of a brother was to be compared to hers of a soul mate, a husband, a father of the children she never had."

And as she went on, Bruno heard a little edge to her voice, perhaps a hint of self-mockery to suggest that however solemn she might sound, she would never take herself quite so seriously. It was a stylized way of speaking that he had heard before. Bruno realized with a sudden shock of surprise that he had heard this exact same tone in the voice of another woman who moved in fashionable circles in Paris. And as the image of Isabelle came into his head, he was even more surprised to realize that it had been days, even a week and more, since he had last thought of her. Could she at long last be losing that potent grip on his thoughts and emotions?

Bruno had known Isabelle first as a local policewoman, one of the star investigators on the team of Bruno's friend Jean-

Jacques Jalipeau, the chief detective of the *département* and known to all as J-J. The love affair Bruno and Isabelle had enjoyed that first magical summer had lingered on despite her move to the staff of the interior minister in Paris, and then to Eurojust in The Hague, and then back to Paris. Each move had come with a jump in rank, and her brilliant career meant she was now spoken of as possibly the first woman chief of France's internal security directorate. Their often interrupted love affair had endured these shifts of location. Even more, it had survived her decision to abort a pregnancy without telling Bruno that she was carrying his child.

"Are you still there?" came an almost shrill voice in his ear, startling him back into the phone call with Ghislaine.

"Sorry, my phone suddenly lost its signal," he replied, trying to remember what Ghislaine had been saying. "The last I heard was your saying how deeply Monique's life had been overshadowed by the death of your brother."

"Yes, and I had gone on to ask whether you could let me know about funeral plans so I could arrange to come down and get a hotel and so on."

"Of course," he said. "And I'm sure you'd like to meet some of the impressive local women that she was close to, like her doctor and a local magistrate who's also a champion rally driver."

"Sure, just let me know when to show up, and thanks, Bruno." She ended the call without giving Bruno any idea of where her family château was located.

He was on the outskirts of town, past the medical lab and the veterinarian's office, close to the junction that led to the town's unmanned train station. He drove on and turned right just before the railway crossing, following the road that led along the floodplain of the Vézère River to Les Eyzies. Where the road took a sudden bend to skirt around a solitary house,

Bruno took a narrow lane to the left that climbed to the hills that loomed over St. Denis. He came to a junction that he recognized. Straight on, it led to the heights of La Peyrière, from where he could turn left to Petit Paris and back to St. Denis. To the right it led to the Grotte du Sorcier, the magician's cave, where he had first kissed Isabelle. He raised his hand in sad salute to what he now knew was a lost love, and for once did not feel that sudden lurch in his spirit. Before he could analyze what he felt about its absence, he noticed a narrow path to the left that was unfamiliar. It was flanked by trees, now naked in winter, and he was struck by the way their bare branches almost intertwined overhead.

He followed it downhill and saw an overgrown grass tennis court through the spaces between the tree trunks. Then after a sharp turn, a charming ancient house came into view. It was a *chartreuse,* rather than a château, smaller and with no hint of fortification. The only unusual feature was that the right-hand side of the building was flanked by a small, round tower with a conical roof like a witch's hat. Bruno guessed from the upper row of windows that it would have no more than four or five bedrooms in the front and perhaps the same at the rear. There was a modest portico on columns above the double doors of the entrance and three windows on each side, all covered by pale blue shutters. Off to one side was a building that had probably once been the stables, now apparently a garage. The *chartreuse* was protected by a low stone wall, topped with iron railings, and the front garden seemed to be lawns and shrubbery with some fruit trees to each side that needed pruning. There was no sign of life, nor of the full-time gardeners Laura had mentioned, but then no garden looked at its best in midwinter.

Bruno wondered how renters would find the place, unless they were escorted there or given a very good map. Nor was there any sign of the full-time housekeeper each of the buildings was supposed to have. Perhaps this was not the right place. He took a quick photo with his phone and sent it to Ghislaine's number with a query whether this had been her family home. He climbed out of his van, strolled around to the side of the building and saw an old barn with an open door, evidently in regular use as a garage from the tire marks, though it was now empty. Smoke was coming from a chimney at the rear, and as he peeked in at the back door he saw a kitchen that was clearly in use, with dishes stacked in a drying rack by the sink, condiments and a half-empty bottle of wine on a table and a wood-fired stove. The housekeeper appeared to be in residence, but had presumably gone shopping or on a social call. Bruno strolled to his van and drove back to town.

Chapter 7

Bruno went next to the sports bar opposite the old gendarmerie, run by two veteran rugby players whom Bruno knew well. It sold excellent draft beer and decent wine, served good pizzas and salad, and the big TV screen was permanently tuned to the Eurosport channel. The place was the obvious refuge for an errant husband who had been thrown out of his home by a furious wife.

"Bonjour, Serge. I'm looking for Xavier," he said quietly as he shook hands with one of the owners, a retired player who was manning the bar. Like most such athletes Serge was not just burly but seemed almost as broad as he was tall and had a broken nose and massive forearms.

"Haven't seen him yet today, but you'll probably find him at his sister's place opposite the tennis club," came the quiet reply. "I hope Xavier gets things sorted out at home—he's not a happy guy. Last night I even confiscated his car keys and made him walk home, and that's not like him at all. He's not usually a heavy drinker."

"Do you know what it's all about?" Bruno asked.

"Trouble at home is all he says, but it doesn't take a genius to work it out. Xavier gets home from Bordeaux and the wife has asked the neighbor to look after her kids for a couple of hours, waits for him to come back from the *mairie,* slugs him with a frying pan and throws him out. Haven't you seen Xavier's face?"

Bruno sighed and shook his head, thanked Serge and turned to leave.

"Christ knows how she learned to hit the poor bastard like that, but I'd hate to have it happen to me," the barman called after him.

Bruno stopped, turned and confessed. "It's probably my fault. She was in my tennis class, and we worked hard on getting the backhand with just the right amount of topspin."

With Serge's guffaws still ringing in his ears Bruno drove to the tennis club, parked his car and then strolled down the street to ring the doorbell of Xavier's sister's home. Melissa came to the door looking tired and drained, a baby in her arms and a toddler clinging to her skirts, but she raised a grin for her old tennis teacher and presented her cheeks for the customary *bise.* Bruno complied and hugged her, told her she looked wonderful, kissed the baby and picked up the toddler to give him a hug.

"You'll find my idiot of a brother in the garden shed," she said. "He's got a sleeping bag and one of those canvas loungers we sunbathe on in summer, and I'm not sure he even deserves that."

"Have you talked to Mirabelle about all this?" Bruno asked. He knew that Mirabelle and Melissa had been best friends and tennis partners at school, and Melissa had been the bridesmaid at her brother's wedding. The women had remained close, taking their kids to the playground together.

"Of course I have, and she did the right thing to throw him out. It's bad enough that my idiot brother was unfaithful, but to give your wife an STD as well? Unspeakable."

"Of course, you're right," said Bruno. "I just hope that this separation is not going to be permanent. There are few things worse for the children than an angry breakup and divorce. I don't know if you've spoken to her about it or not, but do you know what Mirabelle has in mind?"

"She hasn't mentioned the d-word, and she knows her kids miss their dad already, but she doesn't know what to do. She hasn't had a single word from Xavier, not a letter or even a card to say he's sorry. I keep telling him he can't leave her hanging like this, but when did he ever listen to me?"

Melissa pulled up her apron to dry away a tear that suddenly welled from her right eye, overflowed the eyelid and ran down her cheek. "He's a fool but he's my brother and Mirabelle's my best friend and I love those kids. *Merde,* Bruno, do what you can to get them back together. He'll listen to you."

Bruno handed her a clean handkerchief, and when she had dabbed her eyes and then blown her nose, she put it into her pocket, saying she'd wash it before getting it back to him.

"Don't worry about it," he said, embracing her in an affectionate hug, and recalling that he'd embraced her at her wedding, and when she'd shown him her first child. And long before that he'd embraced her to give comfort after she'd lost a tennis match that might have won St. Denis the Dordogne championship. "And if I can't talk some sense into your fool of a brother, I'll see what the mayor can do."

He let her go, walked around to the rear garden and knocked on the door of the shed, announcing his presence and then opening the door and standing over Xavier, who was sitting on the lounger. No book or newspaper in his hands, no sign of any note or letter he might have been writing, no sign at all that he was engaged in the wider world. He was unwashed, unshaven, and his clothes were a mess. But most striking of all was his face. Xavier's nose had been broken and was grossly swollen and red. The bruises that half closed each eye were no longer a stark black but were fading into sickly greens and yellows. His upper lip was badly swollen, and two front teeth had disappeared. Had Bruno not recalled the power of Mirabelle's backhand, he would never have believed such a svelte young woman could inflict such damage.

"Oh, it's you," Xavier grunted, a swollen lip adding a lisp to his voice. "I might have expected it. You or the mayor, anyway."

"We were waiting for you to go see Mirabelle and your children, to tell her you're sorry or at least write her a note."

"She threw me out."

"And I don't blame her, nor does the mayor. Nor would any man with the sense he was born with. You are about as in the wrong as any man can be. Mirabelle's a fine woman, an excellent mother to your children, and she's entitled to hear you say that you are very, very sorry."

"Of course I'm sorry, but she just pushed me out of my own home, slammed the door and locked it."

"She was right to do it," Bruno said. "You not only betrayed her trust and now she's been humiliated before the entire town. You pledged yourself to her till death do you part. And you can't even summon the balls to go and tell her you're sorry."

"She won't listen. She'll just throw me out again."

"You don't know that, and it's a risk you have to take if you want to see your kids again this side of a court case."

"She can't do that!"

"Of course she can, and she'd be in the right. Most of your friends will say the same. Getting so pissed down in the bar that they take your car keys away is not the right way to spend your time, not if you want to clean up the mess you've made." Bruno paused. "You do want to clean up this mess?"

Xavier nodded glumly, a slight wince hinting at the remains of last night's hangover.

"The next few hours are going to determine the rest of your life, Xavier. Do you understand that?" Bruno asked. "They are going to decide whether you have any scrap of respect left in this town, whether you see your kids again, whether your father and your sister ever talk to you again, whether there is any future for you in St. Denis, because you can kiss goodbye being deputy mayor. You won't ever be elected to anything."

"I suppose that comes from the mayor? Or are you making it up?"

Bruno rolled his eyes to the heavens. "If the mayor heard any of this whining self-pity he'd have given up on you already. As of now, we might just be able to save your marriage, but time is running out fast."

"I suppose you've got a plan," Xavier said, in a tone somewhere between a hope and a sneer.

"I've got an idea, but you're going to have to start by coming back home with me and taking a shower and shaving, borrowing some clean clothes and then going to church so Father Sentout can hear your confession," Bruno said. "Or have you forgotten that your wife is a devout Catholic who sings in the choir, goes to church every Sunday and sends the kids to Sunday school?

"And then, instead of spending your money in a bar you're going to the florist to buy the best bouquet they have in stock, and we are going to walk to your house, ring the doorbell, tell your wife you're very sorry and ask for forgiveness. Make sure Father Sentout stands behind you to let your long-suffering wife know that you've been to confession, and he's given you absolution."

There was a long pause, and then Xavier said, "That might just work." He got to his feet. "Why not use the shower here?"

"Because your sister won't have you in her house," Bruno said, his voice as cold as he could make it.

"All my clothes are back at the house," Xavier said. "And Mirabelle won't let me in."

"Let's find out," Bruno said as he held the shed door open. "Come on, I haven't got all day."

Bruno saw Melissa peering from an upstairs window as he pushed Xavier into the back of his police van and drove off, back to his home. She'd probably be calling Mirabelle to pass on the news.

"Why did you put me in the back like this?" Xavier grumbled.

"Because you stink," said Bruno, opening his own window, and the two men drove on in silence.

Once home, Bruno showed Xavier to the bathroom, handed him a towel and from his wardrobe pulled a clean shirt, an old pair of jeans, a thick sweater and an ancient coat. He added his oldest clean T-shirt, socks and underpants and then called Father Sentout and the mayor.

Father Sentout was waiting at the door of the church when Bruno's Land Rover—which he thought might be a little more discreet than the police van—drew up outside. Xavier climbed down from the passenger's seat and marched into the church.

"Father, forgive me, for I have sinned," Xavier almost barked as he took his seat in the confessional cabin. At this point, Bruno went quietly to the church door. He was still able to hear almost every word of Xavier's anti-erotic description of the woman from the Béarn, in the foothills of the Pyrénées, who had tempted him to adultery on the final, wine-lubricated evening of the course.

"In the name of the Father, the Son and the Holy Ghost, I absolve you," the priest intoned after telling Xavier his penance. Bruno held open the church doors so that Xavier and his confessor could march out and cross the road to the florist, where a large and sumptuous bouquet had been hastily assembled.

Xavier marched to the cashier, handed over his credit card, saw his purchase accepted, and with a bunch of crimson roses in one hand and the bouquet in the other, he led the way along the rue Gambetta and up the slope to the place du Temple. The name was all that remained of the town's Protestant church, which had stood until demolished on the orders of Louis XIV, the Sun King, in the late seventeenth century. At the far end of the small square, Xavier, Father Sentout and Bruno turned right up the gentle hill lined with semidetached houses built for the expected baby boom after the slaughter of the Great War.

Xavier marched to the doorstep, rang the bell for a good ten seconds, then stepped back as the door opened and Mirabelle stood upon the threshold. From the corner of his eye, Bruno spotted some flickering curtains, a sure sign that the village gossips were paying attention to this soap opera on their doorstep.

Mirabelle looked magnificent, haughty and regal, her ramrod bearing putting any sergeant major to shame. She wore no lipstick, but her eyes looked enormous, and Bruno made an audible intake of breath at the sight of her. There was no sign of the children.

"I'm coming straight from church, where I made my confession and have been absolved," Xavier declared. "But now I ask you, Mirabelle, to give me the chance to make up for my sin against you, our children and our marriage."

Xavier stood there, awaiting his wife's verdict. The silence lengthened.

Bruno did not turn to look but suddenly realized from the sound of shuffling feet and the occasional bubble of high-pitched chatter that some of the womenfolk of St. Denis had come to witness the spectacle of an errant husband publicly confessing his offense.

Mirabelle's eyes shifted to Father Sentout, and then to Bruno. She held the door open and stood beside it, staring grimly at Xavier, his roses and his bouquet.

"Get in," she said.

Xavier shuffled forward, over the doorstep and into the house. His wife stayed outside for a long moment, looking at Bruno and the priest.

"Merci, messieurs," she said. "I won't forget your kindness." And with a cold smile she marched into the house, quietly closing the door behind her.

Chapter 8

The wintry dusk was falling so fast Bruno knew he would be too late to join Pamela for the evening ride with the horses at the riding school she ran with Miranda. Gilles was in Ukraine for *Paris Match,* and his partner, Fabiola, would be seeing patients at the clinic until seven. It was a weekday, so Félix the stable boy would be at the lycée in Périgueux until Friday evening. Miranda would be supervising the younger riders in the paddock, so Pamela might well be alone, taking all the horses—including Bruno's own Hector—on a leading rein. He knew that he would be counted on to make dinner, since Pamela had already invited Fabiola and the baron, along with Bruno's cousin Alain and his new wife, Rosalie.

Bruno drove home to collect two large jars of *confit de canard,* the duck legs sealed in fat that for centuries had been a proud staple of the local cuisine. He had always wondered why it had taken so long for the *magret de canard,* the breast of duck, to become popular. Local lore claimed the dish had been virtually unknown until 1959 when chef André Daguin, of the Hôtel de France in Auch, near Toulouse, found himself out of beefsteaks. Rather than disappoint the customer, he took a duck breast, scored the skin with a series of slashes of his knife, rubbed in coarse salt and black pepper and proceeded to treat it like a steak. One of the great dishes was born, and Daguin was rewarded with a Michelin rosette.

Bruno was not entirely convinced by this popular legend. Was he supposed to believe that the *magret* was simply discarded until the 1950s? The peasants of southwestern France were seldom rich enough to let the breasts go to waste. He knew that the *aiguillettes,* the long, thin strips of the tender and succulent meat beneath the breasts of the duck, were especially cherished by lovers of good food. To Bruno the idea that people who had been brought up eating the breasts of chicken would have ignored those of ducks defied belief. But it was true that it was easier to store several duck legs in a jar of confit where they would last for months and improve over time. Nonetheless, so widespread was the current popularity of the fashion for *magret de canard* that most local duck farmers usually had a surplus of legs, along with hearts and gizzards, for which Bruno was deeply grateful.

Every autumn he bought duck legs by the dozen, mixed some chopped bay leaves and thyme into sea salt, rubbed the result into the legs and then left the salted legs in a covered dish overnight. The next morning, in a deep pan, he would spoon in enough duck fat to cover all the legs he'd prepared and simmer them over low heat for two and a half hours. Once the legs and fat had cooled sufficiently, he would put as many legs into a sterilized jar as he could fit. Then he would strain the melted fat through a sieve to fill the jar, seal the jars and put them into a big pot of boiling water for thirty minutes to be fully sterilized. Finally, he placed them in a dark corner of his pantry until ready to be eaten.

Six people for dinner, and he, Alain, Rosalie and Pamela would certainly want two legs each, but Fabiola usually wanted only one and the baron's appetite was not what it had been.

That meant ten legs, or one of the larger jars. He had a kilo jar of petits pois in his pantry, and he went out to the garden to dig up a potato plant from the middle row, the one where he had grown fingerlings, the waxy ones just right for the meal he planned. There were other rows for the varieties like russets he would make into mashed potatoes and for the Yukon Golds he would use in stews. But he needed fingerlings to make the *pommes de terre sarladaises* along with a large bunch of fresh flat-leaf parsley and a fat head of garlic. He put these into his van and then made for the young white oaks he had planted on the advice of the baron more than a decade ago.

"Search, Balzac, search," he said, tapping at the ground near a tree that was usually good for an early truffle or two before Christmas. Balzac dutifully trotted up and sniffed eagerly around the oak but found nothing and moved on to the next. On the third tree, the basset hound began to paw at the ground, and Bruno eased him to one side and then used his trowel to dig down just a finger or two more than a hand's width and pulled out a small and knobbly black truffle, just perfect for the dish he planned. He brushed off the soil, congratulated his dog and then used his heel to press the earth back into place, and Balzac celebrated in his usual fashion by giving the tree a token watering.

The baron was bringing some of his own smoked trout to begin, and Pamela always had lemons from her cherished tree to go with the fish. She had also promised to make her special walnut tart for dessert, so Bruno took a bottle of his own *vin de noix* to go with it. The baron was also bringing some red wine, probably his favorite Pécharmant, and Bruno had a bottle of Château des Eyssards to accompany the fish. He would be interested to see what wine Alain would bring, since he was not very familiar with his cousin's tastes. Alain had spent almost all his adult life in the air force as an electronics technician, and it was only recently that he had taken retirement after twenty-five years of service. The two men had then resumed the friendship they had developed in childhood, when Bruno's aunt had realized that by taking Bruno from the orphanage and into her family she would qualify for the generous extra allowances reserved in France for a *famille nombreuse,* with four children or more under the same roof.

Alain and Rosalie, whom he had met when they were both serving in the air force, were embarked on new careers teaching construction skills in the local *collège.* They were neighbors of his friend and confidante Florence in the subsidized apartments that were attached to the *collège* to help attract teachers to work in rural areas. So many young people, whether doctors, dentists or even unskilled workers, were attracted to life in a big city, and cheap housing was one way to try and keep them in the countryside where they were desperately needed.

Bruno loaded his food, his wine and his dog into his venerable Land Rover and set off on the familiar route to the riding school. When he arrived, he was not surprised to find the stables empty. Pamela was a great believer in keeping the horses well exercised, morning and evening. Balzac sniffed his way around the empty stalls and then headed for the kennels where his friends the sheepdogs slept. Bruno left Balzac to his explorations, refilled the water casks and checked on the hay troughs in the horse stalls. He always left it to Pamela to decide how much alfalfa to add to the hay, but her older horses needed its extra protein. He knew she liked to have it ready, so he half filled a bucket with pressed alfalfa cubes and then added water for the cubes to soak themselves loose before letting himself into Pamela's kitchen, which he knew almost as well as his own.

He put his white wine in the fridge and began setting the table. He then turned on the radio, tuning it to the local station, France Bleu Périgord, for the evening news at six. He heard of more Russian threats against Ukraine, worries about rising gas prices, warnings of new troubles in the Middle East. It was one of those evenings when he wondered why it was called news when it was all depressingly familiar.

Bruno expected the others to arrive sometime around six-thirty for the usual *p'tit apéro,* with Fabiola joining them soon after the clinic closed. Pamela and Fabiola would have their usual gin and tonic, while he, Alain and the baron would enjoy one of Pamela's proud collection of single malt scotch whiskeys. Rosalie usually made a single glass of white wine last through dinner. Knowing his friends, Bruno figured they would want to hear about the drama with Xavier and his wife, but Bruno was particularly interested to hear what more Fabiola could tell him about Monique.

Pamela had also been in the Pilates class and might know more. She and Fabiola may even have met Ghislaine, an intriguing woman. Bruno shrugged. The matter was effectively out of his hands, a question of inheritance for the magistrates and lawyers of Sarlat to sort out with Dominic, Laura and the other members of the company Monique had founded. To be honest, Bruno was less interested in the dead Monique than in the very much alive Laura, and for her own appeal rather than because of her delightful basset. She was attractive, interesting, radiated good health, read books and Bruno grinned to himself as he thought how much he had enjoyed her sense of humor.

He was struck by the thought that once again he found himself attracted to a woman from the British Isles, like Pamela, his former lover and dearest friend, although Laura was British only on her mother's side. Should matters proceed happily with Laura, Bruno considered, he would need to be not just honest with Pamela but also kind. Despite his occasional passionate reunion with Isabelle, he was not the kind of man to be comfortable seeing two women at once. And Pamela deserved no less. She had broken off their affair once before because, she had said, while she enjoyed their liaison there was no future in it, and she had firmly said that she would rather have Bruno as a lifelong friend than as a temporary lover. She had no intention of living permanently with any man ever again. Besides, she insisted she was too old to have children, even if she wanted to. And she very firmly did not, while Bruno did.

Bruno, who had long since come to terms with the fact that he was a hopeless optimist where affairs of the heart were concerned, had never taken her remarks entirely at face value. Words had many meanings, he had learned, and whatever might be wholly true today might evolve to allow for different circumstances tomorrow. His next encounter with Laura might be an unintended disaster, leaving not just Bruno but even Balzac in the lurch. He certainly hoped not, so much that he was startled by how much he was looking forward to seeing Laura again.

Bruno pondered this, wondering at the workings of his subconscious mind, and suddenly the reality struck him. The discovery that morning of Monique's suicide, and of her letter describing her pain at the thought of never being able to give birth to a child and become a mother, was the trigger. Bruno, too, had read the studies demonstrating that male fertility also declines in midlife. There was less and less time ahead for him to be a father who could raise his own healthy children and see them into adulthood and hope to have enough time to witness the arrival of their children.

Any children that he might have would still be teenagers, probably still in school, when he reached the usual retirement age of sixty. Time for Bruno no longer stretched unendingly ahead as it once had. If he was to be a father, he should not delay in seeking out a wife, a potential mother and partner for the remainder of his days. Monique's letter, he thought, had come as a warning to him. A warning, yes, but it was also, he told himself, an encouragement, a reminder that for him, too, time would be running out.

At that precise moment, the wall clock gave a pronounced click as the big hand reached six-thirty, and Bruno turned his thoughts to the timing of the meal. Fabiola would want to wind down with a drink after a day at the clinic, so they would probably not start to eat until seven-thirty at the earliest. That meant that he should time his duck legs to be ready soon after eight, so he could start both duck and potatoes at seven-thirty.

Bruno heard the sound of hooves outside and went out to help Pamela lead the horses into the stables, to take off her saddle and all the bridles and help prepare the evening feed. Balzac had trotted out to greet the returning horses and stayed close to his big friend Hector, who bent his head down to nuzzle the dog and then lifted it to repeat the gesture against Bruno as Bruno slipped a blanket over his horse's back.

"A good ride. They're a well-behaved lot, gave me no trouble," Pamela said, "What dreadful crime kept you?"

Bruno explained about Xavier's behavior, the visit to the confessional of Father Sentout and the flowers.

"And this marital guidance is part of your regular duties as a police officer and guardian of the peace?" she asked, her raised eyebrow audible in her voice.

"Not really, but I've known Mirabelle since she was a girl, and she has those lovely kids."

"I assume the mayor took you to lunch and suggested that you take care of the problem in your inimitable way, as he so often does when things are tricky," Pamela said. "I like the old man, but he's always careful to keep his nose clean while steering you into the firing line."

"That's not fair," Bruno said. "Xavier may not be a close friend, but he's a colleague and part of the team."

"Ah, yes, I forget; that old saying about taking one for the team," Pamela said with a sniff. She was standing in the doorway of the stables, hands on her hips and looking angry. "Funny that it's always you who takes the blame. And the bullets. I hope you don't think that Xavier is going to be in any way grateful to you."

"I don't expect gratitude," Bruno replied.

"You saved his marriage, but you made him look like a fool. You may have managed to reverse most of the humiliation that Xavier's wife was feeling after being publicly betrayed, although I can't say I'm at all confident there. Worse, you made the bastard take his humiliation in public. I could say quite rightly, too, but right isn't always wise. Xavier will never forgive you for that, mark my words."

"You're exaggerating," Bruno said, and gave her a fond peck on the cheek as he steered her across the stable yard toward the house. "And there's *confit de canard* to look forward to, and I can tell you about Monique Duhamel, a brilliant businesswoman who committed suicide near here last night, just this side of St. Cirq. You might know her from Pilates. She was one of Fabiola's patients."

"Indeed I did know Monique through Pilates, and I liked her, but I can't say I thought much of the oily little creep she was married to. None of us ever understood what she saw in him. She'd have been better off with one of those suntanned young gardeners she hired." Pamela's chuckle was more lascivious than Bruno had known she was capable of.

He laughed and held the kitchen door open for her, saying that the Pilates class seemed to have taken the place of the old communal wash trough by the river as the gathering spot for the women of the town, and adding that the baron should arrive soon.

Bruno saw with relief that Alain and Rosalie were driving

into the courtyard, with the baron's stately old Citroën following behind. Greetings and embraces were exchanged, wine bottles placed on the kitchen table, and the baron said he'd heard only a secondhand account of Xavier's confession and asked for a full version from Bruno, which Pamela kept interrupting with mocking comments. Rosalie declared that Xavier had got off far too lightly. Alain opened the bottle he'd brought, a sparkling wine from the town vineyard, and began pouring everyone a glass that became a deep purple kir with the addition of crème de cassis.

Bruno gave a short and only slightly self-aggrandizing account of Xavier's confession, the flowers and the apology, the way that Mirabelle's honor was publicly restored with all due dignity and how Father Sentout had done his duty with aplomb. And at that point, the baron echoed a remark that Pamela had made earlier.

"Xavier will come to blame you, Bruno, rather than thank you, and he'll never forgive you for that public blow to his dignity. I've known that young man since he was born, and there's always been something sly about him, something you know but can't quite put your finger on. That's how he seemed to me, anyway. At least he's no longer in line to be our next mayor. Not a woman in St. Denis will vote for him, not his wife nor his sister, and I'm not even sure about his mother."

"You sound very certain about that," said Rosalie.

"I've lived here a long time, seen all the changes, the women going out to work rather than staying home on the farm," the baron said. "They are all much more sure of themselves and their right to their own opinions these days."

"About time, too," said Pamela.

"Couldn't agree more," said the baron, and headlights flashed across the yard as Fabiola drove in. Moments later, a glass in her hand and her eyes fixed on Bruno, she said, "Tell me exactly what happened between you and Xavier and Father Sentout. But first, what happened to that empty container of zolpidem that Monique took?"

"I gave it to Annette at the magistrature, along with Monique's phone, her handbag and the envelopes she had prepared," Bruno said. "But the jar was empty."

"So we don't know if zolpidem was really what that bottle contained?"

Chapter 9

It was market day in St. Denis, and a few minutes before eight Bruno, fresh from his morning run and a shower, parked his police van in the yard of the gendarmerie, put the leash onto Balzac and began his usual patrol. He greeted the stallholders and the early customers with a handshake or a friendly embrace and tried—largely unsuccessfully—to stop them all from giving his dog a second breakfast. He began by making the circuit of the old parade ground in front of the gendarmerie, now a large parking lot except on market days, where there were Christmas decorations on sale alongside stalls of wood carvings, leather goods and secondhand clothes. Then he strolled up the rue de Paris, greeting the stallholders on each side of the street. There were stalls whose vendors were selling herbs next door to stalls with racks of T-shirts and cheap sweaters, followed by the ones he could never understand, where different kinds of holders or cases for mobile phones were on offer. Then came the specialty stalls selling fancy soaps and artisanal honeys, the *saucissons* and the jars of pâté. Bruno had a soft spot for the man selling what he called his "homemade organic loudspeaker." This was a hollow stretch of wood into which a groove had been carved for a mobile phone to be inserted, which somehow amplified the sound to produce surprisingly loud music. Then came other novelties, a magic new formula for cleaning the burn marks from old pots and pans, or making the blackened and ancient cooking utensils that had been inherited from Grandma look clean and new again.

Just after the stall where secondhand books were sold stood the church. The doors were open, and surprisingly loud voices were singing within, which was odd. This was not a Sunday. On market days there were usually only three or four people at early Mass, and that should have ended by now: the stallholders, however devout, were not to be separated from their wares once the customers began to come.

Bruno paused and then looked in, surprised to see the church about one-third full, at least twenty or more people, almost all women from what he could see, singing *"C'est un rempart que notre Dieu . . ."* It was a hymn he half recalled from his orphanage. He spotted Xavier standing beside Mirabelle, a very public statement that the family was together again.

Bruno walked past a hardware stall where a street vendor was trying to sell some new wondrous way of making your age-darkened floor tiles glisten like new. Then he walked on briskly past Ivan's restaurant to the junction and headed across to Fauquet's café behind the *mairie,* where Fauquet nodded a greeting and put a coffee and a croissant on the counter for Bruno before turning back to his conversation with the rest of the bar about the massive collapse of a cliff wall onto a busy road near Excideuil and the almost miraculous fact that nobody had been hurt. A photograph of the rockfall was on the cover of *Sud Ouest,* and Bruno skimmed the story until Balzac gave a little bark of delight.

Bruno turned to see Balzac's daughter, a lovely young basset hound named Gabrielle d'Estrées, come from a table at the back of the café with her owner, Captain Yveline of the gendarmes. Gabrielle, named for a mistress of Bruno's favorite French king, Henri IV, bounded up to her father and rubbed her face against his neck, and Balzac then responded in the same way.

Yveline presented her cheeks to Bruno for the usual *bise* between friends, guided him to an empty table in the corner, out of earshot of the bar, and then said, "I just realized that our greeting is almost like theirs. Do you think we got it from the dogs, or did they learn it from us?"

"Given that they had to learn to do it without having lips to kiss with, I suspect they must have learned it from us," said Bruno. "The test would be to see if English dogs do it, since their masters and mistresses shake hands rather than give the *bise,* although Pamela tells me the English are increasingly adopting our custom."

"I don't think English dogs shake paws when they meet," said Yveline. "Nor do I think humans sniff each other's bottoms when they meet, so I'm not at all sure about your theory of dogs learning from humans and vice versa. Putting that to one side, I didn't know you'd become a recruiting sergeant for Father Sentout until I started getting phone calls about it. And you know Xavier was dragged into the church service this morning. That's one for the books."

"It won't do him any harm," said Bruno. "But I suspect it may not do him much good, either."

"The real question on everyone's lips, however, is not whether Xavier's marriage lasts, but who will take his place as the mayor's chosen successor," Yveline said, with a grin that on any other young woman Bruno might have described as impish. "Bets are being taken, which is why everyone at the bar started talking about the rockfall when you turned up." Yveline paused meaningfully. "Guess who is the current favorite."

"Oh, no," said Bruno as he grasped her meaning. "Not a

chance, it wouldn't be legal. You can't be an employee of the *mairie* as a *policier municipal* and be mayor, too."

"So, resign as a cop. Then run for mayor."

"Remember that I wasn't born here, I didn't go to school here, so I didn't grow up knowing everybody. I don't have a large extended family to vote for me—even if I wanted the job, which I don't, or if I thought I could do the job decently, which I also doubt."

"Spoken like a true candidate," she said, grinning widely. "Maybe I should take a flier on you. Sergeant Jules is handling the bets, and he has you at even money."

"That's illegal," said Bruno, with a bark of laughter. "You ought to lock him up, set an example."

"I can't. The general in Périgueux and two senior cops asked me to keep an eye on the odds for them."

"Are you serious?" Bruno asked, his face going suddenly solemn as he realized she wasn't joking. "This is crazy."

"I don't know how you intend to stop it, but you'll have an uphill struggle with all the rumors out there. People saying you saved Mirabelle's face in that way to make sure of the women's vote, though I think you had their vote when you got the mayor to create that big event to commemorate those young German girls in that wartime grave."

"I didn't get the mayor to do anything," he protested. "If you think that I could, you don't know the mayor."

"I hear you, but when the florist says you were behind it, and Father Sentout says you planned the whole thing—the choir, the service, the bugle call for the dead."

"They're exaggerating," Bruno protested.

"We all know that was you, Bruno, and all credit to the mayor for listening to you."

"But the mayor is going to run again," Bruno said. "I know he was in the dumps when his wife died, but then he took up with Jacqueline and she's taken years off him, years and a good five kilos. He's a happy man again, full of bounce, but with all his old contacts and cunning. He's the best mayor St. Denis could hope to have."

"Okay, so you can have five or six more years as chief of police, he steps down and you're still in your forties and you run as his candidate. You'd be elected in a breeze. I'm not even sure anybody would bother to run against you."

"But I don't have any party affiliation," he protested.

"All the better, Bruno. And since you're not known to be on the left or on the right you don't have any political enemies. And you taught all their kids to play rugby and tennis, you hunt with their dads, and you helped their moms across the road and danced with all the grandmothers at the Christmas parties. Most of what I know about policing I learned from you. And most of what you need to know about politics you've already learned from the mayor."

She sat back and then grinned. "Enough of that. What's this I hear from my spies in Sarlat about a new lady friend?"

Bruno almost gulped in surprise, not only at the sudden switch of topic but at Yveline's knowledge of his interest in Laura. Then he saw that she was looking down with affection at Balzac and Gabrielle lying comfortably intertwined, so perhaps she meant something to do with the dogs.

"You mean the most lovely young basset I've ever seen? You know she's named for George Sand, Chopin's lover? It would be wonderful to see the puppies she and Balzac could make together."

Yveline raised her eyebrows and gave a quietly enigmatic smile, and Bruno was left uncertain whether his ploy had succeeded or whether he was being gently mocked for a clumsy attempt to mislead. Yveline was another member of the Pilates group, so must know Laura.

"Time for another patrol," he said, putting some coins on the table. "Do you want to join me, or are you heading back to the gendarmerie?"

"I have a couple of errands to run," she said. "Just wondered whether you might be free to come around for dinner later this week. I've been feeling guilty, dining at your house so often. Is Thursday evening good for you?"

"That would be a pleasure, and since you're always so generous with the wine you bring—"

"Please don't bring anything," she said, interrupting him. "I'd like to surprise you."

"*Ça va,* Yveline. *A bientôt.*" He rose, nodded and headed out to stroll through the columns that supported the *mairie* and created a dozen or so places where the market stalls could be sheltered from rain. Custom decreed that they were reserved for local stallholders, usually women selling plants or homemade dishes. He greeted them each by name and trotted down the steps and along the quay and riverbank until he came to the old water mill, where the small river Douch ran into the Vézère. He climbed up the slope and crossed the road by the fire station, recalling the long night of the flood and the death of the two Americans in the front seats of the car that was swept away by the rushing river. Bruno and other volunteers had been able to save the mother and child in the rear seats. There was barely any sign left of the angry waters, but Bruno knew he would never again underestimate the river's power.

He mounted the narrow wooden bridge over the stream, then walked past the side of the church, now empty, and along the rows of market stalls, the crowds thinning after the morning rush. This time he entered the *mairie* and took the stairs up to his old office where Colette Cantagnac, who had made herself indispensable to the mayor, the staff employees' union and to Bruno, now ruled. She also did all of Bruno's paperwork, took perfect messages and dealt efficiently with minor matters, which meant that Bruno no longer felt the need for a physical office with desk and chair and filing cabinet. To a degree he never would have thought possible, she had liberated him to the point that his mobile phone had now become his office. If any emergency arose, she could text him.

"Bonjour, Colette," he said, giving her the *bise* on each cheek as she rose. "I got your message. What can I do for you?"

"You have some papers to sign in the mayor's office," she said. "It's about what you are to be paid for those occasions when you were seconded to the spooks." What she meant was that Bruno had on several occasions been seconded to the new internal security department, which was answerable to the Ministry of the Interior, and where Bruno came under the orders of General Lannes. As a veteran bureaucrat and elected official of the staff association of *mairie* employees, Colette had been looking into the long-ignored question of Bruno's pay during these assignments. Bruno had always assumed it was simply his obligation as a member of the army reserves. The mayor believed that the town's budget should reclaim Bruno's pay for those periods, and the interior ministry should recompense him appropriately.

This was where Colette's genius for official rules and regulations came into play. She learned that on such deployments, Bruno should be paid not his town police salary but his salary as chief of police for the Vézère Valley. That rank was recognized by French army bureaucracy as being the equivalent of a captain in the French army, but by the French police bureaucracy as the equivalent of a *commissaire*. And a police *commissaire* was recognized as the equivalent of an army major. That was one problem, which Colette resolved by saying that Bruno's years of military service made him the equivalent of a very long-serving captain, whose pay was almost that of a new major. The second problem was that to give Bruno his back pay all at once would thrust him into a costly new tax bracket.

Colette's solution was that Bruno would be compensated at his usual police pay and the difference would be paid not to him but to the town of St. Denis. The money would be used to finance the construction of a new tasting room for the town vineyard, and Bruno would be suitably compensated with shares in the vineyard, which in these early years was making no profits and thus there was no tax to pay. By the time it was making profits, Bruno would probably be retired and paying taxes at a much lower rate. The tasting room would be built by Bruno's cousin Alain, who would lead a learning-by-doing project of the construction class he taught at the local *collège*. Bruno's windfall would pay for it all.

"I'm not sure I wholly understand all this," Bruno said once inside the mayor's office. "I presume I get some formal document saying that all this is legal."

"The agreement is authorized and signed by the Ministry of the Interior and by the Cour des Comptes, France's senior financial court, and by me for the town council and the vineyard," said the mayor, handing Bruno a very formal-looking document and a share certificate. "I believe future historians will marvel at the bureaucratic genius displayed by Mademoiselle Cantagnac in devising this elegant solution."

"How much would it have been in cash, had that been legal?" Bruno asked.

"Over thirty thousand euros, which would have put you into a higher tax bracket, so you'd lose half of it," said Colette. "I'm also applying for an ex gratia bonus for you for being shot in the shoulder while on duty, but that's still under negotiation."

"Well, thank you, both of you, and to General Lannes and the Cour des Comptes," said Bruno.

"Might I have the share certificate back, please?" the mayor asked.

Bruno complied but asked why.

"We're improving your tax situation again," said Cantagnac. "You are making a cost-free loan of these shares to the board of the town vineyard, until such time as you retire from current employment and your tax status changes."

"So I don't get anything until I retire?" Bruno asked.

"As a member of the tasting committee you are entitled to a considerable number of bottles every year," the mayor added.

"But I'm already a member of the tasting committee," Bruno replied.

"You must learn, my dear Bruno, not to get too bogged down in details," said the mayor. "Isn't it time for another patrol of the market?"

Chapter 10

The market folk knew that they were meant to start closing up soon after the *mairie* clock struck noon and that they were to leave their spot tidy and ensure that all discarded wrapping papers and litter had been cleared. On his last patrol of the market that day, Bruno had just reached the church when his phone rang; the name on the screen was not immediately familiar, but he knew the voice. It was Sabine, in Strasbourg, Dominic's foster sister to whom he'd spoken the previous morning.

"Dominic asked me to let you know he left this morning soon after nine and he should be in the Périgord by six or so this evening. He'd be grateful if you could come to his office and let him know what's going on," she said. "I've emailed you the address and phone number."

"Thanks for the call, but the matter is out of my hands," Bruno said. "I handed all the paperwork, including a letter from Monique to Dominic, to the Sarlat magistrate, Annette Meraillon, and we expect a formal verdict of suicide in the next day or so, which will permit the funeral to go ahead on Friday or the weekend, as your brother prefers." He softened his tone. "I hope the funeral of your foster father went off smoothly. I realize it must be tough on Dominic, two funerals in the same week."

"I'm not sure Dominic reacts to things in the usual way that most people do," Sabine said after a short pause. "He never did, really. I think those early years of being bullied in the orphanage had a big impact on him. I always thought he was a bit odd, and you've probably heard the same from other people by now."

Intrigued, Bruno continued the conversation, "No, I heard nothing about weird behavior, just that Dominic was a private person, not too demonstrative, not many friends. But since he has a cast-iron alibi of being in Strasbourg when Monique died, and we're reasonably sure it was a suicide, we're not looking to question him. But I'm grateful for your help. Are you coming down for the funeral?"

"I never met this wife, and I'm pretty sure he won't invite me to her funeral. He and I have never really got on," she said. "I suspect he came up here only for the reading of the will, to see what was in it for him."

"And was there anything in it for him?" Bruno asked, intrigued less by what he was hearing than by the acid tone in her voice.

"Not a centime. Everything went to the widow, and she can't stand the sight of Dominic."

"You don't sound too fond of him, either," said Bruno. "But it's not easy, spending your formative years in an orphanage."

"Don't I know it," Sabine replied. "I spent the first five years of my life in one before I was put into foster care."

"Me too, the first seven years," said Bruno, feeling a spark of sympathy. "Then my aunt found out that she could get extra money if she took me in."

"Lucky you," she said, with a bitter chuckle. "And I was lucky, getting fostered by the d'Ensingens, but it didn't work so well with Dominic. Anyway, please keep me informed of developments, because Dominic certainly won't."

She ended the call, and Bruno stood looking uncertainly at the phone in his hand, but he saved the number, and quickening his step he headed for the gendarmerie, recalling that with Xavier's problem he had not thoroughly searched Monique's car the previous day. He stopped at the front desk to get the keys from Sergeant Jules, who asked if Bruno had been told of Father Sentout's special service that morning.

"No, but I walked past as it was going on. Was your wife there?"

"Yes, and before she left she said she wouldn't trust Xavier's word as far as she could throw him."

Bruno considered this, then said, "And your wife, Jules, is strong enough to hurl Xavier a long way."

"The farther the better, if you ask me. I never did like him, always stuck up because his daddy was the big car dealer. He never shared much with the other kids in kindergarten. I hope the marriage lasts for the kids' sake, but I don't think it will be a happy one. He's just never satisfied."

"We'll see," said Bruno, making his voice sound more neutral than he felt. And he took the keys from Sergeant Jules, put on a pair of evidence gloves and went off to search Monique's Peugeot.

Bruno unlocked and opened all the doors and the trunk of the car, which still smelled faintly of the death with a hint of tobacco smoke. He remembered the gendarme lighting a cigarette before driving off. The officer in question should be informed that his habit was beginning to impinge on good police work. Bruno began by lifting the floor mats, front and rear, and those from the trunk. He then bent down and peered beneath the front seats, checked the door pockets and opened the glove compartment to find the usual car litter of maps, tourist brochures, tissues, a plastic rain hood and a pair of gloves.

In the driver's door pocket he found a small notebook that recorded the date of every trip to the garage, the amount and cost of fuel bought and the mileage. Most people claiming tax deductions on travel expenses used a similar system. The car had been refueled the previous week with sixty-two liters of gas at a cost of one hundred euros, and the entry noted 10,254 kilometers on the odometer. There were now 10,330 kilometers, but the fuel level was much less than a quarter full. It would not take most of a tank to drive the car fewer than 80 kilometers. It was barely 30 kilometers from Sarlat to the place where Monique took her own life.

There was some cigarette ash on the floor by the clutch pedal, and smears of ash on the external door panel. Monique, he thought, had not been a smoker. Just to be sure, he called Annette, who was having a sandwich at her desk. Had Monique been a smoker, Bruno asked. Never, was Annette's reply. That meant it could only have been the gendarme who drove it back here. Bruno turned on the radio and found a raucous rock station, which again did not sound like Monique.

Bruno ran his fingers along the slides that moved the front seats forward and back and pulled out a half-crushed blister pack of the kind used for prescription medication. There was one pill in it. He put it in an evidence bag, sealed, signed and dated it, and went into the gendarmerie to get Jules to witness the find and to confirm who the gendarme was who had probably smoked while he drove the car back. Could he also check that the guy had used the radio, and could Jules kindly arrange a fingerprint check on the radio buttons? Above all, did Jules think the new gendarme was the kind of guy who would siphon out fuel from a car that was being investigated?

"There is less than a quarter of a tank left and it was filled last week," Bruno said. "The amount of gas bought and the costs and date are in a notebook in the door panel. It looks fishy to me, as if somebody was siphoning off the gas. And the gendarme you had with you, the one who drove it away, did not wear gloves, left his fingerprints all over the place, smoked in the car, left ash everywhere and changed radio channels, so we can't identify any other possible fingerprints on the controls. I don't care how new he is on the job, but that's unacceptable. I'll leave it in your hands."

Sergeant Jules grunted something indecipherable, and Bruno clapped him on the shoulder and left a receipt with the number of the evidence bag. Then he stepped out to the square and called Annette, told her about the blister pack and pill he'd found and suggested he bring it to her for analysis. And when should he expect to see the result of Fabiola's request for a postmortem to check the drugs in the body?

"I'll call the lab and see if we can get a result by the time you get here, or we could meet at the lab if you like," Annette replied. "You sound a bit concerned about this, Bruno."

"I just want to be sure that the pill I found in the car came from the same batch as the ones we think Monique took for her suicide," he said. "Or at least that we can identify it as something prescribed by her doctor."

"Fine, bring it in. I'm working in my office all day," she said, and ended the call. Bruno put his phone away, and at that moment a familiar voice said hesitantly, "Bruno?" He turned to see Yveline, in uniform and looking flustered, which was not at all like her. She gave him a grim smile, saying, "I'd like to talk to you, but not here. There are things I think you need to know about this new gendarme, Villon."

She led him down toward the cemetery and along the path that led to the Domaine de la Barde, now being restored by its new owners, and spoke quietly as if careful not to be overheard.

"The young gendarme who drove Monique's car back here is named Roland Villon and he's a real problem," she began. "I was asked to take him on by an old boss, who said the guy needed careful watching, which would be easier in a small unit like mine. So far we've had two women complaining of indecent assaults during a routine stop, and they complained not to me but to the Police Nationale, so your friend J-J is looking into it. There's also talk of drivers being shaken down for cash to let them off from taking a Breathalyzer test. Now Jules tells me you think he was siphoning gas and may have screwed up attempts to get fingerprints from the victim's car."

"So question him about the gas theft and put a note in his file about smoking in a way that could contaminate evidence," Bruno said firmly. "Get a swab done on his hands for the gasoline. If you find any in his quarters or anything else suspicious, suspend him, and I can arrest him. In the meantime, I'll ask J-J about his inquiry into the indecent assaults and if he wants me to arrange a lineup for the women. Villon wouldn't have been alone on the Breathalyzer patrol. Who was his partner? Do you suspect him or her?"

"That's part of the problem. There are only three people who might have been with him—Jean-Luc, François and Claire Castignac, whom I don't even begin to suspect. She's made it clear that she can't stand him."

"Between Jean-Luc and François, what do your instincts say?"

"These are colleagues, Bruno. I can't work on instincts. I was wondering if you had heard any gossip about it."

"Not yet, but I can make discreet inquiries. We can leave that for the minute," Bruno said. "It seems to me that you may have a bad apple in Roland, but we need to be completely sure. If you like, I can get the Sarlat magistrates to send you a formal complaint about his careless treatment of a potentially suspicious car."

"Talk to J-J first—I need to know what he's planning to do. To be honest, Bruno, I'm in a real bind. Villon is the nephew of a very powerful general at headquarters in Paris, which is why my old boss handled him with kid gloves and warned me to do the same. One or two of the others are a bit intimidated by him. I'm starting to worry about this infecting the whole team."

"A bent cop is bad for everybody," Bruno said. "I'll see what J-J says. If Villon's uncle has real influence, then J-J is likely to handle things himself, which may help. If you're going to discuss this with me again, only do it in person or get yourself a phone that can't be traced to you. Just in case."

"*Merde,* Bruno. We're supposed to be the good guys, and now we have to sneak around like this."

"You have your career to think of. Get that swab done and do the search, and I'll talk to J-J. And let's walk back separately. I'll stop by and say hello to Monsieur Birch, if he's there."

Ten minutes later, Bruno was shaking hands with the red-haired Englishman who had bought the run-down property from the bankruptcy court and who was now taking photographs of windows, doorsteps and other details of the old *domaine,* still a handsome building after many years of neglect.

"Anna and I couldn't hope for a better Christmas present than for the purchase finally to go through," Tim said. "The mayor must really have pushed things ahead at lightning speed."

"After your volunteer work on the night of the flood, you shouldn't be surprised," Bruno replied. "And you have a lot of work ahead of you, so if I can help in recommending good craftspeople, just let me know. Do you have babysitters? I was hoping to get you over for dinner one evening, and we can probably get one of the schoolgirls to watch your boy, or he could stay over with some of the other kids. Just check with your wife when would be a good evening for you both."

"That would be great," Tim said, and Bruno walked on past what would one day be the Birch family's tennis court, then called J-J's cell phone.

"I thought I might be hearing from you, or from Yveline," replied J-J, who held the rank of *commissaire* as chief of detectives for the *département*. He and Bruno were old friends and trusted each other.

"There were no independent witnesses," J-J said. "But since one of the young women making the complaint is secretary to the diocesan council and bishop, and the other is on the staff of the executive council for the Dordogne, their testimony carries a lot of weight. Each of them picked out the photograph of the gendarme we are planning to arrest once the formalities are concluded."

The formalities were what worried Bruno. Neither the gendarmes nor the Police Nationale wanted a public battle. There had been too many cases of what had been known as "the wars between the police" in the past, and nobody wanted to return to those days. Prunier, head of the Police Nationale in the region, would need a great deal of diplomacy in dealing with one of the gendarmes' top generals in Paris about the fate of his nephew, Roland. The general would probably seek a deal under which Roland would quietly resign without fuss, or shift across to the military and be posted overseas. Prunier, on the other hand, would be under pressure from female cops and from the politicians to prove that sexual harassment was treated as a serious crime.

Under French law, however, it would not be up to the police but the *procureur de la République,* the public prosecutor, to press charges. Prunier might seek to hand the matter over to the gendarmes to deal with internally. That was how such difficult disputes had often been handled in the past, but Bruno could imagine the public outcry if Prunier tried such a ploy these days. The media would crucify him; the female lobby would see to that. Bruno pondered what he would do in Prunier's shoes and concluded he'd have no choice but to let the prosecution go ahead. In court, the testimony of the second cop who had been on patrol alongside Roland would be crucial, Bruno thought. In that context, perhaps, he might even be useful.

"Have you been able to interview the two gendarmes yet?" Bruno asked.

"That's what Prunier is discussing with the gendarmes," J-J said. "Prunier has my report, which says there is a serious case from two reliable women, and I have asked to haul in and detain the two gendarmes for questioning under *garde à vue,* holding them overnight with the expectation that the prosecutor will file charges."

"Is Commissaire Gouppilleau involved?" Bruno asked, referring to the senior female officer on the Police Nationale in Périgueux, a woman he had worked with before and admired.

"She interviewed each of the women and took their separate statements, and she made it very clear to me and to Prunier that she demands and firmly expects a prosecution," J-J said. "In fact, what she told me was that she would see that bastard hauled into court even if she had to go into the gendarmerie and drag him out herself."

"Sounds just like her," said Bruno, not bothering to conceal the admiration in his voice for a senior officer who nonetheless had her uniforms carefully tailored and wore spectacularly fashionable shoes around all the police stations. Only out on the streets was her footwear ever the usual functional and unisex black. Bruno let the silence build before asking, "So how do you think this plays out?"

"It's between his career and trying to play nice with the gendarmes," J-J said. "Prunier will move to cover his own ass, as our American friends might put it, and make it clear he expects the *procureur* to press charges, which is also the right thing to do and what every woman cop on the force expects him to do. My job will be to leak, very carefully, that my boss knows that he has done the decent thing, with great regrets about the implications of this for his dear friends and colleagues in the gendarmes. But the interests of the law and public have to come first."

J-J paused. "If you should happen to run into Philippe Delaron of *Sud Ouest,* or one of those women you know on the radio at France Bleu, it might be useful to let them know what I've just told you, from a source close to Prunier."

"Understood," said Bruno. "I'm just wondering how many other women these two bastards harassed or, worse, women without the contacts or credentials to get taken seriously when they file a complaint."

"I'm ahead of you, Bruno. I've already sent a policewoman to go around to the local massage parlors, and I'm awaiting her report. Gabrielle Teyssier, our cyber-tech, is trying to infiltrate some of the online message boards sex workers use to warn one another of dangerous clients, but she hasn't yet found a way in. I'll appreciate any help you can give us in our various lines of inquiry."

Chapter 11

As soon as Bruno ended the call his phone vibrated again. This time it was Sergeant Jules, using his own phone. The message read: "My shift's over. Meet me behind the bank. No helmet, civilian jacket."

This was unusual, but Bruno had great faith in Jules, so stuffed his képi in a pocket, slipped on a civilian waterproof jacket and strolled across the bridge and behind the bank, where Jules sat waiting, his engine running. As soon as Bruno climbed into the passenger seat, Jules took off through the trailer park and then took the road up the hill to Audrix, down to Campagne and heading back toward St. Denis.

"A bit cloak-and-dagger, Jules," said Bruno.

"The new gendarmerie is behind schedule, but because they are merging St. Cyprien with us and extending our territory down south of Belvès, they already boosted our numbers, with three new gendarmes who needed somewhere to live," Jules explained. "We rented a house for them down behind the bus station, one of the places that nearly got flooded. The three new guys each have a room and share a kitchen and a big yard where Jean-Luc and François keep their bikes, and the bastard with a general in his family has a snazzy little sports car."

"I can see why he likes the idea of free gasoline," said Bruno.

"Yveline asked me to find a way to check his hands for traces, but we'd have to launch a formal inquiry for that, so I thought we'd just take a little stroll and see if we run into any nosy neighbors."

"Do you know who owns the place?" Bruno asked.

"My wife's cousin," Jules replied. "His wife will meet us there. Our three young gendarmes are on a familiarization tour around St. Cyprien, now that their gendarmerie is being closed and their staff is coming to merge with us. So they won't disturb us."

Natalie was built on the same heroic proportions as Jules and his wife, and her lips were clenched grimly together and her forearms bulged as she stood with meaty hands on even meatier hips glaring in cold anger at the mess of her kitchen made by three young bachelors without any adult supervision.

"I want them out," she snapped at Jules. "I don't care how much rent the gendarmerie is paying, I won't have my place turned into a pigsty. Immaculate, it was, when they moved in. Immaculate."

Bruno had seen worse, but not often, usually after an artillery barrage. The sink and draining boards were piled high with dirty dishes, and the floor needed scraping as well as scrubbing. The stove looked as though human sacrifices had been recently performed, and mouse droppings were everywhere. The windows had never been opened nor washed, and there was a general smell of rustic rot that made Bruno think Natalie had been admirably precise when she had referred to a pigsty. After a quick glance around, he backed out of the kitchen and went into the old barn. It had traditionally been used to dry leaves of tobacco, but the three men used it as a garage. There were two racing bikes leaning against one wall, one ancient moped and a rusty Mazda Miata with its hood up, presumably belonging to Roland.

What caught Bruno's eye, however, were the three battered metal jerricans that looked as if they might have seen service in World War II. Each could contain twenty liters of fuel, and Bruno remembered that until 1943, when the Allies had learned to copy this German invention, these robust and reliable cans had helped explain the superiority of German logistics in the war's first years. The French, British and Russians had lost too many tanks and trucks to lack of fuel because they didn't have this kind of almost indestructible can. The Americans, however, briskly copied the German product and made nineteen million of them by 1945. Bruno had two at home, one containing diesel and the other regular gas, just in case, so he had a good idea where Roland had probably obtained them. He tapped each of the cans with a knuckle. Each one was full to the brim. Better still, each carried a chalk mark he recognized.

"Sorry and regrets, madame," he said to Natalie. "We won't let these idiots get away with this. But now we're needed elsewhere."

Leaving an aghast Natalie frowning grimly behind them, Bruno directed Jules toward the small industrial park of St. Denis, alongside the railway line on the north–south route from Périgueux to Agen, with connections to Paris, Marseille and Italy. There were lumberyards; companies making and maintaining swimming pools; warehouses for sewage pipes, tree trimmers, vineyard vats and a lot more and small factories making doors, windows and prefabricated garages. It was also home to the splendid new *déchetterie,* a state-of-the-art refuse-and-recycling center, a pioneering venture in this part of France whose presence was a tribute to the mayor's political skills. There were special containers for paper and cardboard, for all forms of glass, for metal cans and for what few forms of organic refuse were not given to the chickens, ducks, goats and livestock kept by many of the inhabitants. Bruno was entirely typical of his neighbors in this regard. Whatever food he did not eat, his dog would devour. And if his dog rejected it, his chickens would certainly enjoy it. He had even seen some of his neighbors feed chicken scraps to their chickens, something that discomfited him on a philosophical level.

Bruno's objective, however, lay just a little farther along this road, so he asked Jules to stop the car and wait. Bruno walked on to a vast site that was identified by a massive sign announcing the arrival of LES RÉCUPÉRATEURS. Cynics might suggest that this was only a fancy new name for the town's traditional junkyard. But the squad of young volunteers who ran the place were convinced that they were the beating heart of the recycling revolution that would save the planet from its wasteful ways.

In front were ancient bicycles and bidets, lawn mowers and loungers, winepresses and an elderly table around which the volunteers sat on a variety of chairs drinking endless cups of coffee or mint tea. The great warehouse inside contained used clothes for men, women, children and babies; furniture both ancient and modern; light fittings, crockery, cookware and kitchen utensils. The walls were covered with prints and paintings, many of them homemade. There were antique stereo systems, tape recorders, ancient desktop computers, video players and vast collections of VHS tapes.

Bruno made a point of stopping by every two weeks or so, enjoying some herbal tea and gossip with the volunteers. He enjoyed their camaraderie, their easygoing company and their common conviction that they were doing their bit to save the planet. Before leaving, he would always browse the large book section to see if there was anything that caught his interest, including the occasional book in English that was not too difficult for him to read. He had learned that one of the best ways to improve his English was to pick up English-language versions of the comic books of Astérix the Gaul and his friend Obélix and their dog, Idéfix, Dogmatix in the English editions. But this time, he had another purpose.

"I remember buying a couple of jerricans here a year or so ago," he said. "Do you have any in at the moment?"

"We did have three," said Valérie, rolling herself a cigarette with practiced twirls of her thumbs as she spoke. "But we sold them just after we opened yesterday morning, to that young gendarme who thinks he's God's gift to womanhood. Silly guy is so full of himself it's unbelievable. Didn't even try to bargain, as if we'd do him any favors. He was in a helluva hurry, and with a very fancy new set of wheels. You could have had them for a euro each, but he paid ten for the three. I tried to rub out the chalked price when I saw him heading over."

"That would have been Roland," said Bruno. "I think he usually drives one of those cheap Japanese sports cars."

"Sports car," mocked Rollo. "A kiddie car with pretensions would be more like it. Besides, he's got a rep, that guy."

Valérie leaned forward and put a gently restraining hand on Rollo's arm to stop him from saying any more.

"Were you after some more jerricans, Bruno, or are you asking for a police reason?" she asked, her voice neutral.

"If any more jerricans come in, I'd be grateful if you could put them to one side for me," said Bruno. "Apart from that, have you any new English-language Astérix books?"

"Yes. *Astérix et les Ecossais,*" she said. "I put it on the shelf under the counter for you. Help yourself."

He thanked her, went to take the comic book, handed her a five-euro note and waved away the change, thanking them and wishing them well before strolling out to the access road.

"We've got the bastard," Bruno said as he climbed into Jules's car. "He paid ten euros for three jerricans yesterday, sometime just after they opened, probably around nine or so. That fits with the time you turned up with him, and then he drove Monique's car to the gendarmerie, so he'd have seen that the tank was almost full. He knew the owner was dead so he saw the chance to get one hundred euros' worth of fuel and stopped off to buy the cheap jerricans."

"Cunning little bastard," said Jules, with a wistful, almost envious tone in his voice. After a moment, he added, "Nearly wish I'd thought of it myself. It's not as though the dead woman's going to miss it."

"Could you call Yveline on your phone?" Bruno asked. "She needs to know about this, and we'd better work out whether I call the magistrates to file the charge against him or you do. I don't mind if you and Yveline want to keep it in the family."

"I was thinking about that," Jules replied. "Might put a big black mark on Yveline's career with that uncle of his in Paris. And if I do it, they might take a closer look at my length of service and push me into retirement."

"What's so bad about that?" Bruno asked.

"The wife doesn't want me hanging around, under her feet all day," Jules replied. "She'd probably divorce me just to get a bit of peace."

"You'll be hunting all day in the season, looking after the garden all summer, could even write your memoirs with all those stories you tell of the old days. You've got a gift, the way you keep the hunting club laughing."

"Yes, well, after a few drinks those guys would laugh at anything. And it's one thing to spin the old yarns, put on a funny voice, get them waiting for it, but it's all very different when you try to write it down. And after all these years even if I wanted to write a love letter it would probably end up reading like an official crime report."

"You don't want to give up, do you?"

"No, Bruno, I don't."

When they arrived in St. Denis, Jules told Bruno, "This is your case. So either you go in and tell Yveline or you file a written report that will have to go to the magistrates in Sarlat and to our headquarters in Périgueux. Which is it to be?"

"Yveline first," Bruno said. "She's the chain of command and needs to be told. And she may be able to deal with this internally."

"Not with the other business hanging over the stupid bastard. Hitting on the bishop's secretary. You couldn't make it up."

As Bruno opened the van door, about to step out, his phone vibrated. It was Philippe Delaron, local newshound. Bruno rolled his eyes and sat back in the car seat, facing Jules.

"Philippe, I presume this is a business call."

"Yes, but it's for Jules as much as for you, Bruno, and I just saw you go past in his car," Philippe said. "I just had a call from Natalie about demanding the eviction of her three young gendarme tenants. She invited me to take some photos, and it does look like a bomb hit the place, so we'll probably make it a lead in tomorrow's paper."

"Give me five minutes to brief Yveline," Bruno replied. "Then she can decide if she's going to talk to you or refer you to the press office to give their usual no comment."

"Merde," said Jules once Bruno hung up. "I didn't think she'd bring the media into this."

"You can't blame Natalie. It's one way to ensure the place gets cleaned up and repainted. Let's go give Yveline the bad news. Theft of gasoline from a vehicle in police custody plus leaving the place like a pigsty. If it was up to me, I'd make them spend all night cleaning up and their next days off repainting the place."

"They should pay for it," said Jules. "I don't care who his uncle is." Then he paused. "I was never planning on going higher than sergeant, but Yveline's career has barely begun and she could go all the way." He paused again and then glanced at Bruno. "So long as she makes no powerful enemies."

"Which this might do, you mean?" Bruno asked. "Starting with Roland's uncle in Paris? That depends on who the general thinks is to blame, Yveline as local commander or J-J and the Police Nationale, where there is a very strong-willed female *commissaire* who is not going to let this be hushed up. I'll file my report on the theft of gas to the magistrates in Sarlat, with one copy to J-J and another to Yveline."

"And I'll suggest to Yveline that J-J tell these three young guys to work all through the night cleaning up the house," said Sergeant Jules. "That could get us some decent publicity if we get Philippe Delaron to take some pics of them washing windows and scrubbing floors."

That was exactly what Yveline decided the three young gendarmes should do, starting that evening, and if Philippe chose to take photographs of the cleanup, so be it. Once Roland's other two housemates had left the room, she formally informed Roland that the charge against him for theft of gasoline had been sent to the Sarlat magistrates with a copy to the gendarme general commanding the Périgueux HQ on boulevard Bertran de Born.

Bruno had barely walked halfway back to the *mairie* before Annette called to ask why a fuss was being made about a tankful of gas.

"It was Monique's car," Bruno explained. "A young gendarme was driving it back to the gendarmerie, saw the tank was full and stopped off to buy some jerricans and siphon the gas out. Have you heard nothing about a young gendarme behaving badly?"

There was a pause before Annette replied, "Oh, you mean the business with Célestine, who works for the executive council? The case J-J was working on? Now I think I understand why you're making a fuss about a few liters of gasoline."

Bruno knew that Annette was a friend and tennis partner of Josette, a policewoman who was J-J's aide and driver, and Josette would certainly know about the women being stopped and harassed by a gendarme. Bruno had learned that the informal communications system among women in the law was just as important as the official chain of command.

"You know Célestine?" Bruno asked, making it sound as if he knew her. He didn't, but Bruno knew that Annette was a member of the women's committee of the Socialist Party, the center-left group that had a majority on the *département* council. It was a near certainty that Annette would know her.

"Yes, of course, but she only said that she'd filed a complaint. And there was another woman involved. Someone with the church. Yes, that's it—she works for the bishop," Annette said. "Did you hear anything about a problem with some powerful relative of the gendarme involved?"

"Yes, a general at the HQ in Paris. It's the same young gendarme in the gas theft."

"Really?" she said, and then she paused. "Well, in that case we'd better make sure this gasoline business gets immediate attention. Leave it with me. And I'll look forward to seeing you in Sarlat tonight."

"Have I forgotten something?" Bruno asked. "What's up?"

"Yes, you're supposed to join us at Monique's place," she replied. "Dominic is on his way back from Strasbourg and is expecting to see us all at the apartment, you included."

"But I'm no longer involved. I gave my statement and assumed that would be the end of it. A straightforward suicide, three separate notes—did you check for fingerprints on the folds?"

"Too busy, sorry, but I can let you have the lab report

tomorrow. I think you should turn up tonight, if only for courtesy. And Rebecca Weil and Laura both said they were looking forward to seeing you again, as am I. We were planning to go on to dinner at l'Octroi, which I know you like because of the traditional Périgord menu, and it would be lovely for you to join us. My treat, since I've eaten your food more times than I can count. And please bring Balzac, since I miss him and I hear that Laura thinks he's lovely."

"Where is Dominic's apartment?"

Annette told him.

"Has Becca held the reading of the will yet?" he asked.

"No, that's not until after the funeral."

Bruno had been planning a simple omelette from his own hens and a winter salad made from his own garden of butternut squash, parsnips, spinach and red onions. He would have followed that with some of Stéphane's Tomme d'Audrix cheese and a glass or two of wine from the town vineyard while reading a new-to-him thriller, *Meurtre Chez les Magdaléniens,* by a local author, Sophie Marvaud, set deep in the region's prehistoric past.

But Annette was a friend, and he looked forward to seeing Rebecca Weil and Laura again, and he was curious about Dominic, to whom he had not even spoken since that aborted phone call the morning of Monique's death. He should at the very least convey his condolences.

"Who could resist such a dinner?" he said. "The three most interesting women in Sarlat, and the mysterious Dominic. I'll be there as soon after six as I can make it."

Chapter 12

Bruno parked opposite the cemetery and then strolled down the slope of the rue Gaubert, Balzac on a leash. As he came to the Plaza Hotel he saw Laura with her own basset hound on the other side of the road. He smiled and waved as he and his dog crossed to meet them, Balzac wagging his tail with evident enthusiasm. Laura, wearing a stylish overcoat that almost reached her ankles, gave a cheerful wave, and her basset hound turned to watch the two males, human and canine, approach. The dog had a front paw elegantly raised, almost as though she expected Balzac to bow and her hand to be kissed. Bruno noted that her tail was also wagging, but in slow and stately rhythm.

"Bonsoir," Laura said, presenting a cheek. "Annette said you'd agreed to come, I'm so glad. And such a pleasure to see Balzac again. I spent part of the day looking to see if George Sand and Balzac had been friends in real life. I knew they were contemporaries, and then I found that she'd said of Balzac that he was 'a serene soul with a smile in it.' That must be a good omen, and my mother says that your Balzac's genes are entirely worthy of my basset."

"That's excellent news," Bruno said. "I hadn't known that

Balzac and Sand were on such good terms. An extraordinary period for French literature, and I know she was good friends with Flaubert and with Victor Hugo."

"And with Alexandre Dumas," Laura said. "They collaborated on various essays and projects, and she called his boy her spiritual son."

"I never knew that," said Bruno, impressed. "But if Balzac and your Mademoiselle Sand produce a litter, in honor of Dumas I think we might call the first son d'Artagnan."

"And then we have the names of all the three musketeers, so that's Porthos, Athos and Aramis, along with Richelieu and King Louis. So we're fine for boys' names," she replied, grinning, evidently enjoying this. Then she gave a mock frown. "But after Queen Anne, Constance and Milady, I run out of names for girls."

"There's a Mercédès in *The Count of Monte Cristo,* and I think I recall a Valentine," he said.

"Mercédès is a wonderful name for a basset. By the way, we can take the dogs up to the top floor, where there's a roof terrace. And this event is just to welcome Dominic back, say how sorry we are for his loss and show some sympathy and solidarity. No business, and above all no talk about the will."

"Understood," Bruno replied.

The elevator would have been intimate for only two humans. With two bassets it was impossible, so Bruno took the stairs. By the time he reached the top floor Laura had taken the dogs to the terrace and hung up her coat. She escorted him into a large living room that ran the whole length of the building. Rebecca and Annette came forward to greet him, and Laura began to introduce him to various colleagues, all of them women except for the senior gardener. The remaining man, barely the same height as Laura and looking to be in his twenties, had to be Dominic. He came forward to shake Bruno's hand, asked what he would like to drink and waved airily at a table filled with drinks and glasses. Bruno took a glass of wine, and said, "Please accept my condolences. It's kind of you to do this—it must have been a long and tiring drive."

"It wasn't too bad. Not too much traffic and I listened to Brahms," said Dominic. "Thank you for taking care of matters yesterday. Is that your basset hound, on the terrace with Laura's dog?"

"Yes, he's called Balzac."

"Easy to remember, which makes a nice change from Laura's creature," said Dominic. "I assume you know everybody here?"

"No, I know Annette very well, but I only met Rebecca and Laura yesterday and don't know her colleagues at all."

Dominic made no response to this but eyed Bruno coolly as Bruno made some forced conversation about the pleasant room and how splendid the views of the old town must be in daylight until Dominic turned to greet another arrival, and Bruno sidled away to where Annette and Becca were huddled together.

"I really have no idea why I'm here," he said.

"To make sure Dominic doesn't start demanding to know exactly what's in the will, of course," said Becca. "That's for after the funeral, in the privacy of my chambers, with a couple of sturdy ushers on hand to ensure everything stays civilized."

"I thought you told me they were married under separation of wealth," Bruno said.

"Yes, but that seldom stops aggrieved spouses from complaining that they've been cheated out of their inheritance by some unscrupulous lawyer."

"What do you do then?" Bruno asked.

"Advise them to hire a lawyer of their own," Becca replied with a smile. "It will make no difference, but it's good for business. Do you know that Abraham Lincoln once said that he remembered how in his early days as a solitary lawyer in town he almost starved? But in the nick of time a second lawyer arrived, and they both then prospered."

They introduced Bruno to the other women who had worked with Monique, including two each from the Périgueux and Bergerac offices. He asked each of them if their territory included St. Denis, and they shook their heads and told him to ask Laura, who looked after most of the properties to the west of Sarlat. She seemed to have disappeared, so he made small talk until she came out of the kitchen with a tray of nuts and cocktail snacks.

"Thank you, my dear," said Dominic, a proprietary tone in his voice. Laura's expression stiffened, her nostrils flared, and she put the tray down on a table with a sharp clatter that briefly stilled all other conversation.

"Dominic, you know that Monique did not like being addressed that way, and I don't either," she said firmly. She turned her back on him, found herself facing the bewildered gardener, flashed him a brilliant smile and asked what she should be planting at this time of year. Bruno felt like applauding.

"Winter greens and lamb's lettuce," the old man stammered. "And broad beans."

"Sorry, Laura," Dominic said loudly. "I'm just back from the house where I grew up in Strasbourg, and everyone in the family spoke like that all the time. I just fell back into the habit."

"That's okay, Dominic," she replied casually, almost tossing the words over her shoulder. "But you're down here again now."

The buzz of conversation resumed, and Dominic began talking to some other of Laura's colleagues.

"Laura's right, of course," the woman from Bergerac said

to Bruno. "Monique hated it when Dominic started talking as though she was a little dormouse of a housewife." She threw Bruno a challenging look.

He smiled at her, and asked, "It may be a little out of your area, over in Saussignac, but do you know Château de Fayolle? They make good wine. My name is Bruno, by the way."

"I'm Nadine, and I know who you are from *Sud Ouest*. La Fayolle is not one of ours, sadly, and besides, it's a working vineyard where the wine has to come first, and that really doesn't fit with what we offer. But it's a lovely old place—I love the lunches they do in summer with that glorious view over the lake. What brings you here this evening?"

"I was the policeman who found Monique's body yesterday morning, then came to see Annette and Becca to sort out the formalities. Deaths mean a lot of paperwork. And Monique had left letters for Laura and Becca . . ." He broke off. "That reminds me. Excuse me a moment."

Bruno turned and walked across to Annette. "Have you given Dominic his copy of the letter yet?"

"No, there wasn't time. Becca and I got here just before you, and he'd only been in the place for a few minutes, barely long enough to wash up. I thought I'd give it to him when we leave."

"The sooner the better, I suggest," Bruno said. "I can take care of it if that's easier for you."

"Well, you were the one who found the letters. Why not?" From her shoulder bag she pulled an envelope holding one of the photocopies that she'd made and gave it to him.

Bruno thanked her and strolled across to Dominic, who was standing at the table where Laura had placed her tray, nibbling at something. "Could I have a moment?" Bruno asked. "Monique left you a letter, which we had to read and check for fingerprints. That's why I'm about to give you a photocopy. Perhaps we should go into another room?"

Dominic led the way into the kitchen and said, "Call me Dom, by the way. My Strasbourg family always did because it's the German word for a cathedral, which is where my foster father worked. Just a joke." He held out his hand for the envelope, opened it and started to read.

"I'll leave you to read it in private," Bruno said.

"No, no," Dominic replied. "After all, you've already read it. Police reasons, I assume."

"The letter makes her plan to commit suicide pretty evident, but we still have to clear up a couple of formalities," Bruno said. "The postmortem, checks on the pills she took, the usual issues."

"Where was she found?" Dominic asked, folding the letter to return it to its envelope.

"Near St. Cirq, at a well-known scenic spot overlooking the valley, between St. Denis and Les Eyzies. I gather she knew the area well from an old school friend who lived near there. It probably brought back childhood memories."

"She wouldn't have seen much to remember in the dark," Dominic replied, his voice flat. "You called me in Strasbourg not long before eight yesterday morning, when it was barely daylight. When do you think she got there, to that place?"

"We don't know for sure," said Bruno. "It could have been anytime the previous day, Sunday. Nobody at the *conciergerie* heard from her all day. You may have been the last person to speak to her when you left for Strasbourg. We know from her phone that on Saturday afternoon she called her lawyer, Rebecca Weil. That's all I know except that your wife had been dead for six to eight hours when I found her yesterday morning. We don't think she spent much time there before taking the pills, because the heater had been turned off and the fuel tank was almost full."

"Yes, that's very like her. She hated leaving engines running. A green thing. We'd talked of getting an electric car . . ." His voice trailed off and he stood still for a moment, staring into the middle distance, and then he turned, looked Bruno in the eye and said, almost aggressively, "You read this letter, of course."

"Yes, of course. And those she left for Laura and Madame Weil."

"Laura, is it? Already? You move fast, Monsieur Bruno."

Bruno stared silently at him, just raising an eyebrow, until Dominic took a deep breath and muttered, "Sorry, I'm not myself."

"I understand. We should have the postmortem by late tomorrow, after which the body will almost certainly be authorized for burial by the magistrates," Bruno said.

"So that's it, it's all done and dusted, clean and tidy. But there's been no serious inquiry whether it really was a suicide, or whether there was somebody who had a lot to gain from her death? You've read her letter, so you'll know it wasn't me who would benefit."

"Monsieur, there is no evidence of anything but suicide, after her miscarriage and subsequent depression, and the mode of death is also classic suicide. It is not easy to force somebody to swallow a lot of pills."

"But could somebody have forged those letters, and perhaps collaborated with someone else to forge the will? That's theoretically possible, is it not? Worth a moment of your time to investigate, perhaps?"

"It's not my decision, monsieur, but that of the investigating magistrate and the public prosecutor," Bruno said patiently. "You are at liberty to ask them to make further inquiries if you have any evidence that points to anything other than suicide."

"That's very convenient," Dominic said, almost sneering. "The person who stands to gain most, who is also the person who could have forged those letters, is close friends with the lawyer who arranged the will and with the investigating magistrate. Does it not make you think, tickle a suspicion?"

"If you have any evidence to support such a conspiracy theory, you should contact Chief of Police Messager here in Sarlat. This is not my jurisdiction, even if I believed it," he said. "Madame Weil will be in touch about the reading of the will."

"That involves only me, I presume, or at least me and the lawyer," Dominic said, suddenly sounding reasonable again. The man's moods were mercurial.

"I wouldn't know," Bruno said, looking him in the eye. "That's not my department and none of my business."

Dominic raised his eyebrows. "And yet you are very friendly with Annette, the magistrate, with Weil, the lawyer, and with Laura, the business partner. That's very interesting."

"I met the lawyer and Laura for the first time yesterday, monsieur, in the course of my duties. That's all. Good evening."

Bruno turned, paused only to tell Annette why he was leaving and went to the balcony to fetch Balzac, where his dog was sprawled out comfortably on his side, facing George Sand, their back legs tucked into one another. He paused, smiling, when he heard movement behind him and turned to see Laura looking indulgently at the two bassets.

"Going so soon?"

"Dominic made some unpleasant insinuations about my friendly relations with you, Becca and Annette. It came right after he read his wife's letter, in which she made it clear the business goes to you and the other women who built it up. So I'm leaving. The only question is whether I take Balzac home or we meet at l'Octroi as planned."

"Why don't you take both dogs down and then I'll follow with Annette and Becca, and we'll see you at the restaurant? I think everybody else has had enough, too."

Bruno put the leashes on the two dogs and led them out to the hall, putting his head around the door of the sitting room to wave goodbye. There was no sign of Dominic. He took the elevator down with the dogs and began strolling slowly to the bistro. They made a very good sauce *rouilleuse* there, he recalled, using the flesh of a peeled and roasted red bell pepper, egg yolk, crushed garlic, olive oil, lemon juice and some strands of saffron. It went wonderfully with fish, but he wondered if it might also work with chicken. They also made a very good walnut tart, and he remembered their *aiguillettes* of duck in a raspberry vinegar, such a tart and bright change from the way he liked to cook them with honey and mustard, sweet and comforting.

He turned to watch for the arrival of his three dinner companions. "This place was named for a medieval tax," he said when they were seated. "Whatever was brought into town for sale at the market, food or goods, had to pay a small entry tax, *l'octroi*. This was the site of the place where the tax was charged, although I'm not sure this is the original building."

"I told the others why you thought it best to leave, Bruno," said Laura. "I don't know if you were watching, but I thought Dominic drank nearly as much as the rest of us combined."

"Does he often drink too much, or was this evening a rare event?" he asked. "He was probably tired after the long drive."

"I don't recall ever seeing him in that shape," said Becca. "And Monique never even hinted at anything about his drinking."

"He can't really have thought that Monique would leave him the whole business when he never contributed anything to it," said Annette.

"I drew up the marriage contract," said Becca. "It had full separation of goods, which meant he could expect nothing that Monique had owned before the marriage, including the company and the building. When they married, Monique wanted to give him the right to live in the marital home, the apartment we just left, and he was given a ten percent share in the notary business while he works there full-time—but the cousin who inherits may not want him to continue working. That's it. No share in the estate agency nor in the concierge business. The country house is owned by a family trust, so it stays in the family. I made that marriage contract as tight as a gnat's ass, as my long-ago American boyfriend used to say. But that's another story. Anyway, Dominic agreed to that contract and he signed it, so he's known all along he was not going to inherit her wealth."

"Unless he thought he could change her mind, over time, or perhaps by helping her become a mother," suggested Annette.

"So why did he suddenly become so hostile to me once he'd read Monique's letter?" Bruno asked.

"Maybe just to see how you'd react. He seems the kind of man to enjoy playing those kinds of fatuous games," said Laura. "I'm surprised he didn't go on to say that I and all the other women in the company obviously had a clear financial interest in bumping her off."

"The letters were all typed, or at least came from a printer," said Annette. "So where is Monique's laptop? In her office or at home?"

"At home here in Sarlat or at the country house?" said Becca. "I presume she ran it through the office printer, so there should be a record in its memory, telling us when it was printed. Laura, maybe you should go back and check whether the laptop is in Monique's office and whatever the printer can tell us."

"It can wait till morning," Laura said. "The office is locked."

"Yes, but Dominic will have Monique's keys, so he can come and go as he pleases," Becca said. "And he seems to be in a suspicious mood."

"*Merde,* there is nothing to suspect and nothing to find," said Laura. "It's just a will that hasn't been changed in years. And I'm not going out into the cold again. It can wait till morning, and I'm hungry for some solid food, probably the duck."

As she spoke a waitress came to take their orders. One by one, they all ordered the menu of the day: onion soup, followed by the *aiguillettes* of duck with raspberry vinegar that Bruno had remembered, with *pommes de terre sarladaises,* followed by the cheese board and a caramel mousse. A carafe of the house red wine seemed fitting.

"What's to stop him from writing a new will and forging Monique's signature?" asked Bruno.

"If a will hasn't been properly filed and recorded and witnessed in accordance with the law, the courts are not likely to accept it unless there is very good reason to do so, and I do not believe there is," said Becca. "There are no direct heirs of the body—that is to say, children who are being cheated out of their inheritance. And the marriage contract specifically says that Dominic played no role and has no investment and no interest in the company."

"And even at the time of the marriage Monique was no longer the majority shareholder," said Laura.

"Not that such considerations have ever stopped a ruthless lawyer," said Becca, with a beaming smile.

"You should know," replied Annette, laughing, as the steaming tureen of soup was laid on the table and wafts of garlic rose to enrich the atmosphere.

Chapter 13

The next morning Bruno rose with dread, gearing himself to face the test the mayor had set. But his ordeal would not begin until just after ten in Périgueux, and it was now just before seven and there was a brightness glowing in the sky to the east. He put on his tracksuit and running shoes and set off along the familiar ridge with Balzac at his heels, racing to keep up. The air was very cold on his face and hands, but he knew his blood would soon warm and began punching the air with his fists, working his shoulders, and as soon as he reached the peak of the ridge he began jumping up and down as he waited for Balzac to catch up. As he trotted back, he felt as warm as toast and happily jumped into his shower as soon as he turned the tap on, knowing the water would run cold for perhaps thirty brisk seconds before it began to flow hot.

Twenty minutes later he was sitting on his horse, Hector, and walking out of the stables with Pamela and Miranda, each of them with two more horses on a leading rein. Bruno's cousins, Alain and Rosalie, followed on the oldest and slowest horses as they learned to ride. In Rosalie's case, it was easy, since she had been raised on a farm in Normandy and learned to ride as a child, but that had been more than twenty years ago, and she was taking it slowly and keeping Alain company, since he had never ridden before coming to St. Denis.

Bruno smiled as he turned and saw the twin plumes of mist coming from the horses' nostrils as their breath rushed out into the chill air. It would be one of those magical mornings where the river would be steaming once they reached the ridge from which they could look down onto the valley and the bridge. It was a sight Bruno always enjoyed, the slightly warmer temperature of the river reacting against the colder air by sending up the mist that made the bridge and the tops of trees seem to float weightlessly. The sight took his mind off the impending ordeal in the Périgueux studio of the France Bleu radio station, where he was to spend an hour being interviewed and answering listeners' questions about the life of a country policeman.

It had been the mayor's idea, to promote the commune of St. Denis and the way its custodian of law and order answered to the mayor and town council, rather than to the more familiar hierarchies of the gendarmes or the Police Nationale. In Bruno's case, most of his predecessors until 1958 had been *gardes champêtres,* rural guards, whose main job was to stop poachers. They had been founded in 1791, shortly after the French Revolution, to replace the servants of the landed aristocracy as the upholders of law in the countryside. In 1958 de Gaulle returned to power with a new constitution and a range of modernizing reforms, which included replacing the old rural guards with local police.

But Bruno was more than just a town policeman. Bruno had been promoted to chief of police of the Vézère Valley, from Limeuil where the Vézère flowed into the larger Dordogne River, all the way to Montignac in the north. This gave him a nominal authority on police matters over his municipal police colleagues in Les Eyzies and Montignac, which Bruno tried to exercise as lightly as he could. Bruno privately thought the whole structure to be flawed and almost unworkable, since he knew the mayors of those towns were just as jealous of their authority as the mayor of St. Denis. Bruno suspected that his mayor wanted this radio interview to reinforce Bruno's authority up and down the river.

Bruno would do his best, but he thought it a vain hope. Politics being politics, and mayors being mayors, and budgets being budgets, Bruno knew that his mayor was engaged in a constant jockeying for funds and powers in the various committees and budgets with his rivals. The mayor of Les Eyzies came armed with the prestige of the National Museum of Prehistory and most of the prehistoric caves in their spectacular scenery. The mayor of Montignac was draped in the splendor of Lascaux, the greatest prehistoric cave of them all with its incomparable cave paintings and the multimillion-euro budget of the high-tech new museum to show them off. The mayor of St. Denis, by contrast, had his wits, a good rugby team, the town vineyard and a renowned market that had just celebrated its seven hundredth anniversary.

Bruno had previously met Marie-Do, the charming host of the morning show and a woman of formidable talents, able to conduct intriguing and informative interviews with politicians, cooks, winemakers, cave explorers, sporting heroes and heroines, archaeologists, pop stars and children. Could she make anything interesting from an hour with a village copper? He very much doubted it.

"You know we'll all be listening and rooting for you, Bruno," called Pamela, from somewhere behind him. Lost in his own thoughts, he'd wandered on ahead, forgetting that the horses on a leading rein behind him would block the trail for the others. He quickly steered Hector to one side with a gentle pressure from his knee, and the other horses dutifully followed so that Pamela could come up alongside.

"I suppose you're a bit nervous about this interview," she said. "I wouldn't worry about it, if I were you. Marie-Do has done hundreds of these things. She'll see you through."

"Yes, but it's not just her. There are calls from the public. So some guy I tackled a bit too hard on the rugby field or who I arrested for drunken driving or gave a parking ticket . . ."

"Stop it, Bruno. You don't give parking tickets and you leave driving offenses to the gendarmes. Of course, there could be people you beat at tennis, or those tourists whose camping car you had towed into the gendarmerie when they parked and blocked the road."

"That was to save them from being beaten to death on the spot by our friends and neighbors."

"And have you picked your favorite book and favorite song? She always asks for those."

"I was asked for one song by a man and one by a woman, so Françoise Hardy's "Tous Les Garçons et Les Filles" and Jacques Brel's "Chanson des Vieux Amants." And the book is Jean-Pierre Babelon's biography of Henri IV."

"Your favorite king—no surprise there."

"The only French king to be immortalized in a dish, to give us *poulet* Henri Quatre. And it's actually two dishes in one, because your first course is the cooking liquid as a soup, and then the chicken and vegetables are the main course."

"Are you sure he actually said he wanted every French family to have a *poule au pot* every Sunday? It always sounded made up to me."

"He said it to the Duke of Savoy: 'If the good Lord keeps me alive, I will ensure that there will be no laborer in my realm who does not have the means to have a chicken in his pot every Sunday.' I asked Father Sentout to help me find the source, and it was a Jesuit classical scholar, Jean Hardouin, citing letters of the Duke of Savoy."

The conversation had taken them down the bridle trail and to the turn into Pamela's paddock and then to the stables. Once they dismounted, Pamela told him not to bother putting the horses in their stalls; she'd see to that. He'd better not be late. She reached up to give him a kiss for luck with her lovely soft lips, calling after him as he turned away to his Land Rover, "Don't worry, Bruno—it's only the honor of St. Denis at stake."

He was halfway to Périgueux when his phone vibrated and he saw it was the mayor. Bruno debated with himself whether to answer. On the third ring, he thought he'd better.

"Whatever you do or say, absolutely no politics," said the mayor. "Good luck. The whole *mairie* will be listening, and most of St. Denis, including the schools. But don't for a moment think you're under any pressure, Bruno."

"Thank you, Monsieur le Maire, but I'd better hang up," said Bruno, thinking the mayor was in one of those moods where he might start spouting about Bruno facing the loss of life or limb for France in many a foreign field. "The traffic is getting tricky. *Au'voir.*"

Bruno pulled into the lane that led down into the radio station's parking lot close to the riverbank, beneath the building. Had he forgotten the name of the historian whose book he wanted to cite? Babelon! "By the waters of Babylon, we sat down and wept," he reminded himself. That's how he'd remember. And if Marie-Do insisted, he could sing the Jacques Brel and the Françoise Hardy. As he walked into the empty elevator, he suddenly realized he'd neglected to read that morning's *Sud Ouest* for the local news. The elevator doors opened, and he was in the main entrance hall. He gave his name and asked the smiling young receptionist if he could scan her copy of the paper, and she looked outraged.

"Don't you remember me, Bruno? You taught me to play

backhand," she announced, rising and coming around her desk to give him a hug.

"Dorothée," he almost sang out, delighted at seeing her again. "What a lovely surprise to see you, and how beautiful you are! Big-city life agrees with you. And how is that twin brother of yours, still at university?"

"Yes, in his third year, still playing rugby, and I'll tell him you asked after him. But didn't you know me on sight?"

"I was in such a dither, a bit nervous, and then realized I hadn't even looked at the paper. Any news I should know about?"

"Nothing special and you're in good time. I'll just tell Marie-Do you're here. In the meantime check out page five. There's a story about gendarmes having to clean up a house they'd left in a mess, and that sounded like you."

"It is me," he said and reached for the newspaper as the girl disappeared. He had time to learn that the landlady had been mollified by the promise that the cleanup efforts would continue through the night. The threat of eviction had been repealed. Given Bruno's opinion of the young man whose uncle was a general, he was not altogether pleased at the gendarmes' reprieve. Dorothée reemerged to escort him back to the studio to be greeted with a hug by Marie-Do and accept some coffee. He was placed in front of the microphone opposite her and listened to the news bulletin on the hour while Marie-Do spoke quietly on a separate mic to her producer sitting in another room.

"Bruno Courrèges," she began. "A big France Bleu welcome for the chief of municipal police for the Vézère Valley; former senior sergeant in the combat engineers, awarded the Croix de Guerre for pulling trapped soldiers from a burning armored car while under fire; shot again earlier this year in the shoulder by Russian gangsters in a mysterious incident around which rumors swirl; keen hunter and horse rider and also tennis and rugby coach for the kids in St. Denis; and I know you to be an excellent cook. And you are just about inseparable from your delightful basset hound, named Balzac. Dear Bruno, how on earth do you find the time for all this?"

"Good morning, Marie-Do, and the answer is I wish I knew," Bruno replied. "It all fits into the day somehow, just as you manage to squeeze the news, the weather, the sports results, the recipe of the day, a joke and a horoscope into your brief time on air. I suppose time doesn't matter that much when you're having fun."

Marie-Do winked at him, the sound engineer gave him a thumbs-up, and Bruno breathed a sigh of relief at clearing the first hurdle. The second was tougher.

"I didn't know you were an orphan, abandoned at a church while you were still a babe in arms," Marie-Do said. "You spent seven years in a church orphanage until your mother's sister in Bergerac was able to take you in and raise you with her own children. Has that experience marked you, Bruno? Is that why you are still unmarried, even though you take enormous plea-sure in being the sports teacher to all the kids of St. Denis?"

Bruno plastered a smile on his face that felt more like a gri-mace. "Two of the things in the world that give me the greatest pleasure are sports and watching kids blossom into interesting and capable adults such as yourself. It's great that our program runs all year-round, as we have rugby in the winter and tennis in the summer. I think it really helps everybody in the valley that the children grow up knowing me as Bruno, and not as some anonymous authority figure with a gun and a uniform."

"So this makes up for being a child abandoned by the mother you never subsequently met, with no idea who your father was?"

"I don't know, Marie-Do, but I think I've known kids who

had a tougher, more grueling childhood than I did, even if they did have their parents around. But I can tell you what I recall as the worst moment of my childhood—it was in the orphanage, where I had made a special friend of the dog in the kitchen. And one day the priest in his lesson solemnly told us that animals have no souls, so we would find none of them in heaven. It broke my little heart."

At that point, there was a station break, a brief weather report that said the cold spell would go on, and they were back on the air. Marie-Do at once asked about the structure of the Police Municipale and how they worked with the gendarmes, who had traditionally been under the Ministry of Defense, and the Police Nationale, who came under the interior ministry.

"I am under the authority of the elected mayor and council of St. Denis, and respect the authority of all the other mayors in the valley," Bruno said. "It sounds complex but it works, because it means that the detectives in the Police Nationale *and* the gendarmes both have access to our local knowledge and can benefit from the trust that we have built up by being a permanent part of our community."

"I have heard, Bruno, that you don't just help raise all the kids through sports, but you dance with all the mothers when their daughters get married, you stand godfather to half the kids, and at the funerals you carry the coffins of the grand-fathers, most of whom you knew through the hunting clubs."

"We are members of a living community, so I think we in the local police tend to be well known, and therefore perhaps more trusted than the detectives and gendarmes who come in from outside."

"I see what you mean, but it all sounds a bit macho, Bruno, rugby and hunting, a man's world."

"I wouldn't say that to a certain local girl if I were you, a brilliant sportswoman, you know the one I'm talking about.

She won a silver medal playing rugby for France at the Tokyo Olympics."

"I stand corrected, Bruno, but we have a caller on the line who wants to raise a different point about some of your connections to the community. The floor is yours, caller."

"Bonjour. My name is Georges Luchan, from Nontron. I'm a retired teacher and member of the Greens, and I want to know why, with your position of trust and your admirable work with children, do you still spend time slaughtering helpless animals?"

"Partly, sir, it's because I have come to believe that most hunters are in their way just as green as you, but in a different way. We certainly know more about animals because we study their ways, and we know that any balanced ecology needs predators to keep that balance. You know yourself that in France we were getting so overrun with deer, with more than two hundred people killed in automobile collisions with deer and wild boars, that the government had to raise the traditional limits on how many we could hunt to get the numbers back under control.

"The fact is, monsieur, that we hunters have a problem," Bruno went on. "Back in 1970 there were two million French people with hunting licenses. We are now down to one million, and we have far more work to do because your policies mean we have to deal with a population explosion. In 1970, we shot thirty-six thousand wild boars in France. But with the boar population explosion, in 2020 we shot more than eight hundred thousand. That's nearly twenty-five times as many, just to illustrate the sheer scale of the challenge. Back in 1970, we shot two hundred thousand roe deer. Last year we shot, with a great deal of official urging, three times as many, six hundred thousand—that's the scale of the challenge. You Greens campaigned hard for the restrictions on hunters that led to the population explosion, and that meant baby deer starving to death because there was too much competition for the available food. Your good intentions had very grim results."

"Next caller," announced Marie-Do.

"Hello, I'm Gabrielle from Bergerac," came a childish voice. "And I want to know why you eat foie gras when it means the poor ducks and geese have to be force-fed and stuffed."

"Bonjour, Gabrielle, I eat foie gras because I like it, and the ducks and geese don't have to be stuffed. More and more farmers are producing foie gras by letting the birds eat freely, as much as they want, without force-feeding. The point is that ducks and geese are migrating birds, and to make their long flights up to Scandinavia or south to west Africa, the birds need lots of energy. They store it in their livers, which routinely swell to three and four times normal size in migrating season. If you don't like that system don't blame me. It was *le bon Dieu* or Mother Nature who invented it."

And so it went on, with requests for Bruno and the other local cops to police the rubbish collection points and stop people from dumping old fridges in the woods. But every second question came from somebody declaring themselves to be Green or vegan. The youngest asked in a piping voice how Bruno could kill his own chickens.

But then came a familiar voice from St. Denis, Alphonse, the elderly hippie who had started a commune in the hills above the town nearly fifty years ago, lived in a geodesic dome and made the best goat cheese in the valley. Despite his long hair and multicolored clothing Alphonse had become a respected citizen, regularly reelected to the council for his good sense and kindly ways.

"Bruno, I'm glad to be able to talk to you because we've known each other for twelve years and more. So when some of your questioners seem to think you are a Green-hating, meat-eating, blood-lapping barbarian, in the pay of Big Oil, I'm happy to tell them you live one of the greenest lives I know. You grow your own vegetables and fruit, raise your own ducks and chickens, even your own truffles. You make your own *vin de noix,* and you're a popular man at our local old people's home because you and your hunter friends are the ones who bring them what they really want to eat, that lovely venison."

"Thank you, Alphonse, it's good to hear your voice, and I think I'm right in saying you were the first Green candidate ever elected to a municipal council in the Périgord."

"That's right, Bruno, I was an elected Green councilor before we even had a proper Green Party here."

The last caller asked if it was true that Bruno still went to the traditional pig killings on the farms.

"No, but only because it has been declared illegal, after the abattoir companies hired expensive lobbyists in Brussels to get themselves the monopoly across Europe for slaughtering all livestock. And I have not been to an illegal pig killing," Bruno said. "In my experience—and in my work I have had to visit many abattoirs—the farmers did a much cleaner and more humane job. It's just an extra cost the farmers have to pay, and that means so do we."

The hour came to an end with the chimes announcing the next news bulletin, and once they were off air, Marie-Do said, "Somebody planned that. You were ambushed, and I'm sorry. We just didn't expect the Greens to be so well organized, even getting the children to be word-perfect, which doesn't often happen."

Bruno smiled at her. "It's fine, Marie-Do, I'm not complaining. They were reasonable questions and they listened politely to my replies and gave me a fair hearing. I'm not sure how many of your usual listeners stayed on once they realized that a well-organized Green campaign was underway. And I wholly agree with about eighty percent of what they stand for. But when it comes to hunting, or the pressures on farmers, I think I know what I'm talking about and they don't."

Dorothée gave him a big hug when Bruno emerged from the studio and handed him a cassette tape of his interview.

"I don't think it was my finest hour," Bruno said, after thanking her and thinking privately he'd never replay it.

"In a way it was," she said. "You kept your cool, you stayed polite and courteous, and you answered everything in what seemed to me to be a reasonable way, even though it became more and more clear that they had planned that campaign, almost like they wanted to put you on trial," she said. "So thank heavens. I think of myself as green, but I like foie gras, and although I eat meat and chickens and fish, I really don't like abattoirs. The brother of a school friend worked in one near Sarlat and had to stop. He couldn't stand it."

At that point the producer came into the lobby, saying he was glad he'd caught Bruno before he left the station because he wanted to apologize for Bruno being put through what he called an inquisition.

"The Greens just flooded the station with calls to make sure they got through and other callers could not," he said. "They obviously planned to ambush you, but I think you held them off pretty well."

"Really?" said Bruno. "I never thought of the Greens as being quite that organized. But if you get a call from a friend of mine on *Sud Ouest,* would you tell him what happened? That they mounted a deliberate campaign to block your switchboard and put me in a pillory? It's hardly what you expect from people who believe in free speech and democracy."

"I'd be glad to," said the producer. "We had eight studio lines open, and our switchboard guy tells me they didn't just block that lot, they jammed all the other phone lines coming into the station. They must have had thirty or so people lined up to do it."

"We'd better look at the Greens of Périgord with new respect," said Bruno. "This took careful planning and military-style discipline. So I take my hat off to them, even though I feel like I've been used as a political punching bag for the past hour."

"Hold that thought," said the producer, pulling out a small recorder from a pouch at his waist. "That's just the kind of sound bite the media loves. Now, tell me again."

Bruno repeated what he'd said almost word for word, and the producer said, "Perfect. We'll get that on the air right away. I think this time we might just get our retaliation in first."

Chapter 14

Back in his car and checking the calls and emails he might have missed while being interviewed, Bruno saw one from J-J's private number, not from the office of the *commissaire* in charge of detectives, and called him back.

"Well done, you stayed calm and polite, you had the facts and won a victory on points," said J-J. "But what was the radio station doing letting only the Green calls in?"

"They had organized a massive phone attack blocking all the lines into the station. Anyway, the producer said he's going to make a complaint about it on the air. But I never thought of you as a media critic, so thanks for the call."

"That's not why I'm calling," J-J said. "We need to meet. Are you still at the radio station? And driving your Land Rover?"

Intrigued, Bruno answered yes to both questions.

"Give me five minutes and I'll join you in the parking lot."

In less time than that, J-J's car was there. He clambered out and let his driver take it back out onto the road that led to the bridge over the Isle, the river that ran through the city. J-J walked toward Bruno's vehicle, glanced around and then climbed into the passenger seat.

"Sorry about this, but things are moving fast on this case

of the well-connected young gendarme," J-J began. "Your old rugby chum and my boss, Prunier, was at some official dinner last night, and a senior member of the *département*'s executive council took him to one side and asked when were the police going to take up the appalling case of the gendarmes sexually molesting a young woman on his staff. The politician said he was under—and I quote—'intolerable pressure' from other women on the council and on staff."

Bruno was about to speak, but J-J, still smiling, raised a hand, palm forward, to silence him.

"Wait, Bruno, because while I was digesting this, by some strange coincidence, I got an anonymous phone call from someone who tells me you have got Gendarme Villon to rights on another count altogether. I was told about theft of gasoline from a vehicle in police custody, interference in evidence in a possible homicide, behavior unbecoming to a gendarme, blah-blah-blah. So we got a search warrant and hit the place the gendarmes were renting early this morning. Roland Villon is now under *garde à vue* in the Périgueux jail, and we are not stopping there."

"Those charges are chicken feed," said Bruno. "What about the young women who were molested? The story is spreading. I heard about it from Annette, the magistrate in Sarlat."

"Remember I told you that we had a female detective asking around the massage parlors?" J-J replied. "We are now looking at several other cases to be taken into consideration, because seven other women picked his face out from a range of photos. And guess who Villon has hired as his lawyer? Somehow, Roland is well enough plugged into the network of our less scrupulous lawyers to have hired the lowest of the bottom-feeders, Poincevin himself. I think you've had a run-in with him before."

"Yes, in those gang wars between the Chinese and the

Viets," said Bruno. "Poincevin was on a fat retainer with the Chinese, ready to turn up and get their boys out on bail. So what does this mean?"

"Well, it could get nasty, and since the gendarmes will not want a stand-up fight with the Police Nationale, there is always the possibility that my chiefs might agree to a compromise and make this about you. It depends how far Roland's uncle is prepared to go to defend his nephew. Given the amount of dirt that we can throw on Villon, and the politics about the women's issue, that would be a very high-risk gamble for the uncle. But you'd better realize, Bruno, that you might just become the fall guy in this battle of cops against gendarmes."

"How do you mean, 'fall guy'? I'm not in the wrong here."

"I know, *mon cher*, but in the higher interest of good relations between the interior ministry and the defense ministry, you might find yourself somehow pushed into the wrong. Believe me, Bruno, this is serious."

"So what do you advise?"

"First of all, make sure of your allies—the mayor, for sure, and his old friends in the Senate. But particularly make sure the women are on your side: Annette and Yveline, of course, and Amélie, that jazz-singing woman who was in the justice ministry. And then there's Isabelle. Let them all know what this is about. And tell Isabelle to call me on the same nonofficial number I used to reach you."

"That's it?"

"Not at all," J-J said. "The key thing is that you find some nontraceable way to print out an anonymous letter to the minister of defense, spelling out in detail what Roland has been up to, and you sign it from 'the angry women of Périgord' or something like that. You send it to the minister, and at the bottom of the letter you note copies have been sent to *Le Monde*, *Le Canard Enchaîné*, *The New York Times* and the *Financial*

Times of London. If you really want to drive them nuts, add that a copy is being sent to the president's *adjoint judiciaire* at the Elysée. That will get the minister's special attention. For God's sake make sure you use gloves when you touch the paper and the envelope. Make a copy of that anonymous letter, and send it to the minister of the interior."

"*Mon Dieu,* J-J, have we come to this? That an honest cop has to resort to anonymous letters to get some justice?"

J-J shrugged, opened the car door and turned as if to leave, then stopped himself, glanced back and said, "You play with big boys, you'd better learn to play by big boys' rules, Bruno."

J-J clambered out, then paused as he was about to close the door and said, "You know I'm on your side when it comes to hunting, but you ought to know that the opinion polls say two-thirds of French people don't feel safe in the countryside in hunting season. And nearly eighty percent want hunting to be banned on Sundays so they can take a walk in the countryside without being shot. We French have come a long way from our peasant roots."

"I know," said Bruno. "Even though the training sessions we do for young hunters mean that deaths by hunters have gone down from forty a year to six in the last twenty years."

"*Au'voir,* Bruno. Take care."

Bruno drove back to St. Denis knowing that J-J was right. French opinion was turning against hunters, mainly because France was no longer a rural country. Before World War II, twenty million people, half of the population, lived in the countryside, most of them in farming families. These days, 84 percent lived in urban areas, and only 16 percent in rural districts, and the people in the countryside were disproportionately old. The population of St. Denis had recently been rising again after generations of decline, mainly because of retired people from the north and east of France moving to

Périgord and the southwest, where the weather was kinder and the house prices low. Parisians found it hard to believe, but a two-bedroom modern house with full insulation on the outskirts of St. Denis could be bought for one hundred thousand euros.

He smiled at the thought of the admirable way many of these newcomers tried to adapt to rural life. Francine, a widow whose husband had been a hunting friend, had a couple of years ago started offering lessons to the newcomers in how to raise their own chickens, what to feed them, how to pluck and prepare them for the oven. Bruno had sometimes thought that on his own retirement he could start a small business offering to help such new arrivals in planning and maintaining a vegetable garden. But one of his burly friends on the town's current rugby team, whom Bruno had trained in the sport for many years, had now started his own such business and was doing well.

Stop it, Bruno! he said to himself, knowing he was letting his mind wander when he should be thinking about J-J's warning. He had a private phone that he normally used for personal matters, but that could easily be traced. He pulled into the tennis club and with a kiss on each cheek greeted the pretty Bernadette, a former pupil who was now one of the club's teenage stars. Without asking, he opened the drawer of the reception desk to borrow the club phone, which he used to call Isabelle's discreet personal phone. He left a message, giving her the number J-J had given him.

"Sounds like you're arranging a romantic assignation, Bruno," Bernadette said, with that worldly air that teenage girls learn to achieve soon after puberty.

"If only, *ma belle,* but you know my heart remains with you . . . and all my other beautiful pupils," he said, giving her a wave as he left. He went to the *mairie,* batted away the congratulations on his radio interview and repeated to the mayor what J-J had said. The mayor scribbled down some details about Roland Villon and his victims when Bruno told him that Célestine worked for the executive council which governed the region, and the mayor would almost certainly have met her in the course of his duties. Nor did Bruno forget to mention the bishop's secretary. The mayor promised to raise the issue with some old friends in the Senate. And on the mayor's advice, Bruno then went to his former office and told the same story to Colette Cantagnac.

"I'm familiar with the matter since I know Célestine quite well," Colette said. "And I think J-J is right to suggest that the staff at ministerial level might find it easiest to blame you. He is also right that an anonymous letter to a minister which claims to be copied to *Le Canard* and *Le Monde,* let alone the international press, is certain to get serious attention. And then when some of the mayor's old colleagues in the Senate raise the same matter . . . Hmmm, have you talked to Annette?"

"Yes, and she was already familiar with the matter since she knows one of the women involved through the Socialist Party."

"You mean Célestine," said Colette. "I'd better make a few calls to some colleagues in Paris. And leave the anonymous letters to me, Bruno. I know just how to draft them. I'll prepare something and let you see it before I have them mailed from Périgueux, or maybe from Cahors."

Not for the first time, Bruno marveled at the underground network of female officials in Paris and the regions, often working at supposedly secretarial jobs way beneath their competence and skills, who helped invisibly to keep the French ship of state afloat and to fend off collisions. He had never guessed at the extent of its existence until Colette arrived in St. Denis, but he supposed it was not very different from the way he and other sergeants in the French army had kept in discreet but constant touch, just to ensure that their officers did not get them all into too much trouble.

It was a strange world, he thought, in which many human activities reminded him of a swan, which appeared to be floating serenely through the water when beneath the surface its legs were paddling furiously. He assumed that the average salary of himself, Colette, the mayor, Isabelle, J-J, various senators in Paris and council staff in Périgueux and magistrates like Annette was probably thirty, maybe forty, euros an hour. Then the lawyers who would inevitably get involved would demand at least three hundred an hour for their services. So this squalid little escapade of Gendarme Villon would probably end up costing the French taxpayer tens of thousands of euros.

And it wasn't over. He walked out through the square, down the steps to the quayside where it was quiet and used his burner phone to call Amélie, magistrate, youth worker, jazz singer and former ministerial aide in the justice ministry when the center-left had been in power. She still had a wide range of contacts among the permanent staff of the ministry. He explained that he was acting on the advice of J-J, whom she knew. He'd barely begun when he was interrupted.

"Is this about the problem with Célestine?" she asked.

"Ah, you know about it?"

"Of course I do, I was at law school with Célestine and then we did a Young Socialists' summer camp on Ile de Ré. She was at Château des Milandes when I did my Josephine Baker concert. She's a great friend of Annette's as well, so I know what's been going on. What's the latest?"

Bruno explained about the young gendarme's uncle and J-J's fear that Bruno could end up being the victim.

"We won't let them get away with that," she replied cheerfully. "I know the people at Justice who do the liaising with the gendarmes, so I think we can start a little rumor about nepotism and then drop a word in the ear of a friendly journalist. I'll see what Isabelle says. I've got a gig this weekend at the Caveau de la Huchette, and she's planning to come along, so I'll see her there."

"What are you singing?"

"It's a tribute to Dinah Washington, the Queen of the Blues, so I'll be doing 'Baby, Get Lost' and 'I Wanna Be Loved,' and I've always wanted to sing her 'Big Long Slidin' Thing.' It's hilarious, a nonstop double entendre about having an affair with a trombonist."

"This Saturday?" Bruno said, wondering if there was any way he could slip away for the weekend. But he knew he'd better stay focused on this business.

"Next time I see you, I'll sing it, just for laughs, though I'll probably lose a bit in the translation. Maybe you should get Pamela to help out—how is she, by the way? Give her my best, and don't worry about this gendarme business. We've got your back, Bruno."

"Good to hear, take care of yourself, have a great concert, and thanks, Amélie. Big hugs."

Bruno hung up and looked up, startled to see he'd walked the whole length of the quayside and was almost at the aquarium. He turned and strode quickly back, wondering if he should go to the riding school to pick up Balzac or check in with Yveline and Sergeant Jules. He trotted up the steps to the *mairie* and saw Philippe Delaron climbing out of his car and waving, saying Bruno was just the man he'd come to see when he couldn't reach him by phone.

"It's about Georges Luchan, the Green guy who was on the radio with you this morning. He's the one getting the blame for trying to rig the program by swamping the station with calls. He's now claiming that you lied on air when you said you hadn't been to a pig killing. And he's sent out an official press release to announce that he's going on channel three this evening to show the film that proves you a liar."

"He'd better watch his step," said Bruno, suddenly feeling a spurt of anger. "I said I hadn't been to any illegal pig killing since slaughtering on the farm was banned. And that's true, because Stéphane and I were asked to make a film at his farm for the national folklore museum, reenacting the traditional event, because it was always a big moment on the farm, with all the neighbors coming to help. They wanted us to do it in the traditional way, and so we did," Bruno said, warming to his theme.

"We had to build the fire to boil the water, then hog-tie the pig and raise it off the ground, head down, before we cut the throat and collected the blood. Then we used a straight razor to shave off the bristles because they would traditionally be made into a shaving brush. Then came the butcher with his special skinning knives, making sure we didn't cut the urethra before slitting the stomach open. That was the moment when all the kids went 'oooh' as the intestines spilled out like an avalanche, steaming as the heat of the innards reached the open air." Bruno recounted helping the children wash out the intestines in the stream. And he insisted that the kids weren't squeamish. They had been raised on the farm and had seen it before. "You remember Stéphane's daughter, Dominique, maybe five or six years behind you in school, Philippe? She's the one who taught me about cleaning out the intestines when I first arrived here, and now she's at Grenoble University, all grown up."

"So you don't think it's a problem," Philippe asked, "that you said you hadn't been to a killing, but by your own account you took an active role."

"I said I hadn't been to an illegal killing. But this was legal, with special permission from the agriculture ministry, and the local land agent was on hand to make sure we did everything by the book, just as the museum wanted. The land agent is the man in charge of enforcing the rules on farms, and he wanted me there because I knew him well and had known his son in the army."

"What happened to this film? Can you still see it?"

"At the folklore museum, certainly. It's one of those films they show about the crafts of the past in that little cinema they have. I have an old DVD of it at home somewhere, if you know anybody who still has a DVD player. We all dressed up as best we could in nineteenth-century gear, the women and little girls in long dresses, me in gaiters and boots and a leather vest, and the makeup artists gave me a fine set of side-whiskers."

"Why the fancy dress?" Philippe asked.

"It was not fancy dress, it was a costume. The folklore museum likes to re-create the old ways whenever it can. I was delighted to be asked, but I think it was Stéphane who arranged it. Anyway, we'd better tell channel three to drop the idea, since it wasn't at all illegal."

"Can you prove that?"

"I'm sure the museum can, and I recall something on the DVD about this film being made with the approval and participation of the agriculture ministry for historical purposes."

"So you have no regrets?"

"About making the film? Not at all. I'm proud of playing a role," he said. "But I certainly have regrets about the bannings of killings on the farm, the way it had always been done, until those bureaucrats in Brussels were persuaded to leave it all for nice, modern hygienic slaughterhouses to enjoy their monopoly. Except that far too many of them are not hygienic and not even very clean, but I doubt if the Brussels bureaucrats have ever seen the inside of one, so they neither know nor care. The old farmers were much more hygienic."

"Maybe you'd better get in touch with the museum," said

Philippe. "Just to be sure they'll back you up. Or if you can find it, take that DVD of yours along to the TV studio. That way they would have to listen to you."

"Okay, but in the meantime why don't you call Stéphane? He's in the film, too. And the real story is that the Greens tried to swamp the radio station with calls. Do you know about that? So much for the Greens believing in a full and free discussion."

"Well, you put them on the defensive this morning because you knew what you were talking about and that embarrassed them," said Philippe. "Then it got worse when France Bleu put out an apology to all those people who had been trying to join the debate but were blocked because the Greens had plotted to take over the phones and dominate the show. So now the Greens want revenge, and they think they can get it by proving on TV that you lied to the children."

Bruno glared at him, and Philippe stood his ground and gazed back steadily at Bruno, notebook and pen at the ready.

"Well, did you?" he asked.

At that moment Bruno's phone vibrated. Keeping his eyes fixed on Philippe's face, he answered it with his name and rank.

"Bruno," came the mayor's familiar voice. "The planned joint inspection of the progress of the work on the new gendarmerie has been put forward a little. The gendarme general finds himself available, and we'll see you there at the site as soon as you can join us."

"I'll be right there, Monsieur le Maire. I'm just assuring Philippe Delaron that we had official permission to reenact a traditional farmhouse killing of a pig when the national folklore museum asked us to make the video for them. You'll remember because you were in the video, too, playing the role of the barber who came with a straight razor to shave off the bristles."

"I remember it well, Bruno," came the reply loud enough

for the young reporter to hear. "In fact, I still have the brush that we made from those bristles and use it every day that I shave."

"I'll be right there," Bruno said and then closed his phone, glared at Philippe and said briskly, "Just for the record, Philippe, any more questions?"

Chapter 15

Although everyone had got used to it, the old gendarmerie in St. Denis was an unusual sight, a structure intended to suggest 1950s modernism. It was, however, rendered in a brown sandstone that always reminded Bruno of the desert forts of the French Foreign Legion that he'd seen in his boyhood comics. Behind it was the associated apartment block, four stories high, built on the understanding that the modern gendarme would be a family man, no longer prepared to tolerate the nineteenth-century military-style barracks that had been his traditional quarters. But the apartment block was now to be transferred to the town to house low-income families as the new and much larger gendarmerie rose on the outskirts of town. The new gendarmes were to be provided with modest but well-appointed single-family houses.

"Ah, Bruno, always a pleasure," said the general in charge of gendarmes in the *département* of the Dordogne, reaching out to shake Bruno's hand. Tall and slim with a pencil-thin mustache and his hair gray at the temples, General Maurice Mouleydier always reminded Bruno of some film star from old movies whose name Bruno could never recall. His officers were wary of his reputation for politicking, but his men liked him and seemed to believe that he liked them. Bruno was not so sure, and he noticed with surprise that the general was alone and appeared to have driven himself from Périgueux. That was unusual.

"The construction delays have been overcome, and we're confident that your men will be able to move in this spring, maybe even in time for Easter," said the mayor. "Certainly by the end of May."

"I do indeed hope so, but this makes matters difficult for us," said the general. "These delays have been very disappointing, particularly the unfortunate business with the sewage system."

"You hired those contractors against our advice," the mayor replied. "Their track record was not reassuring, which made us look a little more closely into the connections or rather into the—er—background of these contractors. After all, we were asking ourselves why on earth you wanted to hire them."

"As we always said in the army, time spent in reconnaissance is seldom wasted," said Bruno, who had spent some hours looking into the family links between the general's wife and the contractors the general had wanted.

"You assured us that my gendarmes would be fully installed in time for the New Year, and that's clearly no longer possible," the general said, plunging ahead without regard to Bruno's hints. "You must realize that presents us with a problem. We already see that with this embarrassing business of these three young gendarmes having to rent private rooms. We may have to rethink the plan to close St. Cyprien and enlarge the gendarmerie here in St. Denis."

"Your contractors were to blame for the delays," said the mayor flatly, staring fixedly at the general. "And it is on the record that we warned you not to hire them, that they had a poor track record."

"Well, perhaps, but that has yet to be determined," the general replied. "But that could mean more delays, and we may be forced to look again at our plans. And as you know, some of my colleagues in Paris always thought that we should perhaps put the new regional headquarters south of the river, in Belvès rather than St. Denis."

Bruno had an uncomfortable feeling that the colleague in Paris was likely to be the uncle of Roland Villon and that Villon was a part of this discussion even though his name had not been mentioned.

"I brought the original contract along for reference," said Colette Cantagnac. "It says clearly in appendix two that the target date for completion is June the first, next year, nearly six months away. It also says in appendix three that local contractors shall only be hired with the consent of the mayor of St. Denis, and only with that consent is St. Denis at all liable for any failings of the said contractors. So it's clear that we are not liable. You are."

"Well, you know what lawyers are like," said the general. "We ordinary people understand that it's better to get along without them, with a good commonsense understanding of things that are in the common interest. You have an interest in keeping the gendarmerie in St. Denis, and we have an interest in having the most amiable and understanding relations with you, in a town where my gendarmes feel welcome and appreciated by the locals."

"That's right, sir," said Bruno. "And what a good relationship it has been over these many years. Sergeant Jules is only one of your three, or is it four, gendarmes who found a wife here in St. Denis. You're almost family, and we understand the power of family ties. And we're fortunate that the vast majority of your gendarmes have been exemplary in their behavior here."

Bruno was not going to come out and say plainly that all of them, the mayor and Colette, he and the general, knew that the issue here was Villon and that the general back in Paris wanted to threaten St. Denis with the loss of the gendarmerie, which would be a serious economic blow to the town.

"You know, it's interesting that the contract to which you refer was drawn up by a lawyer who is an old political friend of mine, and indeed the one who inherited my seat in the Senate after I served my term," said the mayor. At the sound of the word "Senate" the general's eyes narrowed. "Perhaps you'd like me to give my old friend a call and see if the senator agrees with your interpretation of the contract that he himself wrote?"

"We need not call in the senator just yet," said Colette, in her most matronly voice. "There's a very good young lawyer who works as an adviser to the executive council. You know who I mean, Bruno—Célestine."

"That's a good idea," said Bruno, thinking this was starting to feel like a game of power. The general had raised the stakes with a subtle threat to move the new gendarmerie elsewhere. The mayor met the bet with a hint of calling in his Senate friends. Colette raised the stakes by bringing in the executive council, and Bruno now raised them again.

"And why not bring in the bishop, too?" he asked, with mock innocence. "There are a lot of wise heads on the diocese council."

The gendarme general looked at them with a faint but puzzled smile, as though not sure what point they were trying to make.

"Are you aware, *mon général*, that Gendarme Roland Villon has this morning been arrested and charged with sexual assault by the Police Nationale and is now under *garde à vue* in Périgueux?" Bruno asked. "Perhaps your office has not yet been formally informed? I presume he would have contacted his colleagues to ensure that he had the advice and support of a good lawyer."

The general's jaw dropped. Evidently this came as most unpleasant news to him.

"This is not a matter for joking, Monsieur le Chef de Police," he said stiffly.

"It is not a joke, sir. I heard this from Commissaire Jalipeau himself," Bruno said. "The arrest was made this morning."

"But Jalipeau did not think to consult me, or to inform the captain in charge in St. Denis of the arrest of one of her gendarmes? This is outrageous!"

"I believe this is the day off for our *commandante* of gendarmes, sir," said Colette. "She may not be aware of it."

"Did Jalipeau not inform anybody? This is extraordinary," the general exclaimed. "It breaches every rule and tradition of etiquette among the forces of law and order. Excuse me, *messieurs-dames*." He turned away, pulling a phone from his pocket, calling a number, and when it was answered, he said, loud enough for Bruno to hear, "Prunier, is that you?"

The reply was inaudible, but it was clearly not the commander of the Police Nationale in Périgueux.

"Where is he?" the general went on. "I don't care if he's in a conference, I need to talk to him immediately." Another pause. "Very well, tell him as soon as he comes back that I'm awaiting his call on a matter of utmost urgency."

The general stood, fuming with anger, his back ramrod straight as he gazed at the ranks of almost completed houses of the new gendarmerie, whose future was now evidently in doubt. His phone suddenly vibrated, in the way that Bruno's did, and with the same timbre. Bruno would have expected it to ring with the tune *"Pour la patrie, l'honneur et le droit . . . ,"* the hymn of the gendarmes. Perhaps he had been issued with the same type of phone that Bruno had been given by General Lannes.

"Prunier, I am told by the chief of police Courrèges in St. Denis that your Commissaire Jalipeau has this morning arrested one of my gendarmes. If this is true, why was I not informed?"

There was a pause as the general listened. Then he said, sharply, "What the devil do you mean you've been calling me all morning? I've been driving down here to St. Denis for a meeting with the mayor, and my phone hasn't rung once. Maybe you were calling the wrong number. Anyway, is it true about one of my gendarmes being arrested without my being informed, let alone consulted in the usual way among colleagues?"

More silence, and then the general said, "Two charges of what?" Another pause and the general's face turned slowly white. "You're saying this involved a young woman who works for the bishop?" There came a longer pause, and the general's face began turning pink and then darkening to red. "And another young woman is the clerk to the executive council?" Another pause. "Right, I'll drive back up to see you at once."

The general turned on his heel to face Bruno, Colette and the mayor, saying grimly, "Now I understand your references to the bishop and the council. You will excuse me, Monsieur le Maire."

"Sir, your phone," said Bruno. "It's the same model as mine, a French government issue. And I had the same experience of it neither vibrating nor ringing. Unless you are actively looking at the screen, you don't know when you have an incoming call. There's a mechanism that silences both the ring and the vibrations, and it kicks in after you have reduced the call volume several times. That may have been the problem with your phone this morning, sir."

"*Quelle connerie de merde,*" the general snapped. "How do I fix it?"

"Go into Settings, select Sound and Vibrations, and turn up the volume for both calls and notifications. Then it will ring, unless you select Vibrate."

"Oh, *mon petit Jésus.*" The general almost wailed as he followed Bruno's suggestion and then looked at the screen. "I have dozens of missed calls. What an idiotic system."

"Yes, sir, I entirely agree," said Bruno, his voice full of sympathy. "General Lannes and the whole interior ministry all say the same, but we're stuck with these French-made phones."

"If I may add a brief word before you go, General," broke in the mayor. "Please make sure you check the penalty clauses on our contract and check with a lawyer before taking any rash decision. If you abandon this new gendarmerie, we will keep all the houses and you will have a gigantic hole in your budget, and that would never do. But, of course, I look forward to a long and happy relationship with your gendarmes here in St. Denis."

Once the general had gone, the mayor looked a little confused and said as if thinking aloud, "Why on earth would a general drive himself?"

"And do so in an unmarked and anonymous car that I'm pretty sure is not his own?" asked Bruno. "It looks like the kind of car they use to shadow people."

"Or to avoid people," said Colette. "I hear that he has a *petite amie* somewhere near Villamblard, you know, the Château de Barrière, the medieval one they're trying to restore."

"Ah, Count Wulgrim de Taillefer," said the mayor. "The man who launched the study of the archaeology of Vesona, the Roman tower in Périgueux. He had most of his property and treasures looted when he fled the Revolution and did not return until after Napoléon's coronation."

"So the exiled aristos thought any coronation meant it was safe to come home?" asked Bruno. "Even if not the Bourbon king on the throne?"

"Let's not get sidetracked, *messieurs,*" Colette said firmly. "I know you think the contract is solid, but could the gendarmes really renege on the enlarged new gendarmerie here in St. Denis? My job here depends on it."

"Somebody has to do Xavier's job," said Bruno. "I think his political dreams are over. But the administrative work, you'd be just right for it."

"Let's not get ahead of ourselves," said the mayor. "And traditionally a deputy mayor has always been an elected member of the council. In any event, Xavier remains an elected councilor until the next election."

Colette snorted. "I'll be surprised if he has the nerve to show his face in council after this. We all know what happened and I heard that Xavier's father is furious about it all, and he's the man with the car business and the money."

At that point, Bruno's phone vibrated, and he heard the baron's voice, asking, "Can you turn on the radio? There's a discussion all about you on the lunchtime call-in show, starring that bastard Louis, the retired cop from Montignac."

"What's Louis saying?"

"That you got his dog killed, the one he liked to claim was the best hunting dog in the valley."

"Does he say the dog was shot by Arab terrorists?"

"Of course not, Bruno. This is Louis. I'm trying to listen. We can talk later."

"Who is this Louis?" asked Colette.

"Now retired, the former municipal cop in Montignac who

always thought he should have been made chief of police for the valley because he was older than me." Bruno explained what the baron had told him.

"But the job didn't exist before they wanted to reward you," Colette said. "Some people in the union wanted to make a fuss about it, but the orders came from on high."

"Wiser counsels prevailed," said the mayor. "I'll get the radio station to send us a tape so we can listen to the whole thing."

"I suppose this is the follow-up to the Greens blocking the lines into the station to embarrass you," Colette went on. "Maybe we should rally some supporters of our own, maybe the hunting clubs, or some of the kids from your tennis classes, better still the girls' rugby squad. You know how people around here love the idea of girls playing rugby. And we'd better get you some support online, Bruno. That's the real battleground these days, not the airwaves. I'll get the computer club on it."

She turned away, pulled out her phone and began talking. Bruno and the mayor looked at one another, each of them startled at the way Colette seemed so familiar with the relentless advance of technology into the politics and public life of a small village in deepest France. Bruno had a sudden twinge of sympathy for that hapless German infantryman in the trenches on the Somme in 1916 who was the first soldier ever to see the future waddling on tracks across the barbed wire toward him in the shape of war's first tank.

"I'll get onto the old folks' home," said the mayor, a sudden enthusiasm in his voice as he pulled out his own phone, evidently eager to join this multimedia campaign. "If those Greens think they can mount a mass attack on the airwaves, they have yet to be on the receiving end of a coordinated assault by the old folks of St. Denis."

Bruno went to his car and turned on the radio to listen to

Louis's grumbles, just in time to hear the voice of Marie-Do saying, "Next caller, please."

Then came another familiar voice, as his colleague Juliette, the cop from Les Eyzies, declared, "You do talk a lot of rubbish, Louis. Your dog was shot by Arab terrorists in the course of a highly dangerous operation, an operation which succeeded thanks to Bruno. Moreover, it was not a case of Bruno taking a job that should have been yours. Bruno saved you from being fired for drinking too often on the job. The reason you grumble about him is that he's a good cop and you never were. And I speak as a policewoman."

"Hello, caller, could you identify yourself, please?" Marie-Do asked. But by then, Juliette had gone, and another voice, a man's this time, came on the line, saying, "I'm from Montignac, Louis, and I'm not sure that I ever saw you entirely sober when you were on duty, except when you had a hangover. Or when you were hunting. So tell me, as a fellow hunter, why are you agreeing with those ignorant Greens and joining their attack on Bruno?"

"I'm not criticizing Bruno's hunting skills, but he's from Bergerac originally and these city boys don't really understand our life here in the countryside," Louis said. "And all that time Bruno spent in the army turned him into a real military spit-'n'-polish type, and we're not like that here in the Vézère Valley."

"What a lot of crap," the caller said. "It's not spit-'n'-polish types who win the Croix de Guerre, as Bruno did. Nor drunks, Louis. And as someone who lives in Montignac, I have to say I'm very glad that you've retired."

"Next caller, please."

"I'm a hunter, but I also consider myself a Green, and like most hunters in the valley I have a lot of respect for Chief of Police Bruno, not just for his military record but for the way he organized the weapons training for hunters up and down this valley. It's no accident that the number of hunting accidents has fallen dramatically. It's because people like Bruno made their fellow hunters take the training, and the exams, very seriously."

A new voice came on the line. "I'm calling from the retirement home in St. Denis, where we all think the world of Bruno, who spends his spare time teaching the local youngsters to play tennis in summer and rugby in winter. I wish I'd been able to play rugby when I was a girl. And from what I hear about you, Louis, from my cousin who lives in Montignac, you spent half your working time and all your time off in bars and drinking, unless you were out hunting. I'd rather have Bruno's kind of policing than yours."

Bruno smiled as he shook his head in appreciation. He had recognized the voice of Mireille, a retired schoolteacher of formidable size and a very gifted pastry cook whose fruit pies were famous in St. Denis. In fact, she'd probably interrupted her baking of tarts for the old folks' Christmas party for all the village children. And that reminded Bruno that he'd better check the condition of the Father Christmas costume he was expected to wear.

Chapter 16

Bruno was still listening to Louis on the radio becoming less and less coherent as he was mocked by his questioners. Driving into St. Denis, Bruno even started to feel sorry for the retired cop. He parked a discreet distance from the gendarmerie and went into the residential block to ring Yveline's bell with a short-long-short, trusting that she'd recognize the Morse code for SOS.

"We just had a visit from your general," he began when she opened the door to welcome him in. "He was threatening to cancel the contract to move into the enlarged gendarmerie, and that was before he learned that J-J had arrested Roland. He's now racing up to Périgueux to confront J-J's boss in the police *commissariat,* and I don't think this will end well. I hope your job isn't at risk?"

"Bonjour to you, too, *mon cher,*" Yveline replied, with more of a wry grin than her usual smile. She said Bruno was just in time to join her in a late lunch, and he saw from the sea of wrapping paper, rolls of Scotch tape and scissors that she was spending her day off wrapping Christmas presents. Whoops, he thought to himself, that was something he'd neglected to even think about.

"I don't know if my job is at risk, Bruno, not these days," she said. "Ten, twenty years ago Roland's crimes would have been hushed up, and I'd have been eased out to Corsica or the wilds of the Massif Central. But twenty years ago I'd never have been a *capitaine* at all, let alone at this young age, with a highly visible and powerful woman *commissaire* in the police HQ in Périgueux, who, I am reliably told, left Prunier no option but to let J-J go ahead with the arrest."

"Twenty years ago Célestine would not have been in such a powerful position in local government at such a young age," Bruno said. "And the diocese council would not have been run by a young woman. But this is now and the rules are different, even if we aren't sure how different they are in places like the very top of the Gendarmerie Nationale."

"I'm not sure about that, either, but a lot of gendarmes would say if a young gendarme goes wrong, his commander is to blame," she replied. "I may even at times have said something like that myself. In the meantime," she went on, steering him into the kitchen, "I'll set the table and put out the salad and I'll let you make one of your lovely omelettes. There are some of your eggs and garlic and Stéphane's cheese in the fridge."

Once the table was set and the salad tossed, she came to watch as he grated the cheese, chopped some fat heads of garlic very fine and, since she didn't own a garlic press, used the flat of the knife to flatten them. He put her largest pan on the heat with a spoonful of duck fat and a little butter, threw in the garlic and used a fork to whip four eggs into froth, added a generous spoonful of water, salt and pepper and whipped them again. Once the fat was about to spit, he swirled the shredded garlic around it again, poured in the eggs and used his left wrist to turn the pan this way and that while his spatula kept lifting the edges of the eggs to let the uncooked liquid run onto the hot metal of the pan. Then he added the grated cheese from a Tomme d'Audrix, folded over half the omelette to cover the cheese, let it rest and then flipped it to give the merest hint of brown to the other side and then halved and served it, half an omelette each.

"Why does mine fall apart while yours looks like it's been professionally wrapped?" she asked, pouring him a glass of red wine from the town vineyard.

"Practice," he said. "*Bon appétit.* But let's think of your position. It's a pity Gilles is still in Ukraine—it's the kind of story he would handle really well. As things stand, maybe you should have a word with Annette, who knows the law in this area."

"The law is one thing," she said grimly. "The top tier of the gendarmerie is something else entirely. The one thing they fear is not being in control, not knowing what's going on, and getting ambushed like that makes them feel dreadfully exposed."

"That's exactly what happened to J-J and Prunier," said Bruno. "Ten, twenty years ago they could have reached a quiet deal with your general, but with powerful and media-savvy women in their own top ranks they can't get away with that anymore."

"We gendarmes have not yet progressed quite that far," she replied, and then paused before going on, almost hesitant. "Do you think they'll keep Roland in jail until the trial, or will he be allowed out on pretrial release?"

"Call Annette and ask her," he replied. "And you'd better use my phone, just in case."

Annette said it would depend partly on her boss, the grandly titled *procureur de la République.* But since he was a civilian official, close to the executive council where Célestine worked, she suspected he'd want a quick trial and keep the gendarme in custody.

"He makes friends on three fronts: with the executive council, with women in the legal system and with women at large, and even with the church. He makes one enemy, the gendarme general whose nephew is a bad boy, and the general might even lose his job if he tries too hard to protect the nephew. That's how my boss will think."

"And if the gendarme general stays in office, my career is over," Yveline said glumly.

"Not if we have newspaper reporters lined up demanding the general comment on the claim that he's taking his revenge on you," said Annette. "And we know just the woman who'd be prepared to say that publicly—a highly respected Sorbonne professor with an international reputation who has several times had essays on *Le Monde*'s op-ed pages, and just happens to be your mayor's lady friend."

"Jacqueline, of course," said Bruno.

"Of course, this will mean that in future every gendarme in France will be on the lookout for your van, Bruno," Annette went on cheerfully. "You'll never be able to drink and drive ever again."

"If that's what it takes, I'll be his chauffeuse," said Yveline, laughing in what sounded like relief.

"Any word yet on Monique's funeral?" Bruno said as Annette seemed about to end the call.

"The postmortem said suicide by those sleeping pills she'd taken," Annette replied. "The pill you found in her car, Bruno, was some anti-allergy medicine she'd been taking in the summer when the pollen count was high. And so, taking into account the letters she left behind, the *procureur* has signed off on suicide as cause of death. That means her next of kin, Dominic, is now free to plan whatever funeral he sees fit. No word yet what or when that will be."

"What about my gendarme, Roland Villon?" Yveline asked.

"Above my pay grade, but my boss is on the way to Péri-gueux for a meeting with his boss, the chief prosecutor. From what I hear, it's an open-and-shut case for the two women we know about, and now we've heard of several more women coming forward. Got to go, we can talk later, or when I see you at your dinner tomorrow, Yveline."

Yveline ended the call and handed Bruno back his phone, which at once began to vibrate. Another call was waiting, and he answered, seeing from the screen that it was Julien from the town vineyard.

"Bruno, you know Maurice Galantin, the man who writes about wine for *La Croix;* you met him at a tasting last year. He just wrote me a disturbing letter."

Julien went on to say that when Galantin left the vineyard the other day after an early tasting, he was stopped on the way back to town by two young gendarmes and ordered to blow into a Breathalyzer. If he preferred not to, the gendarmes said, he could go on his way for two hundred euros in cash. Galan-tin said he would not take a Breathalyzer but would wait for the arrival of a doctor who would take a blood test that would prove he had not swallowed a drop of alcohol. As a wine writer, he told them, he sipped, tasted and then spat. After a brief dis-cussion between gendarmes, he was waved on. He noted that there were no identifying numbers on their uniforms, so he wondered if they were genuine. But he has a good memory and is prepared to come back for a lineup and is sure he can pick them out. They were both in their early twenties, one slim and dark haired and the other burly and fair haired, and the latter was wearing an expensive watch that Galantin recognized as a Rolex, or at least a very convincing copy.

"That's outrageous, Julien," said Bruno. "I'm here with Yve-line, their boss, and she heard all that and looks pretty angry. Could I drop by the vineyard and pick up the letter? Don't let anybody else handle it. And then Yveline will accept Galantin's offer to attend a lineup."

"There's a PS," said Julien. "He gave his driver's license to the dark-haired one when he was stopped and was careful to pick it up by the edges when he got it back and kept it in a plastic envelope in case the gendarme's fingerprints were still on it."

"Better still," said Bruno. "Do you have a phone number for him?"

Julien read out the number, and Bruno thanked Julien and then called the number. It began to ring just as Yveline said, "The only fair-haired one is Roland, and he does wear a very expensive-looking watch. A solid citizen who writes for *La Croix* is going to be very, very hard to deny."

The phone call was answered, and Bruno gave his name and rank and said he'd just heard from Julien at the town vineyard. Was Monsieur Galantin still prepared to identify these two men in gendarme uniform?

"Very much so, and I still have my driver's license in its plastic sheath, so the fingerprints should still be there. I'm tasting in the Bergerac vineyards for the next couple of days, so I can easily come to Périgueux or wherever you need me to be."

"I'll fix it and call you back," said Bruno. "And thank you for being a good citizen, and a pretty smart one."

He hung up, looked at Yveline and said, "Are you sure you want to go ahead with this, surrendering your own gendarmes to a Police Nationale lineup? A lot of gendarmes won't like it."

"Tough," she said. "I can't have crooks on my team. This is my responsibility. Let me call J-J myself."

Thirty minutes later, after confirming the meeting with Galantin, Yveline and a dark-haired young gendarme were in her car with Bruno in the rear seat, heading toward the *commissariat de police* in Périgueux. Yveline did not introduce Bruno to him, but later at a junction she asked if the road was clear and used his name: Jean-Luc.

J-J met them in the basement garage, nodding his approval when he saw that Jean-Luc was in civilian clothes. Yveline carried his *cahier officiel,* which contained a sheaf of paper with his complete fingerprints. Galantin had arrived just a few moments earlier, so it took less than five minutes for ten young-to-youngish men, all in civilian clothes, to be assembled in a lineup. Roland Villon was brought up from his cell and ignored his fellow gendarme, choosing to stand at one end of the line. Each of the positions was numbered. Villon was number 12.

Galantin, after being briefed by J-J and shaking hands with Bruno, who recalled having once met him at the town vineyard, went into the lineup room. The other gendarme chose position number two. Galantin, walking slowly, paused at each place to examine the face of each man.

"Done," he said, and then held his tongue. J-J must have briefed him not to identify anybody at this stage. J-J led him into a wide room, where Galantin said firmly, "Number two and number twelve," and gave J-J the plastic envelope with his driver's license.

One of the aides from the technical unit was on hand. Wearing gloves, he used tweezers to slide the license from its plastic sheath, dusted it with fingerprint powder, shook it clean, then placed the license in a small black box, closed the lid and there was a brief flash of light at the edges of the box, and then a piece of paper came from a slot bearing the imprints that had been on the license. The technician compared them with Jean-Luc's prints in the *cahier officiel* and confirmed it was the same man.

Roland Villon had already been taken back to his cell, but the other eleven men were waiting. J-J went into the room where the lineup had been held, summoned Jean-Luc to him and told the others they were free to go.

"You are under arrest for falsely demanding money with menace while wearing an official uniform," J-J said. "Do you have anything to say for yourself? Your superior officer is here, and she will arrange a lawyer to represent you, but for the moment you are in custody and your status as a gendarme and an officer of the law is hereby suspended."

Jean-Luc gazed helplessly at Yveline, then at J-J and back at Yveline again. Her face was blank and somber. He swallowed once, then twice, and said, "It was him, Roland, his idea. He sneered at us if we didn't join in. Everybody does it, Roland would say. I think I recognize the guy who identified us, that wine man from the vineyard, the one who defied us to try. Roland said they'd all be over the limit when they came out from tasting."

"If you make a statement, it may go easier for you," J-J said. "You can give it to me or to your superior officer, as you like. Or you may want to wait for the advice of a lawyer. Up to you."

"I'll tell you everything I know," Jean-Luc said. "I felt in my bones this would happen. It's actually a relief of sorts. Do you know about what Roland did with the women we stopped?"

"That's what got you into trouble, the women," said J-J. "You picked one who works for the bishop and another who works for the politicians who run this *département*. You couldn't have picked two worse victims if you tried. Was it always you on patrol with him? Or was François in on this, too?"

"If you don't know, I'm saying nothing," said Jean-Luc. It was a brief show of spirit, but Bruno was prepared to bet that it would not last, not once the cell door closed behind him.

"Up to you, but you won't get another offer," said J-J, his voice a flat monotone that said he'd heard it all before and neither believed nor cared about most of what he heard. "And if we don't get it from you, we'll get it from François. We've got a car heading down to St. Denis to pick him up, and I expect he'll tell us everything you don't.

"Either you help us now with everything you know, or take your chances with jail, the lawyer and the court," he went on in that same, bored tone. "You're looking at six years, minimum. So good luck with getting any kind of job when you get out. If you get out. Disgraced gendarmes aren't popular in prisons. Still, a good-looking youngster like you can probably find some big, hunky protector to keep you alive, if you're very nice to him."

Five minutes later, having said he didn't need a lawyer, Jean-Luc was sitting in an interview room with a cup of coffee and a pack of cigarettes, with a tape recorder whirring gently in the background as he recounted to J-J the various crimes of Roland Villon and François.

"I blame myself," said Yveline as she and Bruno drove back to St. Denis. "I knew it was a disaster, sending those three young recruits to live in that rented house without proper supervision. But the general insisted that he wanted those new recruits to know the area before we all moved into the big new gendarmerie. That's where I went wrong. I should have put my foot down, put my job on the line if necessary, and said no, even if we had to order some of the veterans off into rentals. Those three youngsters were an unsupervised disaster waiting to happen."

"Did you keep copies of the memos you sent, urging that? And copies of the general's replies?"

"Yes, of course."

"In that case, can we find some deniable way to let the general understand that you have lots of ammunition in writing for any disciplinary action he might be threatening to bring against you?" Bruno asked. "The mayor might be one option, or Colette. She knows more about what she calls office jujitsu than you or I ever will. She'll come up with something. And from what I know of your rules, you now have more than a platoon's worth of gendarmes, so you're supposed to have a junior officer to help out, as well as another sergeant to back up Jules."

"We don't have sergeants in the gendarmes," she said wearily. "A senior warrant officer is known as a *maréchal des logis,* and he has three stripes on his epaulettes, which is why you and everybody else all call him Sergeant Jules. If I have my way, I'll get him promoted to *adjudant-chef* or even major. But you're right about the station rules. We have been understaffed in senior ranks for months. All I have is Jules. They keep promising him an *adjoint* and I've been pleading for a *sous-lieutenant.* To be honest I'd even have settled for an *aspirant.*"

"Would you object if I call around to find out the staffing elsewhere in the *département*?" Bruno asked. "I think you're doing more with fewer staff than other units, and that may be deliberate, to put pressure on you."

"I'm used to that," she said with a bitter laugh. "I think it's easier than that. The problem is you, Bruno. There is not much crime in St. Denis, nor up and down the valley now, thanks to you. We have more people in the valley than in the whole of Périgueux, but only about one-third of their reported crimes. That's why I've been undermanned and underfunded."

"Am I supposed to be sorry?" he asked, grinning.

"Not at all, and it's not all to do with you," she said. "This valley has had a low level of crime since we began collecting data in the late nineteenth century, probably because people were too busy working in the fields, hunting and putting food on the table. Talking of which, at dinner tomorrow night you'll see an old friend and new colleague, former sergeant and now sublieutenant Claire Castignac. She just completed her officer training and will join us here in St. Denis."

As Yveline's car reached the outskirts of town, Bruno's phone vibrated. It was Annette, saying she was meeting Célestine for drinks and dinner at Petit Saïgon in Sarlat at seven, and that Célestine had made a point of saying she'd like to meet him. Would Bruno like to join them?

Chapter 17

The restaurant was on the same street as the building where Bruno had first met Laura and her basset, where Monique had launched her *conciergerie* business and where the previous evening he'd been in the penthouse in which she and Dominic had lived. As he strolled down the street with Balzac at his heels, the building was dark except for that top floor, and Bruno wondered what Dominic might be doing. The man was a mystery to Bruno, a type he'd not encountered before, seemingly mild mannered but swift to anger, and always watchful, as if ready to suspect the worst of those around him.

He must have had a grim time growing up in that orphanage in Strasbourg, Bruno reflected, where he'd been one of the few white boys. Bruno's boyhood had been very different. He could not recall any Black boys at his own orphanage, and only one Arab who was an excellent soccer player and therefore popular. On instinct Bruno didn't much like Dominic but didn't want to judge the man when he knew so little about him. There was an old blues number that came into his head, about walking a mile in the other guy's shoes. Bruno's childhood had not been wonderful, but it had probably been a cakewalk compared with what Dominic had gone through. With a French mother and a German father, neither one of whom wanted him, Dominic must have asked himself if he could ever be at home anywhere.

Bruno recalled the cold and distant tone of that extract from Monique's farewell letter to her husband that Annette had allowed him to read. Dominic could not have read it without feeling a sense of failure, of inadequacy, of having failed the one woman who had opened her heart and her home to him, until she sent him that final, grim screed. And Dominic must have realized that Bruno and Annette had each been required by their work to read his dead wife's cold verdict on his failures as a husband and as a man. And others would have read it, too, staff members in the procurator's office, probably the local police, and there would doubtless have been gossip spreading around the social circle that Dominic had shared with Monique, a circle in which as her widower he now had only the shadow of a place.

Bruno turned his thoughts to Célestine, the young woman he was about to meet. She was already building an impressive political career, which meant that Bruno could probably expect to be dealing with her for the rest of his working life. Cops and politicians might not always like or trust one another, but most of them understood the need to find some common ground and understanding. They were, after all, supposed to be engaged in the same business: serving the people, the public order and the common good. That, at least, was the principle, and most of the politicians he'd known in St. Denis and the region seemed to abide by it, more or less. Or at least they made an effort to try. He hoped Célestine would be the same.

Annette was already drinking white wine at the table with another young woman when he entered. He hung up his overcoat, revealing the civilian sports jacket he preferred to wear when off duty. He kissed her fondly on each cheek and then shook hands with Célestine. She was a young woman of medium height, medium build, neat brown hair with blond streaks, large brown eyes and a full mouth with a wide, albeit impersonal, smile. There was character in her face, he thought, a certain directness in her look and strength in her jaw. She was wearing what he'd come to think of as a kind of uniform, a dark blue pantsuit with a cream silk blouse. It was a sartorial cousin to Annette's dark skirt, turtleneck sweater and sports jacket in brown and gold checks.

"A pleasure to meet you, mademoiselle," he said, bowing his head a little to Célestine before adding, "I'm sorry for the difficult time you've been through."

"An occupational hazard for women, monsieur, but thank you," she said. Her voice was low-pitched but cheerful as well as feminine. "I've read stories about you in *Sud Ouest* which Annette tells me don't begin to do you justice. And this is your famous basset," she added, bending down to caress Balzac, who turned at once from his enthusiastic reunion with Annette to greet a new friend.

"He looks too amiable to be a hunting dog," she said. "But I've read that basset hounds can hunt wild boars. Is that true?"

"Yes, but this one focuses more on finding lost children and black truffles and picking up the *bécasses* that I like to hunt," he replied.

"If you get invited to Bruno's home for dinner, count yourself fortunate, because Bruno is a very good cook. But if *bécasses* are on the menu, be warned," said Annette. "It's not enough to eat the bird itself, you will be expected to pick up the head by the bird's long beak and then bite through the thin skull to crunch your way through the brains."

"My father was a hunter and a serious lover of food," said

Célestine. "And when he and his fellow club members trapped ortolans, they would fatten them up and then throw them alive into a vat of Armagnac to drown and marinade, before being roasted. They were then eaten from the claws and legs up, devouring everything but the small beak. The hunter's head was covered in a large napkin while the dish was enjoyed, which my father insisted was to retain the succulent scent of the bird. My mother, by contrast, claimed that it was to hide the hunter's face and identity from God. She refused the napkin, saying it would ruin her hair."

"Did you enjoy it?" Bruno asked.

"No, it was declared illegal not long before I was born, not that it ever stopped President Mitterrand," she replied before pausing and then saying, "I heard you defend hunting on the radio this morning and scribbled down the figures you cited of the population explosion among wild boars and deer. I checked them and found you were right. Should we bring back wolves and other predators?"

"We may have to," Bruno replied. "Unless the scientists can find a humane way to limit the numbers of the deer and wild boars. But while bringing back wolves can work in a protected area like a national park, I wouldn't want to see wolves at large where humans live."

"You said on the radio that you had a lot of sympathy for the Greens. Do you ever vote for them?"

"I always vote for Alphonse, our own first Green on the council," he said, and then paused. "Beyond that, I'm afraid that I suspect there are two tribes, urban Greens and rural Greens, and they often don't speak the same language, which is very sad."

Bruno turned to Annette, who had chosen the restaurant, and asked what she recommended on the menu.

"*Phở,* which is a traditional soup served at breakfast, is always a good place to start if you're not familiar with Vietnamese food. I'll have *bún chả* Obama, pork patties in a fish-sauce-laced pork broth, fatty and rich, or maybe *bún riêu,* which is a vermicelli noodle soup packed with crabmeat, minced pork, tomatoes and greens, zingy and vibrant," Annette said. "*Bún chả* got a new name when President Obama was photographed eating it with an American chef and food writer; it's actually *bún chả Hà Nội.*"

"The Obama one for me, please," said Bruno. "And the *phở* to begin, and whatever else you think I should eat, and I'll have a glass of that white wine you're having."

"I gather you're the man I have to thank for bringing my attacker, that gendarme, to justice," Célestine said. "And please call me Célestine."

"No thanks needed, Célestine, and please call me Bruno. He's already been charged with one count of theft, another of demanding money with menace, and the assault case against you has now been widened to include several other women."

"Why did it take so long, after my own testimony and that of the woman on the diocesan council?"

"I don't know the details of your case, but I imagine it was partly because the place where you were stopped was not listed on any patrol schedule of any gendarme unit in the region. He was wearing no identification beyond a uniform, and the number of his motorbike had been obscured, so his identity was unclear. And relations between gendarmes and the Police Nationale are not always as friendly as we might like."

"Should they not be improved, or perhaps the two police forces might be amalgamated?"

"Relations should be improved, certainly. Fused into one body, I'm not so sure. Since the days of Napoléon our politicians have been wary of putting all policing powers into one organization, just as they usually like to separate their domestic intelligence agency from the international one. It's the old tradition of divide and rule. But tell me about your work. Do you work for the party or the local government?"

"Both, in that I'm a party member, but now paid by the *département,* and if my party lost control, I'd be expected to resign. My job is to run two task forces, one on the future of public transport in what is a largely rural *département* and the other on ways to recruit doctors and dentists when most of them want to head to the bright lights and big cities as soon as they're qualified. We have to examine possible policies, try to assess how and if they would work, what they would cost, whether they were tried elsewhere and so on. I'm supposed to do that without allowing my politics to influence my recommendations, which is not easy."

"Good luck with finding the doctors," he said, and turned to include Annette. "I'm sure you've heard Fabiola complaining about the shortage of all kinds of medical staff, including nurses. Do you want to stay in that role, Célestine, or eventually run for office?"

"I'll be on the party list for the next *département* election, and I hope I'll be on the list for the national and European elections, and as a passionate European, that's where I want to make my career."

"How did you first get interested in politics?" he asked. "Was your family political?"

"Not very, although they always voted. My grandfather was the militant, one of the children of '68. I was radicalized partly by him and his stories, but also I was outraged by Sarkozy and his conviction for bribing a judge to cover up illegal donations and then the campaign funds scandal. It all made French politics seem so squalid. How about you, Bruno. Are you political?"

"I usually vote one way for the president and the other for the parliamentary elections, but it's difficult now with Macron taking up most of the room in the center, so the left and right each became more hard line. Local elections are easier, where you can vote for a person you know rather than some symbol on TV."

"Annette tells me you don't have a TV. Is that true?"

"Yes, but I do have a radio and a laptop. Still, I prefer reading books, being in my garden or walking my dog—"

"And cooking," Annette interrupted.

"I'm surprised that you haven't asked me what happened with the gendarme," Celestine said. "Aren't you curious?"

"Of course," said Bruno, "but it's not my job to pry, and if you want to tell me, I'm certain you will. Whatever he did, it must have been awful."

"It could have been worse. He opened my car door, groped really painfully at my breasts, tearing my bra and bruising them. Then opened his fly buttons and made it clear what he wanted me to do. I said, 'Never,' started the car and drove away fast, and was as relieved as I was surprised that he didn't follow me. I drove straight to the *commissariat* and told a senior woman cop whom I know exactly what had happened. She had my breasts photographed then and again later when the bruises were more prominent."

"Don't tell me," he said. "I bet she was Gouppilleau."

"You know her?"

"Yes, we worked together on a similar case," Bruno said. "I think she's terrific, and I love her taste in shoes."

Célestine stared at him a moment and then burst out in a laugh, looked at Annette and laughed again when Annette grinned and said, "I told you he was different."

"He certainly is," Célestine said, grinning in return. The good humor lasted through the arrival of the food, the pouring of the wine and the rest of the meal. They had a number of friends in common, from her tennis club in Périgueux to

Marie-Do at the radio station. She poured out more wine for Annette and was about to do the same for Bruno, but he put a hand over his glass.

"Let's not tempt fate," he said, smiling. "I have to drive back, and this is no time to start dodging the gendarmes."

"I'm on foot, since I'm staying the night with Annette before some political meetings here tomorrow, trying to judge whether people are ready for a coalition of all the left."

"Including the Communists and Mélenchon?" he asked.

"It would hardly be a coalition without them, but a lot of people have strong reservations," she replied.

"Including me," said Annette. "How about you, Bruno?"

"I'm not very political, but I don't like the hard left and can't stand the hard right," he said.

"That's less an answer than an evasion," Célestine said. "This is just between us, and I'm curious. I know you were a soldier and spend most of your free time as a volunteer, training young people in rugby and tennis. Give me an idea of what you really think."

"I'd probably be a Gaullist if the old man were still with us, and I'd like to bring back national service. It need not be in the military, but in hospitals, schools, public service. I think it's good for our young people of every social class and ethnic group to learn to mix and train together, yes, and share foxholes, too," he said. "And I don't like the way the internet is starting to replace our newspapers, with their traditional belief in the free press. There's so much fake information circulating that we have to do something about that. I think the national debt has been allowed to get out of hand, and our world is becoming dangerous again, so we need to get more serious about defense. Billionaires should pay more taxes. That's about it."

"Nothing about immigration?" Célestine asked. "Please, I really want to know what you think."

"Some of the hardest-working people I know are the immigrants in our market in St. Denis—the Vietnamese and Senegalese—and one of our best teachers is an Arab from Algeria. The deputy head of our fire brigade is a Tunisian. And our under-twelves rugby team is like a miniature United Nations."

"That's a bit of a platitude," she replied. "For every answer I hear like that, Bruno, I hear three or four others about drug dealers, unemployed deadbeats, rapists, bullies of their own women. What do you really think?"

"Most of the women I know, Célestine," he began, his voice more serious, "like you and Annette, and Annette's friends in St. Denis, Pamela and Fabiola and Yveline and Jacqueline— all smart and well-educated women—have not a single child between them. If women like you aren't having babies, then we need immigrants, or the country grinds to a halt."

A silence fell, then each of the two women spoke at once. Annette retorting, "What about you, Bruno? You have no kids that I know of." And Célestine was saying, "This planet is already overpopulated . . ."

They both stopped speaking, and into the silence Bruno spoke quietly.

"A woman I loved was carrying a child of mine and had an abortion without my knowledge, and told me only when it was over," he said. "It was the saddest moment of my life. I would happily have raised the child myself if I'd been given the option. But I wasn't."

The air grew heavy and awkwardness endured as the waitress came to start clearing away the plates and asking with bright, professional geniality if they had enjoyed their meal. They answered automatically and, chastened, she withdrew into the kitchen.

"Sorry," he said. "I didn't mean to put such a damper on things."

"It was my fault," said Célestine. "I pressed you and got more honesty than I expected."

At that moment in the meal, Bruno became aware of a man, alone, who had entered the restaurant sometime earlier and taken a chair in a corner, details Bruno's subconscious had noted without him registering. The stranger had then studied the menu for an inordinate amount of time while holding it close to his eyes with one hand. It was odd behavior, but not until a second glance did Bruno catch the glint of something reflecting the light from a wall lamp, at which point Bruno realized the stranger was taking photos of their table with a mobile phone almost—but not quite—hidden by the menu.

He rose quickly, went to the table, snatched away the menu with one hand and seized the phone with the other, pushing the man back into his seat. He felt two small knobs sticking out from the sides of the phone.

"Call the police, Annette," he said. "We're being spied on."

With that, he slipped the phone into his pocket and used his arms and hips together to slam the table hard against the man's belly, shoving it as far as it would go, trapping the intruder on the cushioned banquette that ran along the wall. Keeping the weight of his body against the table, Bruno pulled out the phone, saw it was still in camera mode and that the man had been filming him, Annette and Célestine during their meal.

"Give that back to me," snarled the trapped man, unable to reach far enough even to touch Bruno, who by this time had shown his own police ID card to the alarmed waiters. They quickly backed away as they saw it.

"Célestine," he said, "take the phone, note the film he's been taking of us and see what else you can find." He handed it to her and she began exploring the phone with Annette until she turned away to speak.

"He's a private detective, Raoul Condorcet. He has a landline starting with 0553, so he's local, and there are emails from the notorious Poincevin," Célestine said, and looked at Bruno. "There's an email from Poincevin saying this creep gets thirty euros an hour to watch what I do and note whom I see, and his pay goes up to fifty euros for every hour over eight hours in any one day."

"Check some of the older photos," Bruno suggested, keeping his eyes fixed on Condorcet. "Are the cops on their way?"

"I called Messager, who lives just up the hill and is coming himself," Annette replied, referring to the town's chief of police, with an equivalent rank to Bruno. An elderly man, he was close to retirement.

"You can't keep me here," panted Condorcet. The edge of the table jammed hard between his rib cage and his hips was keeping him short of breath. Other diners began taking photos of the odd scene of a man trapped by a table while two women went through the phone he'd been using to spy on them.

"I'm not keeping you here," said Bruno amiably. "The table is. And we're just waiting for the chief of police of Sarlat to tell us if this spying on us is legal. The magistrate who is eating with us thinks you don't have the right to film or record us without our permission, which you didn't ask for and we did not grant."

"This is a public place," Condorcet protested.

"Under French law even in a public place permission is required if your photo is taken when you are isolated and recognizable, and the courts have upheld a limited right to privacy in a restaurant, since you may claim to be renting a table for a specific time," Annette said, just as Messager came through the door in plain clothes, with a young uniformed policeman at his heels.

"Bonsoir tous," he said. "Is this the man you claim was spying on you?"

"*Bonsoir,* Monsieur le Chef de Police," Annette replied. "He was filming us and taking recordings of our conversation, using one of these new directional microphones, without permission. Just listen."

"We'll do that at the station, madame," said Messager. "Bruno, good to see you doing another kind turn, helping this gentleman rise from his table. Let's sort this out at the station." Then he paused, examining the man more closely with a glint in his eye that could have been surprise.

"I didn't expect to see you here, Condorcet," the police chief said, almost amiably. "You may not remember me, just one cop among many at Périgueux, but I remember you, our civilian tech wizard when we were learning to deal with camera phones and computers. So you did your thirty years, got the pension, and now you've gone private." The chief's raised eyebrow was far more cutting than any comment would have been.

Annette insisted on paying the bill, saying she was so often a guest at Bruno's house. At the police station, Messager took statements, confiscated the phone pending a confirmation of Annette's interpretation of the privacy laws and released Condorcet while temporarily keeping his official ID as a private detective.

"I haven't seen one of these directional microphones before," said Messager when Annette showed him how the two small microphones could be plugged into one of several sockets on each side of the phone. She then played back some of the conversation Bruno and Célestine had been having in the restaurant. Bruno texted J-J, asking if he knew that the Police Nationale's former tech specialist was now using his skills working for Poincevin, J-J's least favorite lawyer.

Chapter 18

Bruno was woken at six, the winter sky still black, by Marie-Do from France Bleu. She apologized for the disturbance before informing him that the online web paper of what used to be the far-right Front National in the Périgord was leading its new edition with an attack on him.

He shook himself awake. He could never recall the new name that had sought to clean up the image of the old organization, Ralliement National or Rassemblement, something like that. The founders, led by Jean-Marie le Pen, who had been deliberately outrageous about Hitler's gas chambers being "a detail of history," had been replaced by a smoother, younger and less provocative generation, but some things never change.

"Why? What are they saying?"

"It says you prefer to choose Black or Arab kids for the rugby and tennis teams instead of French boys and girls, and that you brought immigrants like Léopold from Senegal onto the sports committee while pretending to be a French patriot."

Bruno sighed and sat up in bed. "Marie-Do, we've known each other for ten years. You've watched me train your nephew at rugby and your niece at tennis, and she got into the semifinals with her partner who was born in Syria. Why do you take accusations like this seriously?"

"Because of the dozens of letters that come into my station manager when I don't take them seriously. He hates it too; he's Jewish. We're obliged to reflect a wide range of views in the community, and when the extreme right starts to win twenty or thirty percent of the vote, we have to take them seriously."

"You may have to," he said. "I don't."

"That's a pathetic answer, Bruno. You and what you stand for are being attacked. Are you going to stand up for yourself or not?"

"What have they said, exactly?"

She read out the exact passage.

"Okay, are you recording? Then here goes: I want every child that is raised in St. Denis and the Vézère Valley to learn and enjoy sports, playing and watching and supporting. I'm very happy that last year, with teams of Black and white and brown kids, we won the under-twelves and the over-twelves championships in rugby and tennis and were runners-up in basketball. The colors we believe in are the red, white and blue of the *tricolore,* which has always stood for Liberté, Egalité, Fraternité."

"That's great, Bruno, many thanks, and now you can go back to sleep and forget that a third of your neighbors tell pollsters they are ready and willing to vote for them. Bye now."

She ended the call, and Bruno looked down and saw Balzac watching him from his little hutch in the corner of the bedroom. Traditionally, his dog had slept in his outdoor kennel from springtime until late autumn, but when the nights grew cold the dog was welcome indoors. At first Bruno had simply put a large cushion in the corner covered by a blanket, but Giselle at the vet's clinic had told him dogs felt more secure if they were enclosed when sleeping, almost as in a cave. So Bruno had made a movable lean-to shelter where his dog slept the night through, sometimes even longer than Bruno.

He rose, put on a tracksuit and running shoes, and went to the kitchen to open the door and look east. There was no sign of sunrise, and the moon had already set, but there was just enough of its light being reflected from the clouds that Bruno could see to run the familiar path along the ridge. He set off, Balzac at his heels, musing on what Marie-Do had said.

Bruno had little interest in politics, but he knew that the public mood in France was sour, the cost of living was rising, and there seemed to be ever-fewer doctors in rural areas like the Périgord. Not much of this troubled him, since much of Bruno's food came from his garden, his hunting, the chickens he raised and the local system of barter, so the baron ate Bruno's eggs and truffles and he ate the fish the baron caught.

This age-old system of the countryside was not as active as it had been, but Bruno had seen that more and more of the incomers of retirement age were growing their own food, taking up fishing, raising chickens and investing the six to nine months it took to get a hunting license. The newcomers came to realize that all of that represented an engaging way to make friends and integrate themselves into the community, like joining the communal feasts of the town's rugby and tennis clubs. Some had bought shares in the town vineyard and volunteered to spend a few days picking the grapes at harvesttime, which usually earned them a ten-liter box of the resulting wine.

By the time he had reached the edge of the ridge and could stare down at the dark valley below, a rosy glow was touching the clouds as the sun began to rise. He trotted back, relishing the magical way the white-frosted edges of the shrubs and woodland caught the pink light of the emerging dawn. After he had reached his garden, fed and gave water to his chickens, he felt all was well with the world. After a shower and a shave, and dressed in uniform, he made coffee and shared the remains of yesterday's baguette with Balzac. Then he headed out to Pamela's riding school to greet his horse and join his friends for the comforting ritual of the morning exercise.

As the horses came out from the stables, steam almost whistling from their nostrils as they exhaled into the frosty air, Bruno laughed out loud, reminded of the old steam locomotives he had only ever seen in films and photographs. There was a thin layer of ice in the water trough, fanciful swirls of frost on the windows, and all he could see of Pamela's face was her nose peeking out between the scarf that covered her mouth and her huge sunglasses. Bruno could feel Hector trembling beneath him, eager to start running, but they walked from the stable yard and then trotted through the paddock and up the path that climbed the gentle slope around the shoulder of the hill that led up past the woodland to the ridge.

As soon as he reached the open expanse, Bruno felt Hector's muscles start to quiver and then bunch as his horse began that astonishing acceleration from trot to canter to gallop in just a few strides. Bruno rose in the stirrups and leaning forward with his face close to Hector's great neck he felt that unique rocking motion that only such speed could bring. His eyes were narrowed against the wind and his cheeks tingled from the chill as from behind came the thrilling sound of many hooves hammering at the frosty earth. It gave Bruno some faint sense of what a cavalry charge must have been like in the olden days. He heard himself whoop with delight at the sheer thrill of the ride. If he'd had a sword, Bruno thought, he'd have drawn it.

He was still panting as his horse slowed and then stopped just short of the treeline. As he watched Pamela and the others slow their own horses and join him, his phone vibrated at his waist. The screen showed it was J-J, so he answered and left it to his friends to discuss whether to ride back the same way or go down the bridle trail to the hunters' cabin and then back to the stables.

"I certainly did not know Condorcet is now working for Poincevin, nor did anybody else, but I spoke to Prunier and we're going to have a full-scale assessment of whatever technical vulnerabilities we might face. So thanks for the tip, Bruno. How did you find out?"

Bruno explained what had happened during dinner with Annette and Célestine the previous evening and Messager's recognizing of Condorcet. J-J explained that Messager had joined the Police Nationale in Périgueux at the age of eighteen. He retired after thirty years with a pension and then walked into the Sarlat job at the age of forty-eight.

"He's already done ten years there and at some point he'll get another pension," J-J went on. "I don't know whether he likes the job, needs the money or can't stand his wife. Which is it?"

"You tell me, but what about Condorcet spying on us while working for Poincevin? Annette is sure it's against the law."

"I think so, too, but the lawyers are arguing. One says it can't be a privileged conversation between a lawyer and client since Célestine is not Annette's client and you were present. Another says you three should all sue him for invasion of privacy."

"What does the *procureur* say? He's the one who has to decide whether to bring charges."

"He's thinking about it. But because Condorcet is on a police pension, we're authorized to search his home and office. Stay in touch, and Prunier says thanks."

J-J ended the call, and Bruno let Hector follow the others down the bridle trail. The sun was now fully above the horizon. Usually Pamela had some Scottish saying about it, but whether a red sky was good in the morning and bad at dusk or the other way around, he could never recall. At the bottom of the trail he cantered along to join her on the wide path and asked which was which.

"'Morning' rhymes with 'warning,' 'night' rhymes with 'delight.' That's how you remember," she said. "What was J-J calling about? A new crime?"

"No, an old one becomes more complicated," he said, and explained the events of the previous evening. "Isn't this the night when you usually see Annette at Pilates?"

"Yes, at five-thirty, when it's too dark to do much with the horses. But it's not an occasion for gossip, Bruno. It's serious exercise." She gave his forearm a token tap of reproach with her riding crop. "Talking of serious matters, is there a date yet for Monique's funeral?"

"I don't know for sure, but Annette said she expected Saturday. Where's it going to be? In Sarlat?"

"Apparently there's a problem with that," Pamela said. "Because she's a suicide they're edgy about using the Sarlat cathedral, and nobody wants to go to the crematorium up near Périgueux, so they may end up using the church in St. Denis because Monique went to church here as a child."

"Has anybody asked Father Sentout about that?" he asked as they reached the stables, dismounted and led the horses inside.

She shrugged. "No idea. By the way, there was a piece about you on the radio, reporting some attack on you from the far-right people. You don't expect that around here."

"Difficult times," he replied with a shrug.

Five minutes later, having fed and watered Hector and covered him with a blanket, Bruno was on the way back to the *mairie*. Once he arrived and parked in the main square he called Laura.

"Bruno, a pleasant surprise to hear from you."

"Laura, I'm calling about Monique's funeral. Have a place and time been arranged yet?"

"Not that I know of. Dominic is in charge of all that and he hasn't asked my or Becca's advice, nor anybody else's as far as I know."

"A friend of mine heard something about there being a problem with the location. Could you get Annette to let him know, discreetly, that Monique worshipped at the St. Denis church as a girl, and that I'm sure we could arrange the funeral there with a choir and so on for a proper send-off? I'd call him myself, but I seem to be on his bad side."

"Join the club. I'll get Annette to check, and look forward to seeing you, sad an occasion though it will be."

She ended the call, and Bruno let his thoughts linger a moment on Laura, the pleasant tone of her voice, her love of basset hounds, but it was almost time to go down and act as traffic cop for the young mothers with their toddlers attending the *maternelle.* He knew them all from his tennis and rugby classes, watched them grow up, marry, start families, but he could never again think of them without recalling the massed female fury of their attack at this very spot on Casimir, that dreadful ex-husband of Florence and the father of her twins. With Balzac at his heels, he strolled down to the special crossing point from the post office to the *maternelle,* kissed the cheeks of the two young mothers already waiting, walked onto the crossing with one arm raised to stop the traffic and let them cross. Balzac, wholly accustomed to the strange custom of his master, waited patiently by the post office for Bruno to escort all the groups of mothers and toddlers over the road.

"My little Delphine thinks you're some kind of relative, because she sees you more often than she sees her grandpa," said Chantal, a girl whose self-confidence had soared once he'd shown her how to hit a double backhand. She was staring down proudly at the baby in the pram, wrapped in layer after layer of woolly clothes, but still waving her arms and legs as if in delight when she saw Bruno peering down.

"It's the uniform," he said, beaming at the baby. "It always works with little girls, until they get to be old enough to know better."

"And when is that, Bruno?"

"Pretty soon after they learn to listen to their mothers."

Chantal laughed and waved goodbye as he went back to escort the next batch of young mothers across. He probably made half a dozen crossings every morning, and he usually enjoyed the banter. Today, it was of a different sort.

"Didn't like what they said about you on the radio this morning," said Anne-Marie, a hairdresser, waiting to cross the road with her three-year-old in one hand and the five-year-old in the other.

"Bonjour, Ramon, *et* bonjour Gabrielle," Bruno said to the two children, giving each one a kiss on the brow before he kissed their mother's cheeks.

"What did they say about me on the radio?" he asked, seeking confirmation.

"It was about you always giving preference to Black kids because they were better at sports."

"Really?" said Bruno. "How many Black kids do you reckon we have in town, Anne-Marie?"

"Five, three from Léopold and two from Jérôme. And then there's Momu's grandchildren, but they're not Black, more brown."

"And how many white kids?"

"Four or five hundred in the *collège,* couple of hundred in the *école,* eighty or so here in the *maternelle.* That's the point. There aren't enough to make a difference, so what were they talking about?"

"I wish I knew, Anne-Marie. People just make things up."

"That's what my Didier said when he called the station to complain, and Marie-Do put him on the radio to say exactly that. It's all right for us here in the countryside, but my cousin Margo, the one who lives in Paris, says it's terrible in the schools there. Half the kids are Black or Arabs. She'd move back here in a minute, but Paris is where the jobs are. See you later, Bruno."

It was a depressing conversation, he thought as he walked back to the main square with Balzac and climbed the stone stairs of the *mairie* to hear raised voices from the mayor's office. Claire, the mayor's secretary, mouthed the word "Xavier" at him, and he nodded and went to his old office. It was now occupied by Colette.

"What are they arguing about?" he asked Colette, jerking his thumb toward the mayor's office.

"Xavier is still under the illusion that he has a political future in the Périgord," she said, giving Balzac a welcome biscuit. "The mayor is explaining why he's mistaken. Xavier doesn't even have one in St. Denis."

"You don't think this will all blow over?" Bruno asked. "People can forget."

"Yes, but not when there are several other councilors who all think they have a chance when the mayor retires or dies in office."

"Do you have a favorite?"

"Yes, but I'm not saying. Anyway, the immediate issue is less Xavier than the new gendarmerie."

"You forget the mayor's friends in the Senate," Bruno replied. "Imagine the reaction if they start asking questions about a general threatening to cancel an almost complete gendarmerie to protect a nephew from charges of sexual assault, among other matters."

"Your political innocence is touching, Bruno," she said, with an almost indulgent smile. "The cancellation will have nothing to do with the general. My guess would be a worried report from a government surveyor that our recent flood casts serious doubt on the location as appropriate for the enlarged gendarmerie. The gendarmes call for a review. That's how I'd arrange it."

"But that's crazy—the new center is on higher ground than the old one," Bruno objected.

"There you are, Bruno. It makes it even simpler. That means they can say that nowhere in St. Denis is there a fit place for the gendarmes' regional HQ. And then watch all the other towns east of Bergerac start fighting like cats to get this plum for themselves. And some of them have Senate contacts of their own."

"You make me feel like a country bumpkin."

"No, Bruno, just an innocent abroad. You'll learn. Forget that for now and tell me why people suddenly seem to be ganging up on you—the Greens, that sad old drunk from Montignac and now the far right. A soldier with the Croix de Guerre, you should be one of their heroes. What did you do to upset them?"

Bruno explained the case of Dr. Gelletreau's son, seduced by a bored young woman who enjoyed combining her extreme-right politics with Nazi porn, and how Bruno had led J-J to her home, which saw the arrest on serious narcotics charges of eight members of the old Front National's private security force known as the Service d'Ordre.

"They're supposed to have cleaned up their act since then," Colette said. "A new name, a new figurehead, the old guard retired, more moderate policies, no more storming out of

Europe, but the bones of the same old beast remain under the new skin."

She cocked an ear to the hall where the sound of angry voices had faded. Then a door slammed, and feet began stamping heavily down the stone stairs.

"Sounds like Xavier has gone," she said. "In more ways than one. And the real problem is that not only will he blame you for this, but I imagine his wife will probably feel the same way."

Bruno shrugged, even as he recalled the baron and Pamela saying the same. "I simply tried to make Xavier apologize and patch things up, and since she's a keen churchgoer I thought bringing in Father Sentout might help."

"But in the process, Bruno, you became part of her own humiliation."

"But that's ridiculous. I was only trying to help."

"You know the old saying about the road to hell and what it's paved with?" she asked.

Bruno nodded, glumly. "What would you have done?"

"You started out all wrong," Colette said. "If you were going to get involved at all, and I know the mayor was pushing you to do something, you should have gone first to Mirabelle, told her how sorry you were and asked her if there was anything you might do to help. Better still, you should have asked me, or some other woman of my age or older who's seen it all before."

She reached behind her, opened a cupboard door and pulled out two coffee capsules, turned on her machine, put two cups under the spouts, inserted the capsules and switched it on.

"Just because the mayor tells you how well you handle these delicate situations, you don't have to believe him, Bruno. I know you're good at handling all sorts of problems, but I don't think matters concerning women are your strong point. Since you're such a ridiculous romantic, you tend to see us as ciphers of some sort: maidens in distress, or as wonderful mothers, or as grannies-in-waiting, not the complicated human beings we really are." She paused. "No sugar for you?"

He nodded and thanked her, musing on what she'd said, and asked, "Suppose I'd done what you said and asked her if there was anything I could do. What do you think she'd have said?"

"Mirabelle was probably just looking for a sympathetic ear from her old sports teacher, especially a man she'd long thought of as reliable and safe. But what you did closed down her options. You took Xavier to confession, and thus you gave her a grim choice. Allow Xavier back or reject him, and thus reject the rite of confession, which is tough for a believer to do with Father Sentout standing there piously beside you. And you aren't even a believer, which means you cynically used Mirabelle's faith as a bludgeon to force her to forgive that wretched man."

"Ouch," he said. "You're right. I hadn't thought it through. Is there anything I can do to put this right?"

"Almost certainly not, but you may have helped save the marriage by giving them something to agree on, namely that you are the enemy. Now drink your coffee before it gets cold and tell me about any more enemies you've made who will be rubbing their hands with glee at the thought of adding to your troubles by kicking you when you're down."

Chapter 19

Followed by Balzac, Bruno was jogging down the stairs of the *mairie* when his phone vibrated. The number on the screen was unknown to him, and he was surprised to hear that his caller was Dominic. Ducking behind one of the pillars supporting the *mairie,* Bruno answered politely and said he hoped Dominic was bearing up under the shock of Monique's suicide.

"Yes, thank you, but I'm calling to ask you more about the suggestion of perhaps holding the funeral service in the church in St. Denis that Monique attended as a child," he said. "I should say that she was not in the least religious, and while I looked into a cremation, that means asking people to trek out to Bergerac or Périgueux."

Bruno explained that the suggestion had come from Ghislaine, who had kindly offered to have her buried in the family plot, and whether religious or not, such traditions in this corner of France were taken seriously.

"In that case it sounds very suitable," Dominic said. "Is there time to arrange this for Saturday morning?"

"That's very short notice. Let me check when the priest is available. Would you want a full Mass or just a simple benediction?"

"The simpler the better, I think."

Bruno promised to call him back and checked with Father Sentout. The priest explained that he had two funerals on Saturday already but would be happy to hold a simple benediction on Monday or Tuesday morning at ten or eleven and would ask for a donation to the church of two hundred euros. The burial in Ghislaine's plot would have to be arranged separately with the undertaker. Bruno reported back to Dominic, who declared himself pleased that the funeral could go ahead. Then he paused.

"I think I may have unintentionally offended you the other evening, and I wanted to apologize, since you have really been very helpful throughout this sad business and more than doing your duty."

"My pleasure, monsieur, not a problem. You had just suffered the shocks of two deaths in two or three days, with two long drives on top of it. I don't know how you held up as well as you did."

"Well, I really am sorry for my rudeness and very grateful for what you have done for me and Monique, particularly since I gather you're going through difficult times yourself, with the Greens and right-wingers all sniping at you."

"Well, criticism comes with the job sometimes. We can't be popular with everyone."

Bruno gave him Father Sentout's phone number, said he'd see him at the church next week and ended the call. Perhaps he'd misjudged the man, he thought as he put the phone back in the pouch on his belt, then paused. He'd better inform Ghislaine, but it was getting cold beneath the pillars. He climbed the stairs back into the *mairie,* went to the kitchen and closed the door for at least a little privacy. He called Ghislaine and left a message, then called Annette to see if she or Becca Weil had any problems with the days and times.

"That means the reading of the will should be on Monday or Tuesday afternoon," said Annette. "I doubt it contains any surprises, but Dominic may want to vent his feelings."

"I thought Monique made it clear in her letter to him that he'd only inherit the building and a share in the notary business," said Bruno.

"It's not quite so clear. According to Becca Weil the will leaves Dominic very little. Not the ownership of the building and nothing at all of the concierge business. That letter she wrote to him was probably written just before she died. Monique must have been tense and depressed; maybe she'd forgotten the precise terms of the will."

"So her husband could be in for an unpleasant surprise," said Bruno. "I'm not sure how he'll take it. I was just talking to him about arranging the funeral in St. Denis. He was very pleasant, and even apologized for being rude on Tuesday evening."

Annette snorted. "Ha, he is usually careful about the people he looks up to and those he looks down upon. I suspect your status may have improved in his view."

"I don't think so," said Bruno. "He made a point of commiserating about all the various attacks on me."

"You must have run out of enemies, *mon cher,*" she said gaily. "From now on, things can only get better."

Bruno instinctively crossed his fingers as he heard Annette's cheerful farewell after her casual tempting of fate. He hung up and was about to replace the phone in its pouch when it vibrated again. This time it was Ghislaine.

"It seems agreeable, in a ghoulish kind of way, that I now know that my and Monique's remains will remain commingled through the coming centuries," she said. "And thanks to Google, I've been reading up on your various exploits, so I'm suitably awed. I'll come down tomorrow and hope to take you to dinner. I'll stay at the Vieux Logis in Trémolat."

"You could always stay at my place. I have a couple of spare rooms," Bruno said.

"That's very kind, Bruno, but in my business we usually stay at the most expensive place available, since we have such an understanding government that it's deductible from our taxes. I've already booked a room, so we can eat there. The table is booked for seven-thirty. Are there other good friends of Monique that I should invite? Laura? Annette? For God's sake don't invite Dominic. I'll leave it to you to arrange matters, Bruno. I've emailed you a letter for your local priest for you to print out. It's my permission to use my family plot for Monique. Whoops, another call incoming. See you soon."

He called Annette back to convey Ghislaine's invitation to the Vieux Logis, adding that Monique was to be interred at her family plot in St. Denis. "Ghislaine said she wanted to meet Monique's friends, so I should also invite Laura and Becca. Who else would you suggest?"

"She thought the world of Fabiola, and what about Pamela?"

"Pamela. Of course, I should have thought of her and Fabiola. What about male friends?"

"I don't think she had any. There were the gardeners she'd known for years, but they were employees. There was Monsieur Castanet at Castel-Merle whom Monique had known since she was a little girl, and some of the overseas clients became friends. I know that Laura has been busy for the last couple of days writing to all their main clients with the news, reassuring them that the concierge business will continue as before, but probably not here in Sarlat, which will be a blow for my social life. Maybe I should move to St. Denis."

"You'll always be welcome, Annette. People still speak in

awe of you as a rally driver. I've never been so scared as sitting in your passenger seat."

"Nonsense," she laughed. "You were too busy navigating to be scared."

Bruno called Pamela and Fabiola, who both said they'd be delighted to join, and then Becca Weil, who also agreed. He tried reaching Laura, but her line was constantly busy. He sent her a text, asking her to call him when she could. It took a while, and when she reached him, he explained Ghislaine's invitation to dinner at the Vieux Logis.

"What a sweet idea. Will you be there, too? It would be such a treat to have you as our token man."

"I'm invited, but I think perhaps I should leave you all to enjoy a girls' night out," Bruno said.

"No," she said, drawing the word out. "We'll all be very disappointed if you don't come, Bruno, especially me. And I find it very hard to believe you're the kind of man who could ever say no to a dinner at the Vieux Logis."

"Well, there is that," he said, teasingly. "And I suppose somebody has to be sober enough to drive you all home."

"There, you see! You'll be keeping the crime rate down, Bruno. It will be almost like being on duty."

"I certainly hope not. But I think you've talked me into it."

The call ended and Bruno felt that cheery glow that came after a little light flirtation with a woman he found attractive and who evidently enjoyed the banter as much as he had. He put his phone away and went to pick up Balzac from what he still thought of as his own office and was surprised to see Colette Cantagnac waving an envelope at him.

"Special delivery from Paris," she said. "I signed for you."

Bruno took the envelope, recognized the handwriting of his name, thanked Colette and took Balzac with him down to his van, climbed in and drove home.

He and Balzac went into the sitting room, where Bruno opened the chimney flue and built up the embers that had kept the stove warm with well-seasoned wood. He took off his jacket and sat in the easy chair he liked to use for reading and opened Isabelle's letter. Even before he read it, he gazed around the room and suddenly recalled the times they had made love in this room, on the chair and on the floor beside the fire. He recalled once when the two of them had been in the middle of dinner, gazing at each other across the table as they ate, and suddenly each of them rose at the same instant and fell into one another's arms.

He stared into the growing flames in the stove, and on impulse rose and went to his music player and inserted the Jacques Brel album they both had loved so much. He pushed the button to move the CD forward to the fourth song, "Je T'Aime," knowing that the next song would be "Ne Me Quitte Pas," and then the song that always summoned up her face and the way she smiled and closed her eyes as she waited to be kissed.

Bruno hardly needed to open Isabelle's letter to know what it contained, but he was interested in her tone and the phrasing. It began with a note of amiable formality, to inform him that she was to be married, to a man who was some years older than she, very much richer, at least as well connected in Parisian politics and with a family of grown children. Isabelle wished him well, and knew that Bruno would feel the same goodwill for her.

At this point the handwriting changed, became more fluid, evidently written more quickly. Some scent of emotion seemed to lift off the page to touch his heart as he read that neither of them would ever forget or regret the glorious, impassioned tumult of their time together, of what they had known and what they had lost.

"Dearest Bruno," it ended. "Embrace our Balzac and hold him close."

He slid to the floor and held Balzac's warm, familiar body, remembering the day Isabelle had first brought the enchanting puppy to him in St. Denis. And his dog, who would always in a way be their dog, nuzzled affectionately at Bruno's neck as if sensing his mood.

Then Brel's "Chanson des Vieux Amants" began to play, its catalog of angry storms and gentle passions, of two lovers growing old without ever quite growing up.

This would never do, Bruno told himself, disentangling himself from Balzac and rising. He changed into a tracksuit and running shoes and with Balzac trailing behind he raced along the ridge as the wintry daylight began to fade, and below the streetlamps twinkled into life in St. Denis, his signal to turn and begin the trot back.

" 'Embrace our Balzac and hold him close,' " he repeated to himself as the basset hound approached, and Bruno dropped to his knees and took him in his arms. They then strolled back together, where Bruno fed his dog, took a shower, first cold, then hot, and a final blast of cold again, and changed for his dinner appointment in Yveline's apartment at the gendarmerie.

Bruno knew that Annette and Claire, the newly promoted officer, were to be guests, and he was delighted to see that the mayor and Julien, from the town vineyard, had also been invited. Julien was a widower, and the mayor's partner was still in Paris, finishing her term of teaching at the Sorbonne before coming back to St. Denis for Christmas. The thought made Bruno feel guilty about the presents he had yet to buy and wrap, a feeling that was intensified when he saw the Christmas tree erected in Yveline's living room. There were even some wrapped piles beneath the tree.

Julien handed Bruno and Claire a glass of sparkling wine

from the town vineyard, turned into a deep red by a splash of crème de cassis. Bruno used his to toast Claire's promotion.

"Congratulations on your promotion to the officer class, where the air is thinner, the rivalries deeper, and the enemies always aim for you," he said to Claire, after hugging her and planting a *bise* on each cheek. It was the usual informal greeting to new officers. "And welcome back to St. Denis. You're looking wonderful, glowing with health, and we're all counting on you to get the women's rugby teams to peak fitness."

"I'm not sure my new commander is inclined to give me much free time," Claire replied with a grin. "Yveline has a reputation as a slave driver, I recall from my last posting here."

As a young gendarme Claire had been given a temporary posting to St. Denis when a DNA test of an unidentified skeleton found in the woods near a local camping site revealed that the dead man had been her half brother, but of whose existence she had no knowledge. All gendarmes, police and military personnel were automatically tested to be enrolled in the national DNA database.

Bruno had been impressed by Claire's professionalism when dealing with the whole affair and had written a strong recommendation for Claire to be approved for officer training. And here she was, back in St. Denis.

Yveline came up to give him a hug, and Bruno handed her a bottle of his favorite Château de Tiregand, saying, "If I'd known Julien was coming, I'd have felt obliged to bring a bottle of the town wine."

"So we're all fortunate," said Julien. "Although I do expect a little more loyalty to the town vineyard from a significant shareholder and director of the company."

"I am loyal, and the day we can make a Pécharmant I'll be even more loyal," Bruno replied, smiling.

"We could always rent a hectare or two from some generous

landowner," said the mayor. "But not many of the Pécharmant vineyards produce anything as good as the Tiregand wines that Bruno's so fond of."

Bruno was relieved not to be the last to arrive. Yveline asked him to join her in the kitchen, where she looked a little nervously at her oven.

"Just checking," she said, with a slightly nervous laugh.

"I always do the same," he said. "It smells great. What are you making? I can smell it's beef, but I'm also picking up just a hint of oranges, which is interesting."

"Gardiane de boeuf," she said. "I had it once as a girl when I was in the Camargue with my parents and I've never forgotten it. This one has been marinating since yesterday and stewing very slowly for the past three hours. I'll serve it with rice."

She showed Bruno a notepad with each step of the dinner listed with rough timings.

"Good for you," said Bruno. "I used to do that when I was learning to cook. It's the best way to start. It smells wonderful, and I think this will go well with it." He handed her the Tiregand.

"Lovely," she said. "There's a whole bottle of Bouches-du-Rhône red in the dish already."

She had six small bowls ready for the first course, each with half an avocado stuffed with prawns in pink mayonnaise, and a saucepan half filled with fast-cooking brown rice ready to be filled with boiling water and placed on the stove. Bruno nodded approval.

"A dish like this deserves brown rice to keep the slightly chewy texture, so you've really done your homework," he said.

She nodded. "I read that the texture comes from the layer of bran that's kept on during the milling."

The downstairs doorbell rang, and Annette's voice came

over the intercom. Yveline pressed the code to let her in, and moments later the young magistrate was there, also with a bottle of Tiregand.

"Hi, Bruno, it's been far too long," she said, laughing and winking at him, after greeting Yveline and Claire, the mayor and Julien, an order of precedence which made Bruno feel a little younger than usual.

"It's been ages," he laughed. "The only news is that Monique's funeral is set for Monday morning and the will is to be read that afternoon."

She nodded. "And Dominic is unlikely to be pleased. Do you think he'll stay in Sarlat? I'm not sure what rights come with his lifetime lease; he may be able to move away and rent it out."

"I'm sure we'll find out," Bruno said. Annette then turned to greet the mayor, whom she knew well. Bruno turned and saw Claire standing off to one side, looking unsure of herself.

"Come help me open the red wine," he said, steering her into the kitchen, where he began to open the Château de Tiregand that Annette had brought.

"What was the most important thing they told you at officer training school?" he asked her.

"Never look like you don't know what you're doing."

"Guess what we NCOs learn?"

"Go on," she said, smiling.

"An officer who tries to assure you he knows what he's doing can get you into real trouble. So find some way to distract him. Or her."

"Have you forgotten that when we last met, I was a fairly new NCO?" she replied, as Bruno picked up the bottle of Tiregand that he'd brought and began to open it, too.

"It's precisely because I haven't forgotten your background

that I'm confident about your future, at least when it comes to dealing with the troops," Bruno said. "Dealing with senior officers is another matter entirely. Yveline is very good, but she's never been an NCO. That's where you come in. You now speak officer, but you also spoke the other language. You are bilingual. That's one reason why I know you'll do well."

"Is there any other reason?"

"Yes, Sergeant Jules thinks you're terrific, likes you a lot," said Bruno, an opened bottle of Tiregand in each hand, "and you know you can trust Jules."

"That's good to hear," she said as they headed back to the living room. "But it sounds as though I'm coming into a real mess here. The gossip about the two young gendarmes getting arrested is alarming, along with the rumor that St. Denis might not be our new base after all. What do you know?"

"Nothing reassuring, but I'm pretty sure that the mayor is probably better at politics than your generals. The evidence against the two young gendarmes is now overwhelming. So look on the bright side, Claire. You're joining a brigade where the bad guys have been thrown out."

"So, nowhere to go but up. Is that right?"

Yveline's voice came from the kitchen, calling out *"A table, mes amis."* Then she emerged carrying a tray with the first course. She was followed by Julien carrying a bottle of the town vineyard's white wine, a blend of sauvignon blanc and *sémillon.* Bruno thought Yveline's timing was right. He usually reckoned twenty minutes for guests to take their places, pass the bread, pour the white wine and enjoy the first course. Then the table would be cleared, and Yveline would have five more minutes to check on the rice, bring out the big casserole dish and serve the red wine.

And so she did, when the glorious Pécharmant wine was poured to go with Yveline's triumph, the *gardiane de boeuf,* with its daylong marinade of onions, red wine, thyme, bay leaves and the skins of oranges. And the brown rice, cooked to perfection, was its perfect partner. Such a pleasure, he thought, to dine with friends at the first dinner party Yveline had hosted and to know that it was a triumph.

Chapter 20

Dawn was just breaking as Bruno drove into Pamela's stable yard and released Balzac to pay his usual courtesy call on the sheepdogs before trotting in to greet his big friend Hector. From the back of his ancient Land Rover Bruno took a small sack of the biscuits he made regularly for Balzac, and which Pamela had recently requested for her own dogs. It was his day off, so he was in civilian clothes, a sweater beneath his riding coat to fend off the winter chill. He donned his riding boots, went into the stalls to greet and saddle Hector, then saddled Primrose, Pamela's usual horse, and was about to lead the two horses out when Pamela shouted for him to join her.

"It's the radio, about you and some secret slush funds," she said, pointing, and Bruno could hear that the standard early morning news show had been overtaken by something out of the ordinary.

"... the headline, 'Secret Cash for Hero Cop,' sparked curiosity and outrage in the Périgord Noir, with respected Chief of Police Bruno Courrèges accused of being on a secret payroll from the General Directorate for Internal Security that has recently brought him a windfall of tens of thousands of euros. And for General Lannes and the DGSI," she retorted.

Bruno shook his head in disbelief as Marie-Do went on: "Former senator Gérard Mangin, the long-standing mayor of St. Denis, is now on the line with us. Monsieur le Maire—"

"This is a pack of vicious lies," the mayor interrupted, his voice crisp with controlled anger. "Bruno Courrèges, who is indeed a hero as one of the few soldiers to have been awarded the Croix de Guerre in recent years, has not received a single centime, let alone thousands of euros, from state funds. But while still officially on the reserve list of the French army, he has been from time to time recalled to the colors to serve France. When this happens, he is entitled to be paid according to his rank, and as chief of police of the Vézère Valley, he holds the honorary rank of a senior army captain and is entitled to a captain's pay for his days on special duties."

The mayor paused for breath and continued, "However, the fact is that he does not receive any of that money. It comes to our *mairie,* and Bruno receives his usual pay as chief of police, even though some of these missions have involved real danger to his life. Earlier this year, as you know from your own reporting, he was shot in the course of such a mission, and was then injured again while rescuing a mother and child from a car that was being swept away in the floods. He was released from the hospital only last month."

"So you're saying that there is no secret fund coming to the chief of police?" Marie-Do asked.

"Absolutely not," said the mayor. "The council of St. Denis and the mayors of other communes in the valley have all been informed of Chief Bruno's recall to the colors when our security services need his skills and local knowledge. There has never been anything secret about that. I am astonished that a reputable newspaper could have printed such lies, especially since no news reporter came to ask me or anyone in the *mairie* about this, nor has anyone put the question to Chief Bruno."

"The newspaper says they have the information from—I quote—'sources in the St. Denis *mairie,*'" said Marie-Do.

"It doesn't say who they might be, and I for one find this claim difficult to believe. It is interesting that none of the usual regional reporters has a byline on this story, and according to our switchboard, no press inquiries were received at the *mairie* yesterday."

"How many people at the *mairie* knew that Chief Bruno was from time to time seconded to the security forces?"

"Let me be clear," the mayor said. "Every elected member of the St. Denis council and every mayor of all the communes along the valley was aware that from time to time Bruno was recalled to military service and assigned to the Ministry of the Interior, where he worked with the army, with special forces, with the General Directorate for Internal Security, and on occasion with the Directorate for External Security. There are occasions when Chief Bruno's local knowledge and connections have been of real importance to our security services."

"Have you talked to Chief Bruno about this?"

"Not yet. This is the first I've heard of it, and today is Bruno's day off, so he may not even know about it, having better things to do than deal with this fabricated nonsense. And so do I. *Au'voir.*"

Bruno went to pull out his phone, but it wasn't there. Changing into his winter riding clothes, he'd taken off his usual belt, and his phone was presumably resting on the seat of his car where it may have vibrated without his hearing it. And since it was his day off, he hadn't turned on the radio news.

"I think you should be ashamed of yourself, putting yourself in so much danger for no reward at all," said Pamela. "I know all the scars on your body, Bruno. It's an outrageous way to take advantage of you and your loyalty, and I have a good mind to go to town and tell your precious mayor just what I think of his exploiting you."

"Please don't," he said, taking her in his arms and planting a fond kiss on her forehead. "He'd be terribly embarrassed and so would I. The mayor would be so much happier if I turn up in his office knowing nothing at all about it and then he can tell me the story and we can decide what to do, if anything. Knowing the mayor, he'll already have had Philippe Delaron frog-marched into the *mairie* to confess everything that he knows about this story, where it came from and why, and who's behind it."

"I don't trust the mayor any further than I can see him," Pamela grumbled. "And it's outrageous that the *mairie* gets all the money that you earn for putting yourself in danger. And don't you forget what I told you at the time, that Xavier would never forgive you for helping him through that row with his wife. I warned you then that Xavier would want revenge. This could be it."

"Yes, you're very probably right. But for now, let's take advantage of my day off and take out the horses. I've already saddled Primrose for you."

And off they went, each with some of the other horses on a leading rein and with Balzac trotting steadily along behind. It was a chilly day, but as always, Bruno found himself surprised by the speed with which Hector's body generated heat beneath Bruno's riding coat, so much that from time to time he raised the flaps over his legs to let some of the warmth escape. It was a day to canter, with the horses trailing behind, rather than gallop freely, and Hector seemed content merely to be leading the way.

Bruno's thoughts drifted to the mayor's performance on the radio, which had surprised him by the deliberate attempt to mislead. It was true that Bruno was receiving none of the money to which he was entitled, but he would probably do well enough in the long run, from the town vineyard. A single man with no family to support, Bruno knew that his modest salary was more than enough for his needs. And the way he lived was almost miserly. The clothing he wore most of the time was a uniform and boots paid for by the town, which also paid for his phone bill and health insurance. His biggest expense was probably his electricity and water bills, along with wine, occasional restaurant meals and the coffee and croissants at Fauquet's café.

That reminded him. This was a day when he needed to buy the Christmas presents he'd be giving to his friends, or rather to their children. Adult friends and colleagues were usually presented with bottles of his homemade *vin de noix,* made every year a day or two before June 21. He'd collect fifty or so green walnuts, chop them up and put them into a big enamel pot with a lid. He'd add ten liters of local wine, bought in a box from the town vineyard for twenty-five euros, six hundred grams of sugar and a liter of homemade and not-quite-legal eau-de-vie from Joe, who had been the town policeman before Bruno. It was getting harder to find a reliable local supplier other than Joe, now that the tradition that had allowed sons and daughters to inherit the family still had been stopped.

"Penny for your thoughts," came Pamela's voice, teasing him to pay attention and stop daydreaming.

"They aren't worth that much," he answered, laughing. "I was wondering what to get you for Christmas."

"What I need is a good *maréchal* to take care of shoeing the horses now that Fernand is retiring," she replied. "They're getting harder and harder to find."

"Not sure I can help with that. Think again."

"Okay—a massage, once a month."

"Done, and with pleasure. Now I have to hope that none of your friends will ask for the same."

"And what do you want for Christmas, Bruno?"

"I'd like Balzac to father another set of puppies, and I've been thinking that maybe I'd like to keep one. I get so much pleasure watching him with the Bruce and Gabrielle from the last litter."

"Do you think he knows he's the father?"

"I haven't the slightest scrap of logical explanation for it, but, yes, I think he recognizes something in them that's special to him."

"That's a sweet thought," she said as the stables came into sight. "I do hope you're right. And I gather I'll see you tonight at dinner. The Vieux Logis, no less. I'll have to dress up. Have you met our hostess?"

"Ghislaine? Not in person, but we had a very long and interesting talk on the phone about her friendship with Monique when they were young girls. She told me how Monique and Ghislaine's brother fell in love, and that he was killed in one of the Twin Towers in Manhattan on 9/11."

Pamela gasped and her hand came up instinctively to her mouth. "How awful for her! Monique, I mean, but Ghislaine and her family as well."

He took off Hector's saddle and bridle, helped Pamela rub down the horses and check their food and water and then went to the *mairie,* still in his riding clothes, to find out if there had been further developments since the morning's radio show. The mayor, he found, was in Périgueux for a meeting with the prefect about the plans for a leg of the Tour de France bicycle race to come through the Dordogne Valley in the year after next. Bruno went in to see Colette.

"I think I prefer you in uniform," she said, taking a dog biscuit from a box in her desk to hand it to Balzac and then gave him that look he'd come to understand meant she was deadly serious.

"I assume you heard the radio this morning, and I hope the mayor hasn't surrendered some hostage to fortune that may come back and bite him," she murmured so that he had to strain to hear. "Nothing he said was false, but there were some important omissions. That tells us something important, which is that whoever leaked this story only knew a part of it, not the whole thing."

"That doesn't get us much closer to the source of the leak."

"I disagree, Bruno. I think this means it wasn't Xavier, since he as deputy mayor was in a position to know exactly how and when the money would eventually come to you. The leaker is someone who only knows half of the story and assumed the money would come to you directly."

"Ah, I see what you mean," said Bruno. "Those who know the real story knew that the money was being invested in the town vineyard until I retire."

"Exactly, and I know of only one person who might have got hold of only half of the plan—Xavier's wife, Mirabelle. He probably left out some details when he told her. Remember that I told you she'd never forgive you? This is her revenge."

He smiled at Colette and nodded agreement. "I think you're probably right. But it's still my day off and I have things to do. Please thank the mayor for me for what he said. I'll see you tomorrow, when Père Noël visits the market and the choir sings Christmas carols on the market steps."

"I wouldn't miss it for the world," she said.

He went to the attic storeroom to find the Christmas outfit. It was draped over a hanger, protected by a large plastic bag and did not look too bad. But he could not find the red hat with the furry rim and the white bobble. After a search, he found it buried in a collapsed stack of triangular *tricolore* flags on the closet floor, presumably left over from the July 14 festivities. The bushy white beard was in worse shape, but he could patch it with some synthetic spiderwebs left over from an old Halloween party, more realistic than blobs of cotton. He wrapped everything in a large plastic bag he found amid the flags and headed out to his Land Rover, Balzac sniffing suspiciously at the bag as he followed.

There were four children to whom he was especially attached—the two children of retired British diplomat Jack Crimson's daughter, Miranda, and Florence's twins, Dora and Daniel—and he needed to find presents for them. He went to the junkyard of Les Récupérateurs and began browsing in one corner of the huge warehouse among the large numbers of books for children. For Dora he got a copy of *100 Poèmes pour les Enfants* and for Daniel a collection of fairy tales. Miranda's children were older, so the six-year-old got *Les Sciences pour les Enfants de 5 à 13 Ans* and the eight-year-old got a beautifully illustrated book of Greek myths.

There was a shelf for new donations, and he quickly cast his eye along it for anything interesting. There was one evidently old book, and he pulled it out and saw it was by George Sand, an edition of 1876, when her death was marked by a series of new editions. It was not a title he'd heard of, *La Mare au Diable, The Devil's Pool,* and since it was priced at two euros fifty cents, he bought it as a Christmas gift for Laura. Or perhaps, he thought with a smile, he would wrap it as a gift from Balzac for Laura's dog. For Florence he found a carafe for wine that he guessed was older than the baron, and for Fabiola and Gilles, a matched pair of tall candlesticks in smoked blue glass. For his cousin Alain and his wife, Rosalie, he spotted what had to be a copy of a Tiffany table lamp, but he liked the soft glow of the colors. From the supermarket he bought a fat roll of wrapping paper and ribbon and another of Scotch tape, went home and began wrapping.

He had finished those for the children and for his friends of the weekly dinners and was skimming through the opening pages of the George Sand novel when he heard the sound of a vehicle coming up the road below his house. When the sound stopped, he assumed it was some stranger who had taken a wrong turn and would find a way to turn around or reverse all the way downhill. But there was no sound of an engine. Curious, he went to his living room, where through a side window that looked over the road he caught a movement. A figure in a winter coat with a dark scarf around the head was flitting between the trees and then stopping as if fearing discovery before dashing to the next tree. This was odd and, after the bizarre wave of media attacks on him, a little disturbing.

Bruno went to his gun cabinet, unlocked it and took out his double-barreled shotgun, loaded it with buckshot, put on a camouflage jacket and cap and slipped a handful more shells into a pocket. He let Balzac out of the front door and whispered, *"Chasses,"* a phrase his dog associated with hunting, and then Bruno went out through the back door into his courtyard and took cover beside his woodpile and waited for Balzac to flush the game. But instead of the long hunting howl Bruno had expected, there came a friendly bark of recognition, which was followed at once by a woman's cry of alarm and surprise. Bruno unloaded his gun, then left it on the woodpile and stepped out to greet whoever it was that Balzac had found.

It was Mirabelle, Xavier's wife, with an envelope in one hand and the other raised, almost clutching at her throat, and she swayed as if about to faint. She stretched out her free hand and supported herself against a nearby apple tree.

"I came to give you this," she said, closing her eyes as if not wanting to look at Bruno, or perhaps not being able to stand the sight of him. The hand holding the letter shot forward.

"You look as if you could do with a stiff drink, Mirabelle," he said, gesturing for her to sit down on the bench that stood against the back wall of his house. "Come on, take a seat and tell me what this is about."

She shook her head firmly, put the envelope on the bench and then stepped back and said, "It's to say sorry."

"Sorry for what?" he asked.

"The story about you. That was me. The new woman at the *mairie* came to my house and told me I had to apologize to you. But I'm ashamed and didn't want to face you, so I wrote a letter instead."

"Well, it's good that you came because I ought to apologize to you, or so says Colette, the new woman at the *mairie,* because she made it clear to me that in trying to get you and Xavier back together I humiliated you in front of your neighbors. I thought it was a good idea at the time, but I was wrong. So I'm sorry."

"We are a pair of fools," said Mirabelle, who gave a sigh and then sat down beside him on the bench.

"Is that you and me or you and Xavier, or are we a trio of fools?" Bruno asked.

"All of us, I suppose," she replied. "And Father Sentout should never have come with you and Xavier to our house. That makes four of us. I was so mad at you, just as mad as I was with Xavier. More, even. Then I thought of that girl I knew at the lycée who writes for the Sarlat paper. So I told her what Xavier had told me, and that was a way to get back at both of you. What I didn't know was that Xavier had told me only half the story."

Bruno sighed. "Are you happy with him, Mirabelle?" he asked.

"That depends on what you mean by 'happy,' " she replied. "Do I love my children? Yes, totally. I can look at them all day and marvel. It's more than love. If you ask, Do I love my husband? I'm not sure. Sometimes I see his features in my son, and something of him in my daughter's eyes, and say yes. Other times, I wonder. Life is complicated."

They sat in silence for a long moment, and then she asked, "Are you going to read the letter? You look as if you were about to go hunting."

"I thought I might go and see if there might be a plump little *bécasse* up in the woods," he lied, and opened her letter. It was just five lines, saying what she had done, and why, saying sorry and adding that she had been misinformed.

"Well, that's that," he said. "You're forgiven, and now go back to your kids. Who's looking after them?"

"They're with their cousins at Xavier's sister's house. That family connection is one of the completely good things that Xavier brought into our marriage, the way the kids grow up together."

"Give them a hug for me."

"I will," she said, and gave him a quick hug with one arm and then something that was more of a peck than a kiss on his cheek. "Thanks, Bruno."

Then she turned and went off down the road. Bruno sat silently until he heard the sound of her car starting and then fading away. He strolled across to retrieve his shotgun from the woodpile and empty his pockets of shells and lock them both away in the gun cabinet.

He finished wrapping and labeling the gifts, then went to the cupboard where he kept his wines and took out two bottles of *vin de noix* and wrapped one for Mirabelle and Xavier and another for Xavier's sister, Melissa. He added them to the crate that already held bottles for the baron and Jack Crimson, for the mayor and for Colette, for Michel of the town works department and for Sergeant Jules at the gendarmerie, for his cousin Alain and his wife.

Then there were more bottles for Yveline, for Dr. Gelletreau, Stéphane, Ivan at the restaurant, Raoul at the *collège* and Jules and Hubert at the vineyard, for Annette, and Tim Birch at the Domaine de la Barde. He always gave a bottle each to Albert and Ahmed at the fire department, to Father Sentout and Philippe Delaron and Lespinasse, chairman of the rugby club, and Marianne at the tennis club. That left only a dozen bottles for his future dinner guests until he made the next batch in June.

Damn, he'd forgotten J-J at the *commissariat de police,* Horst and Clothilde at the prehistory museum, Léopold and Fat Jeanne in the market, Fauquet at the café, Amélie in Paris and the musicians Flavie and Rod Macrae. He'd just have to make an extra dozen bottles next year. At least . . .

He would also need some extra bottles to take along to several predictable festivities during the holiday season, so before heading to the riding school to help Pamela with the evening exercise, he stopped at the town vineyard to buy a case of four whites, four reds and four of the remarkably good sparkling wine. To his surprise, Alain was there, a tape measure in one hand and a notebook in the other.

"It's for the new tasting room for visitors," said Alain. "They can't make up their minds whether they want to convert one of the old buildings at the *domaine* alongside the château or build something new here by the *chais* where they make the wines."

"What do you think?" Bruno asked. "You're building it."

"There's more scope here," Alain said. "At the *domaine* they'll be cramped for space because they want to offer food as well. And they'll have to go through the usual hoops of approvals from the Bâtiments de France to add or change much. Here

I can have something up and functioning in time for next summer's tourist season, kitchen, dining area and tasting room and toilets. Nothing fancy, all wood on the outside, sloping roof with solar panels, septic tank."

"What did you think of those two tasting rooms I recommended you visit, Château de Fayolle and David Fourtout's place at Les Verdots?"

"Very impressive, but expensive with that circular tasting table, little basins and taps; way beyond the budget I've been given," Alain said. "They want room for eight people to taste at a time, with a sink and refrigerators behind the tasting counter, cupboards for all the glasses, spittoons, a showroom for all the wine varieties and vintages, wrapping table and cash desk. All that with a budget just short of forty grand."

"Yes, but it's free labor with you and the kids you're teaching, and Rosalie can handle the plumbing and you can do all the electronics," said Bruno.

"Have you any idea of the kind of weight we're looking at with all those bottles on shelving, and the space needed so somebody can be washing glasses while somebody else is pouring out the tasting glasses and someone else at the cash desk?" Alain asked, as if he really wanted to know. "It's a big deal, Bruno. The tasting room alone is ten meters by six, the kitchen will be six by six, the bathrooms the same, along with secure storerooms. I should know, because I'm having to do the design along with Michel from the works department."

"I thought we were getting some retired architect to give his advice for free?"

"He'll cast a friendly eye over my plans, but we're going to need insurance on the building and that means a licensed architect putting his stamp on the design, which means he could be liable if anything goes wrong. And since there's a kitchen, there's the fire risk, not to mention food poisoning, drunk-driving liability."

"Who does all the insurance for the *mairie,* all the public buildings, the works department, the retirement home, the bridges, the *maternelle* and the *collège,* all the various liabilities?" Bruno asked. "That should get us a few favors."

Alain shrugged. "Don't ask me. That's the mayor's business."

Before buying the wine, Bruno made a mental note to ask Colette about the insurance and then headed for the riding school.

Chapter 21

There were now seven Michelin-starred restaurants in the *département* of the Dordogne—and several more were close—but Bruno's favorite would always be the Vieux Logis, the one that had kept its rosette even in the lean years. The opportunity to dine there was always a rare privilege for him as well as a gastronomic exploration and delight. He preferred it in summer, when the tables were set beneath the trees, and guests could look over the ornately sculpted shrubs and bushes of the garden. Winter had its different pleasures indoors, a sense of warmth and protection that almost, but never quite, verged on the cozy. Whether it was the musicians' gallery and balustrades or the wallpaper, there was a discreet touch of the Lumières, the Enlightenment, about the decor, as if to tame the excesses of the Grande Epoque, although the bottled water they served was Louis XIV's favorite. All year-round, the waiters and waitresses dressed in black, a subtle invitation to the guests to make an effort to look their best.

Bruno, who was driving Pamela and Fabiola from St. Denis, had arrived a few moments before the scheduled time, thinking it proper that he was the first to arrive to greet the other guests. When he had picked them up, he had been suitably full of praise for Pamela's emerald-green dress that went with her bronze-red hair, and for Fabiola's beautifully cut pantsuit in a dark blue heavy silk. When they reached the restaurant, they went at once to the ladies' room to check that Bruno's Land Rover had not disturbed their hair. Bruno was then greeted by Yves, the maître d'hôtel, who escorted him to the private room that had apparently been booked for their dinner. He was standing at the table alone when Annette, Becca and Laura made their entrance, and Bruno could not but bring his hands together in applause.

Becca was wearing a full-length gown that seemed to him North African in inspiration, and which set off her dark hair. Annette could almost have appeared in court in the heavy black silk dress she was wearing with a high white collar and some esoteric accoutrement that clearly referenced a barrister's band. Laura emerged behind them wearing a long, pale blue dress with a very wide belt in the same fabric of heavy silk that might have been inspired by a Japanese obi, the belt worn around the traditional kimono. The color was a perfect match for her eyes, and her fair hair seemed to sparkle under the chandelier. Her complexion glowed with health, and her mouth was, to Bruno's intrigued surprise, free from any hint of lipstick. Pamela and Fabiola were then shown in to join them.

Ghislaine was the last to arrive, in a sparkling sheath that showed off a well-toned figure, her gray hair piled high on her head. She was accompanied by a solemn-faced woman in her fifties wearing a severe business suit; when she turned to face him, without any hint of smile or greeting, he saw an open-neck collar that revealed a necklace that looked like gold coins.

"Bruno," Ghislaine said, "I'm delighted to meet you in person. Would you please make the introductions?"

After Bruno did so, Ghislaine, gesturing to the stranger, said, "And this is Antonia Laperrine. She is a business associate, a good friend and a very discreet private investigator who has spent the last week looking into Dominic's background. Antonia will tell us more later, but now please enjoy the chef's *balade* of the season. I've asked Yves to choose a wine to accompany each course, and of course all of you are my guests."

Now four waitresses appeared, each with two fizzing champagne flutes in hand. Behind them came a waiter with a tray bearing more glasses and a bottle of Château d'Yquem from 2016. He filled the glasses, then they all retired to the kitchen, the waitresses returning with amuse-bouches of foie gras, lobster tail and caviar on tiny squares of toast.

"Dear friends," said Ghislaine, rising from her seat, champagne glass in hand, "I am happy to welcome you all and would ask you to raise a glass in memory of a woman who was my oldest and dearest friend, and who all of you knew and appreciated, with the exception of Bruno, who had the bad luck of discovering her death."

Bruno was the first to rise, the other women following, raising their glasses as Ghislaine said, "To Monique, may she rest in peace." They all echoed her words and then drank.

When they resumed their seats, Bruno was not sure how to proceed, so he watched Ghislaine, who began with the foie gras, then took a sip of the Sauternes, followed by the lobster, another sip of wine and then the caviar. Bruno followed suit, noting that Laura did the same, while Pamela started with the caviar and then the lobster, leaving the foie gras for the end. It hardly mattered, since the wines seemed a perfect match for each taste.

It also seemed the perfect drink to start each of them turning to a neighbor and talking, some of Monique, others of the champagne or of the restaurant, and somehow the conversation seemed to sparkle like champagne itself until the door opened and four waiters arrived. Each one was carrying two plates of one of the inventions of the chef, Vincent Arnould. The waiters were followed by Yves, bearing a tray on which were eight small wineglasses. Into each he poured a generous thimbleful of Monbazillac from Château Tirecul La Gravière, the celebrated Cuvée Madame.

He announced that the dish was named *foie gras d'esturgeon, tartine de champignons à l'huile de noix,* a modest title for a most elaborate dish which began with a very thin layer of smoked sturgeon, on which was placed an inch-thick layer of foie gras. On top of that was a thin slice of green apple very briefly cooked in *verjus,* then another layer of foie gras, topped with another layer of smoked sturgeon. This had been compressed with weights while being chilled, so that when sliced and served it looked almost mathematically precise. On top of this was a very thin slice of toasted brown bread which was covered in thin slices of white mushrooms and shallots, which had been marinated together in sherry vinegar and walnut oil.

Conversation ceased, save for murmurs of appreciation and muted expressions of surprise and delight, followed by purrs of satisfaction and contentment as the glorious sweet wine was sipped. Bruno was accustomed to dining with women who enjoyed their food, but he could not recall that he ever had been in the company of women so very well dressed and stylish, reveling quite so shamelessly in a dish.

Once the plates were empty, Ghislaine tapped her glass with a knife and suggested it was time to hear the report of the private investigator. Bruno had not expected this, but was intrigued.

"Let me begin by saying I was only asked to look into the background of Dominic late on Monday, so I have had less than a week," Antonia began. "I was greatly helped by a woman named Sabine d'Ensingen, the foster sister of Dominic, and she specially asked me to convey her regards to you, Bruno. The difference is that Sabine was formally adopted and welcomed into the d'Ensingen family and Dominic never was. He made little effort to fit in, and while they raised him, gave him a home and an education, he remained a foster ward. The widow d'Ensingen told me, 'I would not trust the little devil as far as I could throw the cathedral itself,' and claims that her husband when alive felt the same way."

But the husband had a sister, Antonia went on. She was unmarried and childless, a notary who had done extremely well from the expansion of the Paris suburbs. She settled in St. Germain-en-Laye, home to the international school and therefore popular with expats. She spoke fluent English and benefited from the influx of English and German speakers. Dominic spoke both and was taken on as his foster aunt's apprentice while he went to university, got his master's degree in law and then got his *certificat d'aptitude.* After two more years under her wing, he was fully qualified.

"He was in his midtwenties and the sister was twenty years older. Sabine and her mother are both convinced that the relationship was also a sexual one," said Antonia, looking around the table.

When the sister would not make Dominic a full partner in her business, she continued, he left her and found a similar role with another female *notaire* in her forties in Nantes. He remained there for two years, where he married the woman. She later committed suicide, leaving her business and her home to Dominic. At the age of thirty-two he sold them both and moved to Bordeaux, where he found work with another *notaire* in her late forties, a woman with an office in Talence. He did some freelance work for her, but she became suspicious of his intentions, fired him and ended the relationship.

"I have a sworn statement as to her suspicions of Dominic's

behavior and ambitions, and a copy of the letter she wrote to her own Chambre de Notaires in which she described her concerns. These were not taken seriously, as she was thought to be, one of her colleagues told me, 'a woman somewhat prone to hysteria with an unfortunate record of complaints against colleagues.' Dominic then moved to Bergerac and met Monique in Sarlat. I can't prove that he targeted her specifically, but I do think it significant that they met when she realized that time was running out if she were to have children, having put such overwhelming effort into creating and then building her new *conciergerie* business.

"At first, I wondered if we were looking at Monique being murdered, but the evidence is against it," Antonia went on. "At the time of her death, he was already in Strasbourg, more than eight hundred kilometers away. Monique's farewell letters to her lawyer, business partner and her husband leave little room for doubt of her intentions."

At this point Ghislaine tapped her knife against a glass and said: "An interjection, if you don't mind? I received a handwritten letter from Monique by mail in Paris on Tuesday, and it was posted in Sarlat on Sunday. It was a letter of farewell, with kind words about our many years of friendship, a reference to my brother as the love of her life and her determination to end that life. And here is a photocopy of the letter that I made for you, Annette."

She handed it across the table, and then said, "I have to confess that I suspected Dominic had a role in Monique's death, and Antonia's research has confirmed that he was and presumably remains a selfish, ruthless and mercenary man, but he seems to have played no direct part in her death. Her will suggests he is not going to benefit from it. And now I think we are ready for the next course," she said, tapping gently on her glass with her knife.

The next dish was a magnificent *mignon de veau rôti,* a filet mignon of roasted veal, topped with a ravioli filled with the yolk of an egg that was itself topped with slices of black truffle from the Périgord. It was accompanied with *rondelles* of onion and plumes of fresh asparagus that Bruno assumed must have come from a hothouse. The wine was a Château Bélingard, Cuvée Ortus, of 2019, a classic of the Bergerac.

"Mon Dieu," announced Ghislaine, raising her wineglass. "How I wish that Monique were with us here to enjoy this meal. So here's to her, wherever or whatever she might be, angel or spirit, cosmic wanderer, ghost or simple memory that we here may share."

The toast was drunk and then Ghislaine called on Bruno to give whatever news there might be on the inquiry.

"As Annette can confirm, the inquiry is officially over now that the verdict of suicide has been established. One thing I should mention, and perhaps I should have done so earlier, is that the evening that Dominic got back from Strasbourg and read the letter Monique had left him, he started making some strange suggestions," Bruno said.

"What do you mean?" Ghislaine asked.

"He suggested on the basis of the letter that Laura was the person who would benefit most from Monique's death, as though that came as news to him, and that you, Rebecca, would be involved, since you had helped her to draft her will. He even hinted that I might be involved in the plot, along with you, Annette, as magistrate. I put it down to strain, since he'd been driving all day after the stress of his foster father's funeral. He took back the remarks right away, saying he was exhausted and was not himself, but it's possible that he might still nurture fantasies of a conspiracy. He apologized again when I called him yesterday about the funeral being held in St. Denis."

"Thanks for letting us know," said Rebecca. "But I hardly

think he can include the medical examiner in his plot, and that would have been the key person regarding the legal verdict of suicide. I don't know who it was, and I'd guess neither do you. Aren't they on some kind of rotation?"

"It depends whether the circumstances suggest the need for a full-scale postmortem at the police lab in Bergerac or Périgueux, or if the duty doctor can sign off after checking stomach contents to confirm the presence of the pills that killed her," said Annette. "The latter is what happened in this case. Standard operating procedure. I received a copy of the medical report and sent a copy to Rebecca as Monique's registered lawyer. Dominic also received a copy as next of kin."

"Bruno, I'm thinking about what you just told us about Dominic raising suspicions when he got back from Strasbourg," said Rebecca. "What if he was deliberately suggesting that Laura and I were involved to shift attention away from his own role in all this? Look, we all know that Monique slowly but surely became a different woman after she married him, more nervous, more prone to depression, less certain of herself, looking to him for approval, which almost never came. It's something we've all seen happen to lots of women in marriage, that steady decline in self-confidence. And for Monique, at her age, not being able to carry a child to term was a massive blow to her self-esteem. To have a child was why she married Dominic in the first place."

"The more I think about it, that was something he played on, treating her like a piece of fine china, almost like an invalid, helping her into and out of chairs," said Annette.

"You're talking about behavior, caring for a pregnant wife, that a lot of people would think is pretty normal," said Bruno.

"Bruno, this is a thought experiment I'm trying here," said Rebecca. "I'm wondering if Dominic was capable of that degree of patience, of being that subtle and wicked, playing slowly but deliberately on Monique's insecurities until she felt so worthless she did the job herself."

Bruno shook his head. "Sorry, Rebecca, but I'm not convinced. He signed off on a marriage contract with a separation of property, so he knew all along he wasn't going to inherit."

"But if he was confident that he could undermine her self-confidence over time, play on her insecurities, make her more and more psychologically dependent on him, then he could take her to another *notaire* and get her to sign a new will," Rebecca countered.

"I see what you mean," said Bruno. "What does the law do in that case?"

"The most recently dated will is the one that is valid," Annette replied. "Unless there is reason to question its validity."

"So in theory Dominic could have taken Monique to another *notaire* to sign a new will last week," Ghislaine said. "He could have done it in Bergerac or Bordeaux and got it properly witnessed and sent off to be registered. Then he turns up at Rebecca's office on Monday, drops the new will on the table, thumbs his nose at everybody and waltzes off with everything."

"Theoretically, yes, but the letters she wrote to him and to me and to Laura on Sunday make it clear that shortly before she took her own life she firmly believed that the old will was valid," said Rebecca, sounding to Bruno's ears for the first time like a lawyer. "That would mean that any new will could be questioned in law, even if legally registered."

"I suppose that could mean a pretty dramatic lawsuit," said Ghislaine.

"His reaction when he read Monique's final letter to him, which said explicitly that her business would go to Laura and her colleagues and not to him, suggests that he didn't have such a new will in hand," said Bruno.

"Unless he was lulling you into a false sense of security," said Ghislaine.

"My motto has always been hope for the best but prepare for the worst," added Antonia as a discreet knock came on the door.

Two bowls of winter salad were served. Bruno saw shredded kale, carrots and brussels sprouts, diced apples and roasted pumpkin, along with goat cheese and hazelnuts, all glistening with olive oil and giving off scents of fresh lemon juice and ground pepper.

As the door closed behind the waiters, Antonia went on to propose some subtle inquiries among the *notaires* in the rest of the *département,* or wherever Dominic might have reliable contacts.

"I don't think we need to worry too much," suggested Laura. "For me and the other employees, the important part of Monique's heritage is the company, and the majority of the shares are already in our hands or, rather, in our names. Monique was down to holding just under thirty percent of the shares, so even if he did play dirty with the will, Dominic won't have control, and the rest of us can always outvote him."

"Your faith in your fellow employees is impressive, Laura," Ghislaine said dryly.

"In my experience, however, such trust is very seldom rewarded, except perhaps in heaven," added Antonia.

"The Monique I knew would not have gone along with any last-minute changes to her will," said Pamela.

"I agree," Fabiola chimed in. "She was made of sterner stuff than that, an honorable woman."

The salad plates were removed, and in their place came the double-decker cheese tray, which could be carried by a single waiter and then opened to become twice the size. Unusually, it included some British cheeses among the French classics, a Cornish yarg and a Sparkenhoe Red Leicester. Seeing that Pamela and Laura had each chosen them, Bruno followed suit, partly from curiosity, partly because he thought each of them had good palates. Then he noticed that the cheese had come with a dusty bottle of old port, a dessert wine that Bruno had only previously tasted at the table of his friend Jack Crimson.

The yarg was odd, creamy on the outside and then crumbly in the middle, and the Red Leicester was silky in the mouth, a slightly sour taste balanced by a nutty flavor. He enjoyed both cheeses and sipped at the port with pleasure while he wondered which dessert Vincent would serve them. Or perhaps which dessert Ghislaine had chosen for them, since she had evidently arranged the whole meal in advance; there had been no fussing over menus and choices. He had dined very well, felt not at all full and had drunk sparingly. He saw from the watch on Annette's left wrist beside him that it was still some minutes before ten o'clock.

"In the few moments that remain before Vincent treats us to one of his exceptional desserts," said Ghislaine, "I want to thank you all for coming, and I'm sure I speak for all of us women that we were pleased to have a very agreeable gentleman among us. It's always a risk, throwing a Daniel into a den of lionesses, but we didn't have to growl once. Thank you, Bruno. I think it says a lot about Monique that she had such a large collection of intelligent and sympathetic friends, and I know all of our lives were enriched by having known her. And after her funeral, I'll make sure to stay in touch with you all."

Heads around the table nodded, and there were murmurings of "Well said," but Laura raised a hand.

"I think in recent years I probably spent more time with Monique than almost anyone, working alongside her day by day, although I know, Ghislaine, that you and she were friends for nearly forty years. And I know that you, Rebecca, and she were close throughout the Sarlat years, and then Annette joined your friendship, and Pamela and Fabiola widened it with those Pilates sessions we so much enjoyed, and which did us all so much good. Monique was a very special woman and we are all honored to have known her as a friend. I can't think of a better way to remember her than to have eaten here, together, all of us thinking what a fine woman she was and how much she'd have loved to be here with us."

Each of the women said a few words, recalled something especially kind or wise that Monique had done or said, and Bruno suspected that at least one waiter was listening in, since when the last voice had spoken, the door opened. Servers entered with trays carrying what looked like drinks in white mugs, on flat white plates that contained raspberries flecked with cream, and then red rolls of something that looked like sliced beet.

As if on cue, Vincent appeared at the door, and everyone at the table began to applaud, but the chef raised a hand, and said, "I know you've had your cheese course, but I call this dessert my vacherin—a *vacherin aux framboises, sorbet framboises betteraves*. And thank you all for coming, and Bruno, my friend, I think you must be the luckiest man in France tonight!"

As Vincent left to applause, the group was exploring the plates before them, realizing that the white mugs were made of meringue and that they contained a sorbet of raspberries and beet that had been transformed into something unusual and sublime, topped with a vanilla-flavored Chantilly cream.

"I hate to break this perfect mug, but I really love meringue," Ghislaine declared, tapping the side of the tall, white tube until it shattered and the mingled juice of beet and raspberries flowed bright crimson against the perfect white of the meringue. Like blood on snow, thought Bruno.

Chapter 22

The dinner party at the Vieux Logis had gone on a little longer than Bruno had anticipated, then the drive back to St. Denis had been interrupted by a phone call from Kyiv, where Fabiola's partner, Gilles, was waiting for the Russian invasion that he and his hosts were convinced was coming. But it was not coming just yet, they had agreed, and Gilles felt he was free to fly back to St. Denis for Christmas. Fabiola, understandably, wanted to celebrate this news. Pamela and Bruno felt obliged to help drink a bottle of champagne that she opened as soon as they reached the home she shared with Gilles, when his journalism permitted him to be there. Bruno stood, gamely nodding his head, smiling and sipping champagne he did not want as Pamela and Fabiola discussed emergency appointments at hairdressers and beauty parlors, special welcoming dinners and Christmas presents. Then Fabiola burst into tears at the thought her partner would be going back to Ukraine early in the New Year and Gilles was sure that war would follow.

Bruno then had to drive Pamela home, and, given his knowledge that he was to see Laura and her beautiful basset on Sunday, Bruno was a little nervous about how the night would continue. He and Pamela had for some time been deeply affectionate and loving friends, each aware that their liaison had no future, but each far too fond of the arrangement to permit it to end. Pamela had once even ended the affair, saying he deserved the time and space and freedom to seek the wife and future mother of his children that she knew Bruno wanted. When such a woman failed to appear, she had relaunched their arrangement. "Friends with benefits," the young people were said to be calling it.

Bruno had long ceased to be amazed by the foresight, or perhaps the intuition, of women. Millennia of being the physically weaker sex, he thought, must have given them survival skills and levels of understanding far beyond the thinking of most males with their belief in muscles and the skills of the hunt. So he was not entirely surprised when, pleasantly relaxed from Fabiola's champagne, Pamela brought up the topic he'd hoped would not be broached that evening.

"I enjoyed meeting Laura this evening, and I understand you and she have a devotion to basset hounds in common," she began.

Bruno felt himself become instantly sober, every sense suddenly attuned to interpret what was about to follow.

"Yes, hers is named after the feminist writer George Sand," he said, trying to shift the conversation in a literary direction.

"She was impressed that you recognized the name," Pamela said. "And that you had even read some of Sand's books. Who would ever expect a literary policeman, she asked me, and I had to reply that our mutual friend Bruno had hidden depths, and how clever of her to notice them."

Bruno felt these same depths now opening as a chasm beneath him. Seeking to change the subject, he touched upon a theme close to Pamela's heart by replying, "But you know how much I enjoy horses as well as basset hounds."

"Oh, yes, dear Bruno," she said, and while he kept his eyes

on the road he could imagine the mischievous glint in her eye as she replied, "There has never been anything lacking in your animal instincts, which explains why you are so good at hunting, or should I say at chasing game? And there are few men more dangerous than hunters who read," she said. For the first time he could hear the teasing in her voice.

"Seriously, Bruno, I wish you well," she said as he turned into the driveway of the riding school. "Laura is an interesting and thoughtful woman, and unlike me she is one who rather hopes to have children of her own, should the right man cross her path. A literary basset lover who enjoys his food and is a very good cook might be just the thing, so long as he understands her commitment to the business that she helped Monique to build up."

He pulled into the driveway before her house, turned and took his hand from the steering wheel to take hers, saying, "You are an extraordinary woman, wise and kind."

"You're not too bad yourself," she replied, planting a kiss on his cheek and letting herself out of his Land Rover. "Sleep tight, Bruno. And don't forget your duties to the children tomorrow, Père Noël."

The children, thought Bruno, were usually the least of his problems. They just wanted to get close to the choir and grab whatever little snacks or goodies or fizzy drinks had been prepared for them. It was the parents who tended to be the issue—each of them wanted to snap the perfect family photo or Christmas memory on their smartphone. And these days everyone had one: the parents, the grandparents, the uncles and aunts, and the teenagers, and each of them thought he or she was an undiscovered Cartier-Bresson, a born photographer. They would clamber on top of vehicles, crawl beneath market stalls, hang from lampposts, stand on the parapet of the bridge; anything to snap that perfect image.

Cheered by the thought that Balzac would be waiting loyally by the door as he returned, Bruno drove off, turning on the radio for any late news at midnight. He found instead a late-night talk show, and he would have switched channels to get some music, but he recognized the arrogant drawl of one of the guests. It was the lawyer, Poincevin.

". . . the whole relationship strikes me as unusual, odd, perhaps even a little unwholesome. I understand that they are colleagues and are required to work together, to cooperate for the common good. But as the young man's *commandante,* Capitaine Yveline's first duty should have been to her fresh-faced, innocent new recruit. Instead, she tossed him to the wolves."

"And in your view, the wolf would be, er, who, exactly? Are you suggesting that Chief of Police Courrèges is in any way responsible?"

"The question is, What was the village policeman doing—excuse me, Chief of Police Courrèges—giving himself a free hand to meddle in issues of internal training of gendarme recruits? It's unheard of, and many gendarmes tell me so, in the clearest terms."

Bruno pulled into a convenient turnout at the side of the road, kept his headlights on and continued to listen.

"So that's why you say this relationship between the gendarme *capitaine* and Chief of Police Bruno is questionable?"

"More than just questionable, it's scandalous," Poincevin insisted. "Courrèges was an army sergeant and is now a village policeman, given an honorary title because he acts, secretly, as the local eyes and ears of the security services, which is ostensibly not his job. It all smacks to me of double-dealing. You may want to believe in this nonsense of his not seeing a penny of his secret pay from the secret police, but I don't. He's not a village constable, he's a secret policeman. And he has influence, extraordinary and undue influence. That is why some hapless young gendarme recruit is in jail for reacting too amiably to some pretty woman he thought was making a pass at him."

"Not just one young woman, Monsieur Poincevin, there are now several women who have filed complaints."

"Are you surprised, given this village policeman's contacts and influence? I have little doubt that he made sure the gendarme was charged with plausible complaints from all sorts of women and of course one from an elderly and unmarried male wine connoisseur, the type we used to call a confirmed bachelor." Bruno could hear the air quotes in the lawyer's disdain. "Oh yes, this secret policeman Bruno knows how to make things look very bad indeed."

"You sound as though you nurse a personal grudge against Chief of Police Courrèges, Monsieur Poincevin," said the interviewer. "Is that the case?"

"Not at all. I have only met the man once. I was applying for bail on behalf of some Chinese man who didn't know much French and had been arrested after a misunderstanding with a Vietnamese stallholder in the market. Courrèges was rude and very unhelpful, and seemed to nurse some animus against the Chinese fellow, or perhaps against me. I got my client out on bail in the end despite the efforts of the chief of police. This was in the St. Denis gendarmerie, by the way, where he seemed to be running the place, which is not surprising, given his connections to the security services."

"So what's happening to your new client, the gendarme accused of sexual assault? Are you getting him out on bail?"

"Oh, I don't think Chief Bruno would want that to happen, oh, no. He wants the young man locked up until it's time for trial, when all the witnesses have been carefully prepared. Just the other evening he was seen having dinner with one of the women bringing these baseless charges at a restaurant in Sarlat, grooming her in her testimony, I imagine. Bruno is quite the ladies' man in his own right, or so I'm told, with lady loves in Paris and Bordeaux and Sarlat. One wonders how he has time for the secret police work."

Bruno sent a message to Marie-Do asking her to have a full text of the interview sent to him, with copies to J-J, Yveline and Annette, at her earliest convenience in the morning. He suggested the radio station's lawyer should also have a copy, since the station's late-night host did not seem aware of the sub judice rule, which banned public discussion of a pending case.

Poincevin must have known that, thought Bruno. So what was he playing at? Was it some legal trick to get the trial postponed or transferred elsewhere, or simply to buy time? Was Poincevin shooting for a mistrial? How on earth could that be made to work? He'd ask Annette in the morning, but for the moment all he wanted to do was to greet Balzac, take him out for a last walk while the dog watered the garden, then fill up the woodburning stove so it would last all night while they slept. Suddenly he realized that with his mind on other things he'd gone past the turnoff to his house. He drove on, knowing he could take another road and come to his house from the back, a route he sometimes took when returning from Savignac.

As his Land Rover climbed the hill and turned right, he saw a sudden flash of light as a car door opened somewhere near his house. One figure was walking past, another seemed to be getting out of the vehicle. That was odd. Balzac was not barking to greet or warn any strangers. That was even more odd. J-J sometimes dropped by late at night but always called first. Bruno cut his own lights, including the one for the car door, turned off the motor and buttoned up his coat to prevent his light shirt from showing. He picked up some earth, spat on it and rubbed blotches onto his cheeks, forehead and the backs of his hands. He grabbed a tire iron he had in the car to repair flat tires and a large wrench that could probably smash a knee.

Bruno struck off through woods as familiar to him as the streets of St. Denis, coming down the slope behind his house and then skirting to the side away from the usual entrance road. He could see the shadow of a car looming, somebody leaning against it, low voices murmuring. He listened for the second voice and heard that it came from the stand of trees at the head of the road, probably watching for his arrival.

He could get into his house through the back door, unlock his gun cabinet, load and come out firing a warning shot. But whoever was out there might be armed. And there could be a third man, watching the back door. Bruno waited several minutes, simply listening. He identified two voices and doubted that there was a third. There was no hint of Balzac's presence, so they must have drugged, shot or beaten him badly. They would pay for that.

His immediate target was leaning against the hood of the car, facing the entrance road, his back to Bruno. He was about Bruno's height, the shoulders seemed broad, and he was looking up at the cloudy night. Bruno had the tire iron in his right hand, hissed and as the man turned he slammed the iron onto the man's head just above the ear, and then rose to embrace him as he toppled, a dead weight. Bruno let him down gently onto the ground.

Then Bruno slipped into the car, turned on the headlights at full beam and then turned them off before slipping out to see a dazed and dazzled man standing at the head of the entrance drive with his black-gloved hands clamped over his eyes. Bruno went up, kneed him hard in the balls and karate chopped him in the throat, then used the man's belt to tie his elbows together behind his back. He did the same to the first man, still unconscious on the ground.

Next, Bruno went to his police van and came back with

two sets of large-sized handcuffs, which he used to cross lock the two mens' ankles together. He turned on the headlights of their vehicle to illuminate the scene as he took the wallets of the two men and their identification papers.

He was surprised to learn that they were gendarmes attached to the Périgueux motorized brigade on rue Trarieux. He knew the place well. They were supposed to be in uniform when on duty, but these two men were wearing civilian clothes and each man sported tactical gloves in black leather. He pulled one glove from the man who was still unconscious; it was heavy with lead weights across the padded knuckles. The man he'd blinded with the headlights had a telescopic baton. They were planning to do some serious damage, or at least threaten it.

Bruno sighed and began looking for Balzac, relieved to find his faithful companion just inside the unlocked door to the kitchen in a drugged sleep but apparently uninjured. Bruno suspected knock-out drops in his water. He then called J-J's home number and told him what had happened, suggesting that a Police Nationale patrol should come and take the gendarmes away. Then he called Fabiola and the mayor, who arrived at Bruno's house about ten minutes later.

The mayor used his phone to take photos of the two gendarmes and their papers. Fabiola checked the eyes of the one Bruno had hit, who was now conscious, and found no signs of concussion. The mayor then called Philippe Delaron of *Sud Ouest* to come with his camera. Then he called the prefect. She had not yet gone to bed and said she would come directly to St. Denis, on the way alerting the duty officer at the Elysée in Paris to the news of an attack on a senior policeman by two gendarmes in civilian clothes.

Bruno woke the vet and asked him to come right away to Bruno's home and ascertain what drug had been given to Balzac. A hypodermic needle was found in the gendarmes' car with a one-hundred-milligram injector containing ketamine. Almost all of it had been used. Bruno checked his phone. A standard anesthetic dose was five milligrams per kilo, and Balzac weighed thirty-three kilos, so Bruno felt a wave of relief.

By one in the morning, the prefect, the mayor, Prunier, J-J and Philippe Delaron were all standing in Bruno's garden. They were drinking Bruno's scotch to keep out the cold and waiting for the arrival and the explanation of the gendarmes' General Mouleydier who had spluttered in confusion and bafflement when called from his bed by the prefect. The two handcuffed gendarmes had, after a few curses, sensibly kept silent, although each of them was now shivering.

"Do you have an explanation for why two of your gendarmes in civilian clothes and using a private car should lie in wait to ambush the chief of police?" the prefect asked Mouleydier when he arrived.

"The two gendarmes are off duty, madame, and they were not under any orders to come here in civilian clothes and a private vehicle, nor to drug Chief of Police Bruno's dog," the general replied. "I have no explanation for their behavior and the head of their brigade was shocked to hear of this. I have no objection to their being taken by the Police Nationale, questioned and duly charged."

"Is it possible that overzealous loyalty to the gendarmerie after the charging of a young gendarme with sexual offenses might have led to this extraordinary attack?"

"That may be so, Madame Prefect, but I couldn't possibly comment."

The prefect asked Philippe Delaron to back away out of hearing.

"I am under orders to report back your reply to the Elysée

where officials of senior rank are waiting for my report," she went on. "I will give you five minutes to come up with a better answer and then I will leave your career in the hands of the Elysée. We are both aware that another general is involved, the uncle of the young man who should never have been allowed into the gendarmes in the first place. You might want to consider whether your career ends here tonight, or your senior officer takes the responsibility. Five minutes, then it's up to you."

"Thank you, madame."

She turned away and then waved Bruno to join her, walking toward his chicken coop.

"Is there anything more you can tell me?" she asked.

"Only that the same gendarme general has threatened to cancel the new gendarmerie in St. Denis."

"Not on my watch, he won't," she said, glancing at him. "I'm told you came up with the extra evidence that nailed Villon, but I don't know the details. I'd like to hear them."

Bruno explained the attempted shakedown of the wine taster and the lineup, where he confirmed the identifications of Célestine and the bishop's secretary.

"So the testimony of one man was taken more seriously than the testimony of two young women, however well connected," she said, rolling her eyes.

Bruno shook his head. "Not quite. Villon had already been arrested and placed under *garde à vue* by J-J on drugs and theft charges before we heard about the wine taster."

"Point taken," she replied.

"There's another aspect to this," Bruno went on. "Villon's lawyer is Poincevin, known to all of us in law enforcement as an unscrupulous man who would probably sell his own mother if the price was right. He was careful to be publicly elsewhere, on a late-night radio talk show, while the gendarmes were here waiting for me to come home. But I think Poincevin might be involved in this, and other than Villon's uncle, I don't know who else could afford his fancy legal fees."

"I know Poincevin's reputation, but he never quite steps over the line," she replied. "Somebody certainly has, though," she went on, glancing fiercely at the local gendarme general.

Bruno felt a twinge of sympathy for the man who must be feeling squeezed between his own chain of command in the gendarmes and the greater power of the state which was now, thanks to the prefect, taking a direct interest in this squalid business.

"The Elysée was already aware of one aspect of this because of some media questions about threats to cancel the new gendarmerie even though it's almost finished," she said. "Do you know anything about this?"

"Yes, I was there when the general told us the future of our new gendarmerie was suddenly in question," Bruno replied. "He seemed to be furious, but I couldn't tell if the emotions were his own or if he was reacting to orders he didn't like."

"Why didn't you tell me about that?"

"Because the mayor thought you should hear it from his old friends in the Senate. And I work for the mayor and the council of St. Denis."

"And for General Lannes and the DGSI," she retorted.

"Only when formally recalled to the military. And not in this case."

"How the hell did you know about this ambush?" she asked.

"I didn't," he replied. "I took the back way home and saw a brief flash of light as someone opened their car door, although the headlights were out. I came quietly on foot to see what was going on and realized they were waiting for me, lights out, and had immobilized my dog."

"Okay," she replied, "that should do." She paused, looking

grimly at him. "I may need to talk to you again before I make my report to the Elysée."

"No problem."

"And I hope your dog gets better, Bruno."

"Thank you, so do I."

Chapter 23

Bruno was not feeling at his best the next morning as he changed into the Father Christmas costume in the men's room at the *mairie*. He had got to bed at 2:00 a.m. and slept solidly until just after eight. Balzac was still asleep and now breathing normally in the little cave-like sleeping space in Bruno's bedroom to which he'd carried the dog. He had showered, shaved and dressed, feeling grumpy at having missed his morning run. When he got into town he was so late he had to park on the far side of the river. At least he'd remembered to buy the lamb shanks and some cheese from Stéphane's stall for Gilles's welcome-home dinner. He'd brought a sprig of thyme, bay leaves and ten heads of garlic from his garden, purchased a bottle of Monbazillac from Hubert's wineshop and then borrowed the largest bowl from the kitchen in the *mairie* to marinate the lamb in the mayor's fridge. He broke each of the heads of garlic into their separate cloves and added them all to the marinade. On top of the bowl he laid a sheet of paper on which he wrote the word DANGER, adding a warning that nobody should touch this bowl on penalty of Bruno's vengeance.

"Ho-ho-ho," he announced as he plunged into the crowd, wincing at the sound of the handbell he had begun to ring, and wishing he hadn't. The barrage began at once. It was not the cheerful greetings of the children but the constant demands of the adults, each of them carrying a smartphone. Everyone demanded that he smile for their camera, pick up this child or that, turn this way, now the other way, and now this child, and now bend down to put his arms around two children and then stand behind a carriage with a baby that looked understandably terrified, and then start again with the "Ho-ho-ho."

At least there was no foolish attempt at fixing antlers to one of Stéphane's calves this year as a kind of make-do reindeer, a scheme dreamed up one well-lubricated evening at the hunting club. They had forgotten the remarkable capacity of the bladders of young dairy cows, and half the choir had been drenched, and all rushed dripping into the mayor's elevator to reach the bathrooms upstairs. The stench had lingered well into February.

"Is that you, Bruno?" demanded one child.

"Ho-ho-ho," he replied. "Who has been naughty and who has been nice? Did you help *Maman* with the washing up, and did you help Papa wash the car?"

"Papa takes it to the car wash," came one dispiriting reply. Another child said coolly, "*Maman* puts the dishes in the machine."

And then once the choir began, instead of "Vive le Vent" half the children were singing "Jingle Bells," and "Mon Beau Sapin" had become "O Christmas Tree" for some kids and "O Tannenbaum" for others, and Bruno wondered what language the children would be singing in another thirty years. Even that most French of Christmas hymns, "Il Est Né le Divin Enfant," had its English chorus, "Play the oboe, sound musettes." It just proved how ruthless the English had been in their plundering of the French language with its original name for the instrument, *Jouez hautbois, résonnez musettes*!

But Bruno knew the tune he wanted to sing, and as the first notes of the glorious Christmas hymn came, he belted out the words he had known all his life:

> *O Christ, Roi des anges,*
> *Captif dans les langes,*
> *Splendeur pure et sans déclin*
> *Du père divin;*
> *O Christ, Roi des anges,*
> *Voilé sous un corps humain:*
> *Que votre amour t'implore,*
> *Que votre foi t'adore*
> *Et qu'elle chante encore*
> *Ton règne sans fin!*

It didn't seem to matter that Jack Crimson, Miranda and her children, along with Pamela and some other British and American voices in the crowd, were roaring out their words of "O Come, All Ye Faithful" to its grand old rousing tune. Bruno could close his eyes and almost remember the smell of the incense at Mass as the familiar words took him back to the little chapel of the church-run orphanage where he had spent his first years. He blinked to brush away the tears that had suddenly formed, and into the silence he waved his handbell and called out again, "Ho-ho-ho, *Joyeux Noël.* Merry Christmas, everyone."

Then the choir broke into "Douce Nuit, Sainte Nuit," ignoring the solitary protest of the wife of Montsouris, the only Communist on the town council. And she was far more militant and leftist than her husband. She was standing at the edge of the small square above the steps and waving a tall pole that carried a placard that read CHRISTMAS IS A RELIGIO-CAPITALIST PLOT.

At least she's not targeting me for once, thought Bruno, and at that moment she twirled the pole around so he could see the slogan on the placard's other side that read: BRUNO is a SECRET policeman.

And Merry Christmas to you, too, he thought as the choir launched into their farewell song, *"Minuit, Chrétiens, c'est l'heure solennelle,"* and began marching back to the church. They were followed by all the children whom Bruno had to guide on toward the little path past the church to their feast at the retirement home, where the entrance hall was today framed by balloons.

Inside the big dining hall, with a huge Christmas tree in pride of place, rows of tables were loaded with little sandwiches of ham or cheese or pâté, almond tarts and apple pies. There were cakes with a thick layer of jam in the center and cream on top, plate after plate of homemade biscuits and bottles of fizzy drinks. Elderly ladies were lined up proudly like so many soldiers behind the loaded tables gazing fondly at the little ones as they lined up ready to dive into the food.

The parents, knowing from experience something of the chaos that a large number of children in a limited space can wreak, were watching nervously from the back of the hall. But this was a Père Noël with a voice of command, determined that the heroic efforts of the old ladies should not be plundered by a gang of children.

"What do we say to these kind grannies who have prepared this splendid feast for you?" he asked solemnly.

"Merci, grands-mères," they all piped up.

"And what do you wish them?"

"Joyeux Noël," they chanted, more or less in unison.

"Now each of you can take a plate and one little tart and one little sandwich at a time, and a drink, then go back to the far side of the hall and sit quietly while these friendly old grandpas sing their carols for you, and you can join in if you know the words. You can go to the tables to get some food when I give you the word and remember that you have to walk slowly. Wait for it—walk."

The rush was on, at something close to walking pace, but once the tables were reached, little arms became tangled as they were thrust toward the food. Sandwiches slid off plates and splashed into glasses and dropped soggily to the floor until Père Noël had had enough.

"Stop," he roared in a parade-ground voice. "Now each of you step back three paces. Go."

With a mutinous look here and there, interspersed with looks of longing at the still-loaded tables, the children backed away.

Père Noël then made a stately parade, walking up and down between the children and the tables, noting that there were five tables and forty children. He got them to form orderly queues of eight children each, and then they went up to the tables one at a time, and then returned to the far side of the hall. The old ladies were all checking surreptitiously that their table was being emptied at least as rapidly as the table to each side. The grandpas were all standing by the Christmas tree and began to sing in excellent harmony. The children went up one by one to get their slices of cake and to say thank you while the old men went from "Petit Papa Noël" to "Mon Beau Sapin" and rounded it off with "La Fille de Père Noël."

One of the old ladies came across to hand Bruno a plate with a cheese sandwich and a battered apple tart, all that remained of the feast. He put the plate down to clap his hands and ask the children, before they put their coats on, to thank the singing grandpas and the grandmas by singing the carol he knew they had all rehearsed in school:

De bon matin
J'ai rencontré le train
De trois grands rois, qui allaient en voyage . . .
Three great kings, I met at early morn . . .

The market was drawing to a close as the clock on the *mairie* struck noon, and Bruno emerged looking like himself again, the policeman of St. Denis, with the uniform and peaked hat to prove it. The Père Noël uniform was hung up for another year. He still hadn't repaired the shredding white beard. Thinking that a mobile phone suddenly ringing would not help the children to suspend their disbelief, Bruno had left his phone with Colette in the *mairie*. But she had come out to watch the fun, and his phone appeared to have been ringing nonstop ever since.

He had received calls from J-J, Annette, Marie-Do, General Lannes, the prefect, Laura, J-J again and Philippe Delaron. As he looked at the screen it rang again. Annette.

"Thank heavens you answered. Where on earth have you been? All hell is breaking loose," she began breathlessly.

"I was dressed up as Père Noël for the children's concert," he replied calmly. "And it's not very convincing if your phone starts ringing. So, what's been happening?"

"The gendarme general in Paris has resigned, along with the one here," she replied. "And the *procureur* has called in Poincevin to explain his breach of the sub judice rule. And everybody wants to know if you're going to sue Poincevin for defamation, and Marie-Do is worried that you might sue the radio station, too."

"What are the penalties for breach of sub judice these days?"

"Up to a year in prison and a maximum fine of forty-five

thousand euros. But for defamation, that depends on the court."

"I would never sue the radio station. In Poincevin's case that's very tempting. But he's a lawyer, he must have known he was risking a lawsuit."

"I suspect he may have drunk too much at dinner to be cautious," she said. "Some of his words were slurred and the interviewer and the technician both told Marie-Do that he stumbled entering the studio."

"Any other news, or should I answer the other calls?" Bruno replied.

"How is Balzac?"

"He was still asleep when I left this morning after being drugged last night."

"Fingers crossed for Balzac, and if you want me to recommend the best defamation lawyer in France, just let me know."

Next, Bruno called J-J to apologize for not being available and was immediately interrupted.

"I called the mayor and he told me you were with the children. Have you heard the news? Two generals resigning on the same day—unbelievable."

"I heard. And I gather we get to keep the new gendarmerie and Yveline stays on as *commandante.* I was happy to hear Poincevin may be in trouble for talking on the radio about a case that's sub judice."

"My heart bleeds," said J-J, laughing. "I'll believe it when I see it. You know how lawyers stick together."

"What's going to happen to those two gendarmes who were at my place?" Bruno asked.

"Under *garde à vue* until the *procureur* decides what to charge them with, beyond drugging your dog and conspiracy to pervert the course of justice. If it were up to me, I'd offer them a deal under which they agree to be witnesses against

Poincevin and Villon's uncle—unless a deal has already been agreed to in return for the general's resignation. It's not a case the gendarmes would like to see made public."

Bruno then called General Lannes, who said he was glad that Bruno was unhurt, that neither gendarme general was a serious loss and that he hoped Balzac would be fine. That was it.

Bruno then called Laura, who said she could hear that he was fine but how was Balzac?

"I'm glad you have your priorities right, Laura, and I only hope that Balzac will not be a disappointment to George Sand. He might not be at his best tomorrow, but let's go ahead as planned."

"Great. I'm looking forward to it and I hope you'll show me the scene of the crime. May I bring some food or wine?"

"Not much crime, despite what Annette may be saying," Bruno said, laughing. "Why don't we meet for a coffee and croissant at Fauquet's café at the end of the bridge at nine-thirty or so. We can stroll through St. Denis, and if Balzac seems up to it, we can take a proper walk and then I'll make lunch. How does that sound?"

"We'll look forward to it, Bruno. Nine-thirty and we'll bring dessert. Hugs to Balzac. *Bisous.*"

His next call was to Marie-Do, who began apologizing until he interrupted her, saying it was not the station's fault, and that the *procureur* was going through the broadcast not to punish the radio station but to see if Poincevin had broken the sub judice rules.

"I couldn't believe that crap he was saying about you, Bruno, when I played the tape this morning. It was really vicious defamation, if you ask me."

"We'll see, Marie-Do. Anyway, don't worry about me and thanks for getting us the transcripts and see you soon."

His last call was to Philippe Delaron to say sorry, but no comment until the *procureur* decided what action to take. He was fine and his hound seemed to be recovering.

And that was it, the marathon phonathon was over. The market stalls had gone; the cleanup crew had removed all traces of the market debris and the choral concert on the steps except for two little white tufts of fake hair from the beard of Père Noël, which would now certainly have to be replaced. He drove home and changed into working clothes and checked on Balzac, who seemed to be sleeping normally. The bowl of water Bruno had put out for him early that morning was now half empty, so he'd woken, had something to drink and then gone back to sleep.

Bruno tidied the garden and the chicken coop, swept the terrace and the driveway and then cleaned the kitchen, bathroom and living room. He brought in sufficient wood to keep his stove going overnight and the next day and then thought what he might make for lunch. He and Laura would be hungry after the walk, so he'd start with some soup, followed by an omelette with truffles and a winter salad with cheese. He planned to serve it with a bottle of an unusual red wine from Château de la Jaubertie, from its range of *cépages oubliés,* or forgotten harvests. It was a blend of 40 percent Mérille, 40 percent Fer Servadou and 20 percent Malbec. Mérille, sometimes known as Périgord Noir, was an old grape variety, known across southwestern France for being full-bodied with strong tannins. Fer was another local veteran, named for the ironhard wood of the vines, with softer tannins and a distinctive perfume of red fruits. These groups had fallen out of use, partly because of the phylloxera plague of the late nineteenth century but in the Bergerac region more because of the competition from the new wonder crop of the black tobacco that went into Gauloises cigarettes. Bruno liked the idea of reviving the old wines and thought that Laura was the kind of woman who would be interested in them.

The soup would be easy to prepare. He had stock in his freezer made from boiling beef bones, which he would use to make a broth with some stale bread, onions, beets and a beaten egg, and maybe he'd add the portion of chopped cabbage he wouldn't use in the salad. He had some *cabécous* of goat cheese, one of Stéphane's Tomme d'Audrix and a block of aged Cantal. And he'd show Laura where the black truffles came from, under the oak trees he'd planted in his own garden.

The real challenge would be that evening's welcome-home meal for Gilles, at which Jack Crimson, the baron, Pamela, Fabiola and Florence would be present, and maybe Jack's daughter, Miranda, and her children, which would mean Florence's children, too. He called Pamela who would know by now whether Miranda planned to come.

"No, I was going to call you to say Miranda has a date, so Jack Crimson has to babysit, but Florence is bringing Daniel and Dora."

"Well, if Florence's children are joining us, why not Jack and his grandchildren? The kids all enjoy being together, and they've probably missed Gilles just as we have."

"That's a good idea. Why don't you call Jack and suggest it?"

Bruno at once called Jack, who said he'd be delighted to bring his grandchildren. What could he bring?

"Wine and maybe some cheese," said Bruno. "I'm cooking lamb shanks with garlic and Monbazillac. The baron's bringing some of that trout you and he smoked as the first course. Florence is bringing a salad, and Pamela is making her lemon meringue pie. But if you and Miranda's kids are coming, she might be persuaded to make two; we all know it's your favorite."

"And the children's favorite, too. We'll count on you to persuade her, Bruno. And to go with your lamb shanks, I'll bring some Montravel red from Daniel Hecquet. Which Monbazillac are you using?"

"One of Julien's Clos l'Envège. I'd better start on the lamb, but I'll call Pamela first."

Pamela was already making two pies, she assured him, so Bruno set to work. He took the lamb shanks from their marinade, patted them dry and then browned them in duck fat before putting them into his largest casserole. Then four peeled and chopped shallots went into the duck fat to cook through before they went into the casserole along with the marinade. He took a large sheet of parchment paper, crumpled it, ran it under cold water, shook the drops off and then spread the paper over the meat, wine and garlic in the casserole. He then put the lid on the casserole and checked his watch. It would need two hours in the oven at 180 degrees Celsius.

Bruno began to calculate. Gilles was flying in from Kyiv on a flight that reached Paris just before 11:00 a.m. He would then have a comfortable three hours to clear customs and take the train from Charles de Gaulle Airport to the Montparnasse train station to catch the 2:00 p.m. fast train to Bordeaux. That trip of five hundred kilometers took two hours, and the local train to Le Buisson from Bordeaux needed another two hours for the hundred-kilometer journey on the local train. So Fabiola would pick up Gilles from Le Buisson at 6:40 p.m., and they would be back at Pamela's by 7:00 p.m., which meant eating sometime after 8:00. So Bruno should arrive at Pamela's before 4:00 p.m. to exercise the horses, and he'd have plenty of time after the ride to cook his lamb shanks and the vegetables that he'd take from his garden—potatoes, carrots and parsnips.

As he looked at his watch, he heard a sound from the corridor and then a shuffle and a rather wan-looking Balzac padded slowly into the kitchen and looked at his empty food bowl.

He then gazed up at his master with a look of disappointed reproach. Balzac must have caught the tempting odors of Bruno's cooking.

Bruno turned at once to the box where he kept his home-made dog biscuits, made from whole wheat and white flour, wheat germ, eggs, apples, milk powder and baked in the shape of bones. He handed one to Balzac to eat raw, crumbled two more into a saucepan that he filled with milk and turned on the gas to warm it. Meanwhile he took some chopped meat from the fridge and fried it quickly in duck fat with salt. He then stirred the meat into the milk and biscuit mush and set it down before his dog.

Balzac gave a grunt that might have been forgiveness, but Bruno suspected that what it really meant was that Balzac had been through a pretty rough day and Bruno had best ensure he'd do better next time. Balzac then followed Bruno out to the Land Rover, waited while Bruno lifted him onto his usual seat and waited some more while Bruno loaded the stewpot with the lamb and the bags of vegetables and some wine. By the time Bruno drove off, Balzac was asleep.

Once they arrived at the stables, Balzac decided to stay in Hector's stall while Bruno and his horse rode off with lots of other friends on horseback. After his meal, a pleasant doze in Hector's warm and familiar-smelling straw was called for. He had barely drifted off to sleep, it seemed, when the usual sounds were back—horses' hooves in the stable yard, then the panting of Pamela's amiable and welcoming sheepdogs. Then came human voices, boots in the straw, the creak of leather as saddles and bridles were removed and horses were rubbed down. Hector then came slowly and carefully into the stall, and Balzac felt his warm, horsey breath as he was given an affectionate nuzzling by way of greeting. Balzac half turned, gave Hector's jaw an affectionate lick and then tucked himself into the warm straw to doze again. He heard the splashing of water as Bruno washed himself in the stable sink and then the sound of familiar pattering feet and children's voices as Daniel and Dora came to hug him but were then called away to their bath.

Balzac woke again to the sound of a car rolling over the gravel that had no smell of an engine. He knew this magical car which did not stink belonged to Fabiola and here she was with her male friend who had been absent for some time. He could hear shouts of welcome, sounds of human affection, shrieks from children, softer tones from women, hearty male voices of friends that he recognized.

Then they all went indoors to their dinner and Balzac drifted off to sleep again, to dream of that wondrous meaty scent that had earlier awoken him when he was home with Bruno.

Chapter 24

Balzac seemed to be himself again the next morning when Bruno took his basset hound for a brisk, chilly run, skirting the woods to run along the ridge and watch the sunrise before returning home. He showered, shaved and changed into corduroy slacks, a flannel shirt and a down jacket to head to Fauquet's for breakfast, where he had planned what he hoped would be an intriguing surprise for Laura.

He had invited Yveline and Rod Macrae to join them at nine-thirty, and to bring along Balzac's two pups. Yveline was the proud owner of Gabrielle d'Estrées. Rod, the veteran rock musician whose comeback tour had begun at one of the riverside concerts Bruno organized each summer, was the owner of Balzac's son, Robert the Bruce. The proud Scot had named his dog for the king who had secured Scottish independence for the next four centuries by soundly defeating the English at the Battle of Bannockburn in 1314. Bruno thought Laura would be interested to see some of Balzac's progeny, and Rod, just as he wanted them to see Laura's glorious dog.

Yveline was the first to arrive with Gabrielle, walking along the rue Gambetta from the place people were already beginning to call the old gendarmerie. Gabrielle was mainly brown with white legs and paws, with a white muzzle that stretched up to her brow and a black back that continued onto the first third of her tail, while the next third was brown and the final tip was white. He bent down to welcome her, delighted to see that her first greeting was for her father, Balzac, before she turned to have Bruno scratch behind her ears.

Then Bruno saw Rod's lanky figure strolling along the bridge from the parking lot by the bank. The Bruce was too low to the ground to be seen at first. Balzac gave a cheerful "Woof" of greeting when he saw his son, and Gabrielle gave little yips of excitement at seeing her brother.

The reunions were still underway when a gray Range Rover pulled up in front of the *mairie* and Laura emerged, swiftly followed by George Sand, and each of them looked lovelier than Bruno had remembered. Balzac and his two pups turned to examine the newcomer, then Balzac bounded forward to sniff noses, and Yveline and Rod exclaimed at the striking looks of the light-brown-and-white female basset just as Fauquet arrived carrying a tray loaded with a coffeepot, cups, plates and a basket overflowing with croissants and *chocolatines*.

Bruno made the introductions of Laura to Fauquet and the others and the pack of bassets. They all shared breakfast while Laura marveled at the good manners of Balzac and his offspring as they waited, trembling with eagerness and excitement, to be offered portions of the food. George Sand, by contrast, sat back grandly on her hind legs, her head held high and immobile. Her eyes were fixed on Laura, but otherwise she seemed not to twitch a muscle as if waiting, as a grande dame of letters should, for lesser mortals to feed her.

Once Balzac and his young had each been given a corner of croissant, Laura reached across to give her dog a portion, but with the speed of a born pickpocket the Bruce leaped into the air and plucked it from her fingers, swallowing the morsel before his legs retouched the ground. Bruno laughed, and to his great pleasure, Laura exclaimed in surprise and then laughed, too.

"He's a right scallywag," said Rod, speaking English to her and smiling, and Bruno could guess at the mixture of admiration and reproof in the word's meaning.

"I haven't heard that word in years, not since I played with my naughty cousins on family vacation in Cornwall," Laura replied in English, before adding in French. "I suppose we'd call him a *coquin.*"

That seemed to break the ice, and Yveline asked if Laura had any tips on bringing up female dogs. "You're doing just right, bringing her up with lots of male dogs for company. I only wish I'd done that for this one. She seems superior, but I think she's really just shy. I'm afraid I don't know many people who have dogs in Sarlat."

"What games do you play with her?" Bruno asked. "Throwing and fetching balls? Catching Frisbees? Balzac likes running after horses, playing with children and finding truffles. Basset hounds have some of the most sensitive noses in the dog world."

"The Bruce likes chasing rabbits but never catches them, and he seems to like music: sometimes I even think he's trying to dance," said Rod. "And once he gets onto a scent, he'll not let go. The times I've followed him uphill and down dale and catch up to him standing over an old rabbit warren, wagging his tail and proud as punch."

"Mine had real problems learning to go downstairs because of her short legs," said Yveline. "But she'll trot after a scent all day, and she's a born tracker, a perfect hunting dog."

"Your George Sand just doesn't look like a hunting dog," said Rod. "She's too beautiful. All that lovely and soft white fur, I'd hate to see it all muddy and skin scratched by the undergrowth. To me she seems more like a model than a hunting dog."

"Hunting wasn't quite what I had in mind for her," said Laura. "But we do go jogging together around Sergeac, where Monique had her country place."

"Most mornings Balzac and I go for a run," said Bruno. "Like this morning, I needed it. Our friend Gilles came back from Ukraine yesterday in time for Christmas, so it was quite a feast. A run clears out the cobwebs and gets me ready for my shower and shave and new day."

Yveline was on duty and Rod Macrae had to go to the St. Cyprien market, so they said goodbye, and Bruno paid the bill. Laura's Range Rover, some seventy years younger than Bruno's ancient model, was left parked by the *mairie*. Laura helped Bruno load the dogs into the back and she climbed in beside him, gazing in wonderment at the primitive interior of one of the first civilian models Land Rover ever made.

"How old is this car?" she asked.

"It was built in 1954, the year of Dien Bien Phu," Bruno replied. "An old hunting friend of mine bought it when he got back from Vietnam, and he left it to me in his will when he died."

"Then I think it must be the oldest car that I've ever ridden in," she said, turning to see how the two dogs were getting on in the back. "They're both sitting up and George Sand is trying to look out of the side windows, but they're too high."

"Give it a minute," said Bruno. "Balzac will show her how to get up on the side bench and look out from there."

"You're right," Laura said moments later. "Balzac's up and she's followed him. That seems like a good omen."

"Great view," she said as they pulled into his driveway. They sat a moment looking over the valley to the east, where ridge after ridge climbed away. There was not another building to be seen, although many houses and whole campsites were tucked away in the valleys between the rolling hills.

There was another ridge to the west, partly wooded. Due north was mainly forest all the way to the valley of the Isle, the river that ran through Périgueux.

"Which way are we heading for our walk?" she asked.

"We'll start by going up behind my house through the woods and then onto the ridge to the west that has a view of the setting sun and then making a circuit to come back from the east, maybe a couple of hours, ten kilometers, and that way we'll work up an appetite for lunch."

Laura was sensibly dressed in walking boots, heavy trousers tucked into thick socks, with a waterproof jacket over a turtleneck sweater and a woolen hat that he guessed had been bought for skiing. The overall look was functional for a wintry walk rather than fashionable, and Bruno approved. George Sand was well behaved, even off the leash, padding along beside Laura and ignoring Balzac, who forged ahead, occasionally darting off in the woods at either side of the path, scaring those nesting *bécasses* who chose to live dangerously close to the ground.

The reunion of the two dogs had been polite, even cordial, with some wagging of tails as they had sniffed at each other, and George Sand had looked on approvingly as Balzac reunited with his son and daughter. How the dogs understood these family relationships was unclear, but Bruno felt that somehow they did. Now she was content to walk beside her mistress and follow Bruno and his dog.

Bruno was not nearly so at ease, thinking it was some time since he had set out to woo a new woman and he was more nervous about it than he had expected. He knew little of Laura's previous life or relationships, but she was evidently well established in Sarlat, if she had been playing a tavern girl in that reconstruction of the battle that liberated Sarlat from the English in 1370. He was attracted to her but not at all clear what she felt about him, except that he had a fine dog who could make a suitable mate for her basset. Never let it be said that Bruno was not a man happy to build castles in the sky; his biggest issue as a romantic and optimistic soul was trying to live in them. That particular piece of self-knowledge had been hard-earned but was needed to restrain his tendency to project fantastical futures onto unsuspecting women.

Words had many meanings, he had learned, and whatever might be wholly true today might evolve to allow for different circumstances tomorrow. There was no falsehood in this, and no deliberate malice. It was an essential ability of humans to adapt to different circumstances, so characteristic of the species that it was probably ingrained in the DNA. Anyway, this day with Laura might be an unmitigated disaster, leaving not just Bruno but even poor Balzac in the lurch. He very much hoped not, now that he had seen George Sand warm to the two puppies, and to Balzac, perhaps all the more because she seemed now to understand that the pups were somehow his.

Bruno pondered this, wondering what dogs made of pregnancy and motherhood, and suddenly recalled the discovery of Monique's suicide, and her letter describing her pain at the thought of never being able to give birth to a child. Might dogs feel that same instinctive sense of loss?

"Slow down a bit, could you?" came a voice. Startled, he turned to see Laura, trailing some meters behind as they slogged up the steep and narrow path through the woods.

"I'm sorry—going too fast, am I?" he asked. How could he have been so thoughtless as to take this route through the woods where the path was too narrow to walk side by side, so Laura had to plod along behind him like some dutiful wife of an earlier century? He cursed himself, knowing he should have planned this more carefully.

Finally they reached the open ground of the hilltop, and he was able to point out the unimpressive hillock called La Ferrassie, where archaeologists had found the oldest-known human grave, the first deliberate burial of human beings with what seemed to be some ritual and respect, around seventy thousand years ago. The remains of babies and a fetus found here were protected by stones, Bruno explained. Pollen had been found around the neck of a woman, perhaps an intentional remnant of flowers. And a man, with the most complete Neanderthal skull and skeleton ever found, appeared to have been crippled some years before his death. Unable to hunt, he had apparently been fed by his community.

"Maybe the man could have contributed in some way, even crippled, maybe making flint knives or something," Laura said, breathing more easily after the slog up the hill.

"You're probably right," Bruno replied. "They found that his teeth had a strange slanting angle to them and suspect that they got that way when he held animal skins in his teeth while scraping off the hair and flesh with edged flints to make leather garments."

From here they could see north as well as west, and the route back along the ridge was broad enough for them to chat as they walked abreast. From Bruno's interest in archaeology they moved on to Laura's fascination with château life, the transition from the Middle Ages through the Renaissance, the Reformation and the Enlightenment. One of her hobbies was the history of food and cooking, she told him. She had investigated why the Périgord had the reputation as a land of milk and honey even in medieval times, and whether a distinct regional form of cooking had emerged early.

"These were the borderlands between the milk and butter fat of the north and the olive oil of the south," she said. "And here it was duck and goose fat, because this region and our rivers were the midpoint of the birds' migration flights between Scandinavia and North Africa. This was where they came down for water and could be hunted and bred."

"I always like looking at the kitchens whenever I visit an old castle or château," Bruno said. "They're often the largest part of the house, with a dining area that suggests a lot of entertaining."

"The nobles and barons had money," she said, "from taxing the trade along all the waterways, the Dordogne, the Vézère, the Auvézère, the Isle, the Lot, the Garonne, all the rivers that inspired the Romans to call this region Aquitaine, the land of waters. The rivers were the only way to move goods in bulk."

"That would be wine, I suppose," Bruno replied. "Maybe fruit in season, and cheeses, some livestock. What other cash crop did we have in the Périgord to sell in bulk downriver?"

"The real treasures of this region in the Middle Ages were our chestnuts and to a lesser extent the hazelnuts," she replied. "In this part of France the main starch came from chestnuts until potatoes became common in the eighteenth century."

"I thought the Spaniards brought them back from South America in the sixteenth century," Bruno said.

"Yes, and they were widely grown in Spain and in Ireland after Sir Walter Raleigh introduced them in the seventeenth century," she replied. "But they only became common in France in the eighteenth century when a man named Parmentier persuaded the king to wear a potato flower in his buttonhole."

"I read something about that," Bruno said. "Antoine-Augustin Parmentier was forced to eat potatoes when a prisoner of war of the Prussians in the Seven Years' War, a time when France thought they were only fit for pig food. Parmentier lived long enough to work for Napoléon and managed to produce sugar, which the English navy blockaded from reaching France, from beetroot."

They strolled on, chatting happily away about food and history, discovering each other's interests in a natural, unforced way, and putting to rest Bruno's earlier concerns.

By this time, Bruno and Laura were hand in hand, chatting happily about food, their two dogs pottering along behind, side by side, amiably turning to this path or another as they explored together, traced the scents of sheep and rabbits and then trotted back to rejoin their human partners.

"Did you know that one of the reasons for the wars between Rome and Carthage was that Carthage and its region were the main sources of truffles, which ancient Romans esteemed highly?" Laura asked.

"No, that's fascinating," he said. "I read somewhere that truffles were first appreciated by the Sumerians and that Plutarch thought truffles came from lightning striking the soil. Did the Romans have the Périgord black truffles we get in winter?"

"Yes, the Romans had them, but mainly they had Terfez truffles, which had very little flavor of their own but were noted flavor carriers. Juvenal wrote that he thought truffles were produced by thunder, and Cicero called them children of the earth."

"What a pleasure it is talking with you," Bruno said, suddenly noticing that they had stopped and were facing each other, and that Laura was beaming at him, her lips breathlessly apart.

He didn't know whether she had stars in her eyes or they were in his, but before they knew it, they were kissing. Their lips were closed, but hers seemed very full and welcoming as if they had a life of their own. Then he felt her fingertips caressing his neck, and despite the thick layers of coats and sweaters and flannel shirts and vests they each wore on this wintry walk, he was intensely conscious of the sense of her body against his and the way her hand at the back of his neck was drawing him deeper and deeper into her.

Then she drew back, stroked his cheek, took his hand in hers, kissed it and murmured, "Take me to your home, Bruno."

They walked on, not talking, their heads turned simply to look at each other, the dogs following patiently behind. Once at the house, they were about to go inside but turned to watch Balzac proudly showing off his estate to George Sand, escorting her to his kennel and the chicken coops, to admire the stately geese and lively ducks, the avenue of trees nurturing Bruno's truffles.

Bruno and Laura smiled at each other, he opened the door for her to enter and followed, but before he could reach for the door handle, she put a hand on his chest and kissed him very slowly. Then she closed the door, as if to make clear that this encounter and this time and this exploration was for the two of them alone.

Chapter 25

Some hours later, with the daylight just beginning to slowly fade, Bruno and Laura were in dressing gowns in the living room before the stove. They were drinking champagne. He was tending the fire, and she was breaking Bruno's homemade dog biscuits in two. She gave a half to Balzac and then a half to George Sand, and then they each took a sip of the last of the kir from a single glass.

"Hungry?" he asked.

"Yes, I'm beginning to feel a little hungry, but mainly for you," she answered, kissing him again, pushing him down onto the floor and sliding herself on top of him as she loosened her dressing gown and let her breasts trail over his chest, his neck, his mouth, his eyes. He groaned with pleasure until she slid back down again so that her lips were level with his.

"That's just to remind you what lies in wait after dessert," she said, her voice teasingly husky.

"I need to eat to build up my energy for this evening, and I want to cook for you and to go out into the garden where Balzac can help me find a truffle for you, and maybe George Sand might want to join us," he said, kissing her again. "And

I'll bring back some eggs for you that will still be warm from the chicken coop, the freshest you've ever had."

"Excellent idea, so long as I can watch you through the window of this lovely warm room."

Bruno put on his warm clothes and took a trowel from the box of gardening tools in the gun room. Balzac, who knew his master's habits well enough to understand what Bruno intended, went to wait eagerly by the door until Bruno would open it and step outside. Bruno was delighted to see George Sand decide, after casting a short farewell glance at Laura, to join Balzac by the door before the two dogs leaped out into the cold.

Bruno started in the chicken coop, collecting six eggs, three of them still warm to the touch, and went back to hand them to Laura. Then he went to the oak trees he had planted at the eastern end of the garden, where he had light from the setting sun. He began tapping the cold earth with a bamboo cane to wake the tiny truffle fly. There was no sign of movement, so he repeated the action at the second tree, and then again at the third, without success. At the fourth tree, a white oak, his tapping stirred a truffle fly, almost too small to see, but he caught its movement in flight against the sun's fading rays.

"*Cherches,* Balzac, *cherches,*" he said softly, and his dog obediently began sniffing at the spot where Bruno had first seen the fly. Balzac began to scratch at the earth, and politely stood back so that George Sand could follow suit, sniffing and scratching. Then Bruno eased them aside and began to dig, gently, with his trowel in the cold but not frozen earth, and put his own nose down to sniff for himself.

There it was, that special, almost fecund scent of truffle, a scent so close to the sexual pheromones of pigs that many a hunter in the old days had lost a finger or two to a pig that was determined not to give up its treasure to a human. These days, hunters who used pigs to find truffles usually had a bridle wrapped around the muzzle so the pig could sniff but not bite. Dogs had to be trained to recognize the scent, which did not take long, and Balzac's nose was several times more sensitive than any pig's.

It was at that point that Bruno was aware of some movement beyond the hedge at the front of his garden. He thought he heard something, and then saw a brief flash, perhaps sunlight reflecting from a shiny surface. There was not much wind but what little stirring of air that Bruno could feel was wafting from his position toward the hedge, so the dogs would not be smelling a thing.

Bruno then tossed his trowel at the hedge where he'd heard the noise. Balzac shot off like a rocket as Bruno pushed himself into a crouch and then ran to the opening, where he spotted a man wearing some kind of mask and a camouflage jacket who had risen from his knees and was trying to run—or rather to stumble—away. Bruno ran after him, swiftly catching up and then diving to tackle the stranger's legs, the dogs now baying as though he were felling a boar.

Bruno's shoulder, with all his diving weight and momentum behind it, hit the man just below the knee. The masked stranger cried out in pain as he crashed to the ground, a large mobile phone spinning away from his hand to fall with an expensive sound of cracking glass.

Bruno ripped off the face mask the intruder was wearing, pulled up his head by the hair and then smashed his face down into the ground to stun him before he rolled the now-helpless figure over, his face bloodied from a smashed nose. It was Condorcet, the former police technician who was now a private eye. Bruno patted the man down in a search for a wallet or a weapon.

Condorcet stared at him but then tried to shrink away as Balzac's snarling muzzle with bared teeth came within biting distance.

"Be careful," Bruno said, finding a wallet in the rear hip pocket. "This dog's a killer, hunts wild boars. Stay very still and don't upset him.

"Monsieur Condorcet, this time you're clearly guilty of trespassing with illegal intent, not just taking clandestine photos in a restaurant."

Bruno reached under Condorcet's jacket and pulled out a heavy revolver from a leather pouch under the man's armpit. He recognized it at once, the Manurhin MR73 that was standard issue for the gendarmerie and much of the police from the 1970s into the 1990s. This one looked like the nine-millimeter Parabellum model, and all the chambers but one were loaded.

The gun's barrel looked as if it hadn't been cleaned for years, and there was dust and hair around the bullets that Bruno could see. It was long overdue for an overhaul. As he pushed gently at the chamber to check its tension, he felt it shift and rock in place. That was very bad. He shook his head in despair at this mistreatment of a classic firearm.

"If you tried to fire this revolver, it would probably blow your wrist off, if the cartridges were even still able to fire."

He patted down the rest of Condorcet's form, then pulled out his own phone to call Sergeant Jules and ask for two armed gendarmes to take an illegally armed trespasser, and former police employee, into custody.

The phone call over, Condorcet suddenly spoke, his voice hoarse and the blood in his nose making him sound as if he had a heavy cold.

"My mother is eighty-five and alone. Can I give her a call to say I won't be back tonight, but all is well and I'll see her tomorrow?"

"You probably won't see her tomorrow, not after being arrested with an illegal weapon," Bruno replied.

"I know, but that's for tomorrow. She's an old lady. I just want to reassure her for tonight."

Bruno thought about it, then nodded and said okay. Then he pulled a tissue from his jacket pocket, gave it to Condorcet and said, "Blow, or your mother will know something's wrong from your voice."

Condorcet's voice sounded less like a foghorn as he said, "If you open that phone you knocked out of my hands, go to recent calls because I called her this morning."

Bruno called the number and heard an elderly female voice, answering, *"Oui, mon cher?"* and he put the phone to Condorcet's mouth.

"Oui, Maman, désolé," he said. "I'm tied up on a job, but I'll be home for lunch tomorrow, so take care. Love you, *Maman,* and sleep well."

Bruno looked at his prisoner before asking, "You live with your mother?"

Condorcet nodded. "I was married, but she wanted a divorce. No kids. She got the house, so I moved back in with my mother."

Bruno nodded, and said, "I'm going to have to tie you up until the gendarmes come to take you to jail."

He pulled out Condorcet's belt, rolled him onto his belly and used the belt to tie the man's elbows together behind his back. He left Balzac and George Sand watching the bound man and went to his door to reassure Laura that all was well and to stay out of sight. Then Bruno picked up a notebook and pen from the hall table and went outside to join the dogs. Bruno sat on his prisoner's rump so that his own trousers stayed dry and called J-J's mobile number.

"Your ex-tech who now works for Poincevin has just tried to ambush me in my garden while armed with an old police weapon that I don't think he's entitled to have," Bruno began.

"Even if it's legal he needs to be tried and sentenced for recklessness with a lethal weapon. I think he also may have planned to spy on me and take photos. Sergeant Jules is sending a couple of gendarmes to take him in. I suggest we leave him there overnight while I draft a statement, and you can have him picked up in the morning and brought up to your jail."

Speaking words he knew Condorcet could hear, Bruno went on, "He's no genius, so he may not yet realize that we're really after Poincevin, and if he helps us, we might be able to help him. Otherwise with what I'm pretty sure is an illegal handgun he's facing five to ten years, without even counting the other charges."

J-J said that made sense and he'd see Bruno in the morning and hung up. Bruno drafted a brief statement in his notebook of Condorcet's spying, his face mask, his illegal and armed trespass and his attempted escape. He would send it with the gendarmes to Sergeant Jules, who would make a copy.

"Where did you leave your car?" Bruno asked, leaning over so that Condorcet could see him out of one eye. The other was fixed, nervously, on Balzac's snarling face.

"Near the Brin d'Amour campsite," came the gasped reply. "Walked over the hill and through the woods to get here."

"Did you see me out walking, maybe three, four hours ago?" Bruno asked.

"No, I'd just got here when you came out with the dogs."

Bruno finished his statement, signed it, and when the gendarmes came to take Condorcet away, he used his official stamp to certify his statement and gave it to them.

Then he, Balzac and George Sand all gathered to dig out and admire the lovely melanosporum truffle, about the size of Laura's delicate ear. They went back into the house together, and Bruno hugged Laura, kissed her soundly and was privately delighted to see that she was still in one of his dressing gowns.

Bruno said that the trouble was over and that he now proposed to make Laura the finest truffled omelette that she had ever eaten.

"Does this sort of sudden emergency happen often with you?" she asked, her voice light, as if trying to convince them both that she knew this was in the day's work.

"Hardly ever," he said, taking her in his arms. "And it wasn't really an emergency, just an overweight and retired police tech with an old gun that he's probably never fired in anger, and it probably wouldn't have fired if he pulled the trigger. It's certainly been a long time since he cleaned it."

"Are you usually armed?" she asked.

"No, only when we have an emergency, and that's usually left to the gendarmes," he said. "But you should know that I'm a licensed firearms teacher for hunters, and I hunt regularly. I follow the gun laws to the letter, and so do most hunters. So I'll look forward to getting a couple of *bécasses* one day and cooking them for us, maybe some venison. And if you like, I can teach you how to hunt, and you already have a fine hunting hound, even if George Sand will need a little training, and I'm sure Balzac will be very keen to help. Or you might just like to come out with me for the walk and to enjoy being in the countryside."

She looked at him a little coolly, as if surprised by the invitation but with a smile playing around her lips.

"Let me think about that," she replied. "I've never really considered taking up hunting, even though I'm not a vegetarian and enjoy roast venison and rabbit. But I'm starting to feel hungry, and that truffle omelette sounds good."

"Yes, I need to get my strength back," he said, grinning and taking her in his arms.

"And the night is yet young," she said, cupping her hands around his cheeks and pulling his head down to her soft lips.

Chapter 26

The next morning, Bruno woke before dawn, stretched luxuriously and smiled as he caught the hint of Laura's scent on the pillow beside him. He had driven her back to her own car just before midnight, since she had to go home to get ready for Monique's funeral in the morning and the reading of the will in the afternoon. He took Balzac out for a brisk trot in the chill air, returned to shower and shave, then grilled the remnants of the previous evening's baguette while brewing coffee and listening to the radio news. He heard that a large crowd was expected at the funeral in St. Denis of local businesswoman Monique Duhamel.

As soon as the news ended, his phone vibrated, and Sergeant Jules said, "The ex-tech you arrested yesterday with the old handgun, he wants to talk to you. He says he wants to make a deal."

"On my way," said Bruno, and on the way he thought of the other things he'd have to do, from arranging parking spaces to bringing in reinforcements if there were serious crowds at the church at eleven and then at the cemetery.

"Commandante Yveline has already authorized a squad for

you to use for crowd control," Jules said as Bruno entered the gendarmerie. "And Condorcet is waiting for you in the first cell."

Condorcet looked better than he had the previous day. The dried blood had gone, although he had black eyes coming. He stuck out a hand for Bruno to shake as he rose from the narrow bed where he had slept. Bruno leaned against the door and said, "You wanted to talk?"

"Yeah, and with a witness present if you like."

Bruno called for Jules to send down a witness and was pleased to see the new officer, Claire, arrive in uniform with a notebook and pen. He greeted her as she turned on her phone to use for recording. She checked that the recording was working, and Bruno asked Condorcet what he wanted to say.

"I want to be able to get out of here today and go home to look after my mother," he said. "And I think I can tell you enough to get you to agree. I can tell you how and why Dominic's wife lost her baby and how things have been fixed by Poincevin so that Dominic will inherit every bit of property and money that his wife had to leave."

Bruno's eyes widened. "You mean to tell me that Monique's will scheduled to be read today is not the real will?"

"It's real, all right, but it's been superseded," said Condorcet, looking smug. "I know how and when and where it was fixed and what it says. Poincevin planned the whole thing, drafted the will, and he's going to share in the take."

"You say you know how and why Monique lost her baby—you mean it was not a simple miscarriage?" Bruno asked.

"No, it was deliberate, and I was the one who had to get the drugs." Condorcet shrugged. "Simple enough. There are always nurses and young doctors short of money. First, you take a pill called mifepristone. Pregnancy needs a hormone called progesterone so the fetus can start to grow normally. Mifepristone blocks the mother's own progesterone, so basically it just stops the pregnancy in its tracks. Then you take misoprostol. It's best to take it soon after the first pill, but you can use it up to a day, a day and a half, later. This stuff causes cramps and bleeding; in effect it empties the woman's uterus. It's almost like having a natural early miscarriage."

"Did you give her these drugs?" Bruno asked.

"No, and I don't know who did, her husband or Poincevin. I just got hold of the drugs, cost me two hundred euros, no questions asked," said Condorcet with a shrug. "I was told by the nurse who helped me that it's quite common for women to abort a kid without their old man knowing."

"When was this?"

"I got hold of the drugs in the first week in December; they said it was a rush job."

"Did they say why it was a rush job?"

"They thought time was critical. You're not supposed to use these drugs after the ninth week."

"And what week was this? Do you know?"

"No idea, just that Poincevin said it was a rush. I got the stuff in two days, and I assume Dominic gave her the drugs almost immediately. I'm no doctor, but Poincevin and Dominic had been reading up on this stuff."

"Did they say why they didn't want Monique to have the baby?"

"No, but it's obvious—a baby would inherit, or at least share, in whatever Monique left. Dominic wanted it all for himself, except for whatever he had to pay Poincevin, who was also helping to fix the will."

"Did you get paid?" Bruno asked.

"No, I was just on Poincevin's usual starvation wages," said

Condorcet, this time with a brittle laugh. "The bastard. He reckoned I was still in debt, what with the interest."

"Had Poincevin lent you money?"

"Sort of. He paid off the casino I owed money, bought off the heavies who'd already beaten the shit out of me and then threatened to do the same to my mother. I couldn't have that, so I went to Poincevin, because I'd done a fair bit of work for him in the past. He came back and said I owed. So I work for him. He gives me a thousand a month in cash, plus expenses, plus he pays the woman who comes in to look after my mother."

"Are you prepared to testify to this, against Poincevin, in court, and to sign an affidavit?" Bruno asked.

"Lead me to it," said Condorcet, with a bitter laugh.

"So Monique lost the baby," Bruno said. "What happened exactly?"

"Poincevin arranged everything. We all went to Paris. Dominic and Monique were to visit art galleries and concerts one last time before she had to take things easy because of the pregnancy. They went off to visit a woman *notaire* in St. Germain-en-Laye, must have been at least sixty. She was some old friend of Dominic and he called her Clothilde. That's where they got Monique woozy on some other drug, and she signed the new will, leaving it all to Dominic."

"Who witnessed the new will?" Bruno asked.

"Two women who worked for the *notaire*."

"What do you remember of this event with the new *notaire*? Where was it? What was her family name? Did she know that Monique had been drugged?"

"She seemed to know all about it. Whether Clothilde knew or not that Monique had been given drugs, I don't know. She already had the company records of Monique's operation, tax returns, lists of employees, all that. She'd already drafted the new will, leaving everything to Dominic. I have an audio record of the whole thing on that phone you took from me yesterday. I also took photos of the *notaire*'s office."

"Were you and Poincevin listed as the witnesses when the new will was signed?" Bruno asked.

"No way," said Condorcet, mockingly. "No paper trails for Poincevin. He's too sharp for that."

"Where did you stay while this happened?"

"Dominic and his wife were at some hotel in Paris, Poincevin was somewhere else in Paris, and I was in a cheap Airbnb near the *notaire*'s office."

"Why were you snooping around my place yesterday?"

"Dominic told Poincevin that some woman called Laura who had worked for Monique had the hots for you and that could be a problem with the inheritance. They were worried about you being involved, that you might smell a rat about the changes in the will. I was supposed to get photos of you and Laura together to blackmail you."

"A pity you lost your phone," said Bruno, privately cursing himself for forgetting about it and would now have to go home and look for it.

Bruno turned to Claire, asking if she had any questions she wanted to ask of Condorcet.

"You said Monique was drugged in some way when she signed the new will?" she asked.

"She was so woozy I thought she was going to fall over or faint at any minute."

"So when she signed, Monique was not fully in command of her faculties?" Claire went on.

"No way, she could hardly stand up."

"And Poincevin and Dominic and the new *notaire* were all present with you when Monique was visibly drugged and not able to sign of her own free will. Is that right?" Claire went on.

"That's right," said Condorcet. "And I can prove it because I recorded the whole thing on my phone, the one that you knocked out of my hand, Bruno, at your place yesterday. You get that and you'll have all the proof you want—Dominic, Poincevin, the bent *notaire,* woozy Monique. All of it."

Bruno turned to Claire. "Let's get his statement printed out, signed and witnessed, and I'll go home and find that phone, and make some phone calls."

"Can you cancel the funeral?" Claire asked. "An autopsy might be able to find evidence of the abortion drugs Monique was given."

"Good thinking," he said. "I'll leave that with you. Brief Yveline and say we need to do a full autopsy on Monique's body. Call Father Sentout and cancel the funeral. Then get ready to haul in Poincevin and Dominic for questioning. I'll brief J-J while I drive home and look for that phone. I'll also call Fabiola about an autopsy."

"Can I go now?" Condorcet asked.

"Not a chance, not just yet," said Bruno. "But once your statement is signed and witnessed, I'll approve your release on bail so you can see your mother. And if your story holds up, I'll see you get out of this with no prison time. Are you happy with that?"

"More than happy."

Bruno went to brief Sergeant Jules, leaving Claire to brief Yveline, then drove home, calling J-J to update him on the way.

"You sure about this, Bruno?"

"We've got Poincevin's private eye on tape, saying all this, and I'm trying to find this phone he had when he was spying on me yesterday."

Bruno parked in his driveway and went to the area beyond the hedge where he'd tackled Condorcet the previous day. He was feeling ashamed of himself for not remembering to pick it up. But he found it quickly enough, a sopping wet iPhone with a cracked screen. He drove back to St. Denis, checking his watch to see it was eight-thirty. He had time to call Fabiola to explain the urgent need for an autopsy on Monique's body, currently in the St. Denis funeral parlor and about to be moved to the church.

"I have a very urgent question for you," he began when Fabiola answered. "Can you identify in an autopsy whether a woman had lost a baby because she took two drugs called"—he checked his notes—"mifepristone and misoprostol? We have a witness who claims he obtained the drugs to allow Monique's husband to end her pregnancy."

"What?" Fabiola said. "Her husband? The bastard! Wait, let me think. The short answer is that I don't know. I'll have to make some calls. But the funeral is in just over two hours."

"No, I'm having it postponed. Is there any way I can help you, by calling medical schools or something?"

"Leave it to me," she said. "We'll probably have to take the body to the police lab in Bergerac, but I'd better call the forensic expert there first. I'll call you back once I know."

Bruno called Father Sentout to say the benediction was off pending the autopsy, and then called Annette to explain the new development and asked her to inform Ghislaine and Rebecca Weil. He called Laura himself to explain why the funeral would have to be postponed.

"So far it's just an allegation by Condorcet, the same guy that I caught spying on us yesterday," he told her. "But he has a lot of collateral evidence that we can check out through car mileage, phone locations and so on."

"Could it possibly be true?" she said, her shocked tone coming down the line. "His own child? What sort of monster would do that?"

"Maybe somebody whose own childhood was so completely

miserable that he grew up warped or sick or something," said Bruno. "I can't begin to fathom something like that. I have to go but can't wait to see you again."

"Same for me," she said. "Can we get together tonight for dinner? It's my turn to cook."

She gave him her address and asked if there was anything she could do.

"Did Monique call you those days when she went off to Paris, just before the miscarriage? We can probably verify her location from her call records, so if you can give me dates and times of your recent calls, we can cross-reference your call history with hers, in case it's been tampered with somehow. Business aside, I'll be counting the hours until I see you tonight."

"Me too," Laura replied, and as soon as that call ended another one came in, this time from J-J.

"Condorcet may be in the clear," Bruno said to him. "He's been cooperating fully, giving us chapter and verse on Poincevin and the husband and the new will. You'll get the transcript of my interview with him later today. And even if Condorcet is trying to trick us, I have his phone, which should have the time of most of the calls he sent and received. Where are Dominic and Poincevin now?"

"Poincevin is not in his office in Périgueux, nor is he at home. It's the same story with Dominic. Poincevin's secretary hasn't heard from him, but says he has an appointment at the reading of a will at Maître Weil's chambers in Sarlat this afternoon."

"The key is going to be whether Fabiola and the police surgeon can prove the presence of abortion drugs in Monique's body after the time that has passed," Bruno said. "For that, we just have to wait. And in the meantime, I have a promise to keep."

Bruno ended the call and returned home to get his Land

Rover and a civilian jacket before driving to the gendarmerie in St. Denis to pick up Condorcet and head north toward Périgueux. Condorcet directed him to the modest, terraced house near the train station, where he had been raised and now lived with his mother.

"I'll wait here," said Bruno.

"She might be reassured to see you," said Condorcet. "Show her your police credentials and say I'm working with you, that would please her. She doesn't like Poincevin, the hours I keep, all that."

Bruno shrugged and followed him into the property, which reminded him of his aunt's place in Bergerac, the small town house where he had spent his boyhood.

"I know you from your photos in the newspaper," Condorcet's mother said as soon as they were introduced, putting a broom to one side and taking off her rubber gloves to shake hands. Her name was Marie-Claire, and given Condorcet's years since retirement, she had to be in her eighties at a minimum. Marie-Claire looked considerably younger and was evidently mobile enough to take care of her own housework. "You're that policeman from St. Denis, the one with the basset hound."

Bruno agreed that Balzac was his dog and went out to the Land Rover to bring him to greet the old lady. They had moved from the hall into the living room, and Marie-Claire had taken a seat to be able to pat Balzac and tell him what a fine hound he was.

"What job are you on at the moment?" she asked her son.

"Can't say, *Maman.* Bruno would have to answer that."

"It's a bit delicate," Bruno replied. "I'm sorry, but I can't go into details. Your son is being a great help to us in a confidential matter, but I can't tell you any more until the operation has been concluded." Bruno noticed the old woman sit taller at the formal language, a small smile edging its way onto her lips. "We'll try to let him get back here this evening, but it could be late or even longer—I'm sure you understand that police work is round-the-clock. We'd better let you get back to your house-work, madame, although this house looks impeccable to me."

Bruno rose, said goodbye, put Balzac on a leash and waited a moment outside the house for Condorcet to follow him.

"Thanks, Bruno," he said when they were all settled back in the Land Rover. "She said she was proud of me. What now?"

"We drive back to St. Denis and hope that I get some news from the autopsy. Then we decide whether to take you with me to Sarlat for the formal reading of Monique's will."

"But there's the new will that Poincevin and Dominic arranged with the *notaire* in St. Germain-en-Laye," Condorcet said. "That's the latest will by date, so it's the one that counts."

"Unless it can be legally challenged," Bruno replied. "If there is reason to believe she might not have been in full command of her faculties or signed under duress or under false pretenses, any of these objections throws the will open to be questioned in court. And at that point you become a crucial witness because you can testify to Monique's condition and why everybody went all the way to Paris to sign a new will and have Poincevin on hand, even though he didn't witness it. And Dominic's foster aunt is the one to certify it?" He raised an ironic eyebrow. "The whole thing stinks."

Chapter 27

Rebecca Weil's chambers were in a relatively modern part of Sarlat, south of the historic center and near the secondary *collège* named for Montaigne's great friend Etienne de la Boétie. It was suitable, thought Bruno, for a lawyer to be based near a place named for the man who invented the legal concept of the rights of man. The building was three stories high and contained the offices of two lawyers and two *notaires.* Rebecca's were on the first floor, and included a waiting room that could double as a conference room when needed.

When Bruno arrived with Condorcet shortly before two that same afternoon, he saw J-J's heavy jaw drop in surprise. Beside J-J sat his driver and ever-reliable aide, Josette, who gave Bruno a friendly smile, and Laura gave him an even-wider smile along with a little pursing of the lips, as if blowing him a kiss. She was in a row of four chairs in which sat other members of Monique's *conciergerie* team, with a second row behind them, two of whom Bruno vaguely recalled from the reception at Dominic's apartment only six days earlier. Behind them he saw the gardener he had met briefly at the same event, along with other men and some women who Bruno assumed were company employees.

Ghislaine, in the front row and flanked on one side by Annette and on the other by the detective Antonia Laperrine, gestured to Bruno to take a seat next to them. He pointed to Condorcet, shrugged and took two places in an empty row behind Ghislaine, shaking hands with Messager, the Sarlat police chief, who was in the back row with Bruno's friend Romain, the deputy mayor. Bruno recalled being told by Rebecca Weil that Romain was on the board of directors of Monique's company, and the two men shook hands. There was no sign of Fabiola, nor of Dominic, but there were still a few minutes to go when Bruno's phone vibrated and he saw that he had a message from Fabiola to say that she was just entering Sarlat.

"Positive news!" she had written. Looking around and counting the rows and chairs, he saw there was space for thirty or more people in the room. The conference table facing them was empty except for a young woman sitting quietly to one side, a shorthand pad and pencil before her and a machine that might have been a tape recorder. There were three empty seats, one probably for Rebecca, another presumably for her colleague, the *notaire*. He had no idea for whom the third seat might be reserved.

The room had been designed for a certain solemnity, with wooden paneling on all the walls, heavy double doors behind the table at the front of the room and two large doors at the rear, one on each side. There were portraits of serious-looking men in nineteenth-century dress, presumably lawyers or *notaires,* on each side wall. And behind the empty table was a fine landscape that Bruno recognized as the riverside beach at Vitrac, a few kilometers south of Sarlat.

Feet were shuffled and pages turned. Coughs were suppressed and mobile phones were consulted. Some people spoke in discreet whispers and others sighed heavily until the double doors at the rear opened and Rebecca Weil entered, wearing legal robes of black and white with a double-tailed collar. She was accompanied by another woman of a similar age in sober civilian dress. They took two of the seats at the main table.

"Good afternoon, ladies and gentlemen, and thank you for attending the reading of the last will and testament of the late Monique Duhamel, a friend to many of you here," Rebecca began. She introduced herself and the *notaire* beside her, Madame Hervault, and added, "We are still awaiting the arrival of some interested parties, so please forgive this short delay."

She turned and began conversing with her neighbor in a very low voice until the sound of feet coming quickly up the stairs turned every head. The door was flung open and Dominic entered, followed swiftly by Poincevin.

Their arrival was hardly unexpected, thought Bruno, and he kept his eyes on Rebecca, interested to see that it was at this point that the secretary at the side of the table appeared to turn on the tape machine.

"Sorry to be late," said Dominic, taking a seat in the vacant part of the front row, and gesturing to Poincevin to sit beside him. "Traffic."

Rebecca nodded curtly, turned to the *notaire* and said, "Let's begin."

"This is the last will and testament of the late Monique Duhamel, spouse of Dominic d'Ensingen, signed and dated and witnessed this year, on October twenty-first, and formally registered at the national Fichier Central des Dispositions de Dernières Volontés, on October twenty-eighth."

Dominic rose, coughed briefly and said, "Excuse me, madame, but I have here the copy of a later will signed by my late wife on the seventh of this month, at the office of a notary in St. Germain-en-Laye, and formally registered on the sixteenth."

Dominic stepped forward and politely handed a copy of the new will to Rebecca, who lifted the cover page and studied the contents.

"I see," she said after a while. "Would you like me to read the crucial section? It is very short."

"Please do," said Dominic, poker-faced.

" 'In view of my pregnancy, I wish to revoke the last will that I signed and now wish to leave all my worldly goods of whatever kind, *mobilier ou immobilier,* to my husband, Dominic, and to our unborn heir.' "

Rebecca put down the document and said, "Signed and witnessed on the seventh of this month at St. Germain-en-Laye.

"How very sad that after this was signed your wife suffered a miscarriage on December eighth, as you were leaving Paris to return to Sarlat," Rebecca said, her voice noncommittal.

A silence fell.

Dominic raised his head and spoke again, "Very sad for me as well as for her. Saddest of all for our unborn child."

Ghislaine rose from her seat, and said, "You are not in the least bit sad, Dominic. In fact, I believe you rejoice."

There were intakes of breath and then the sound of tires squealing on the street below, a vehicle braking hard. A car door slammed; feet could be heard rushing up the stairs. All heads turned to the door as it burst open to reveal Fabiola standing there, brandishing some official file.

"I have just attended an autopsy, requested by the Sarlat court on the formal recommendation of magistrates, of the late Monique Duhamel. I was her doctor, and she was my patient. We have found evidence that there was no miscarriage, but a deliberate abortion of the unborn child. She had both mifepristone and misoprostol in her system, and there is no signed official form of consent to an abortion on record. So somebody is guilty of the medical murder of her unborn child and is responsible for Monique's own death. Commissaire Jalipeau, do your duty!"

"One moment, madame, if you please," said Poincevin, rising. "And please take a seat, madame. You are overwrought. With all due respect for your undoubted medical skills, you were not present when the miscarriage took place. And in any event, the will that she signed on the seventh of December still stands."

Fabiola turned and, too fast for anyone to stop her, slapped Poincevin's face so hard that he stumbled and almost fell back into his seat. He cowered against the chair, slowly pulled a handkerchief from his pocket, held it against his face and mumbled through it, "I forgive you that assault, madame, you are not yourself."

By this time Bruno was there to hold Fabiola and half pull, half carry her away from Poincevin. He entrusted her to Romain, and then, pointing at Condorcet, he declared: "Maître Poincevin, I have in my hand a sworn statement from this former police technician, Monsieur Condorcet, hired as your private detective, of your payment to obtain these abortion drugs.

"We also have a tape recording of the signing of the supposed new will in St. Germain-en-Laye by Monique Duhamel in the presence of you, Monique's husband, Dominic d'Ensingen, and Dominic's foster aunt, the *notaire* who drew up the new will. All the voices are clear except that of Monique, who is obviously incoherent and apparently under the effect of some drug. The voice of her husband is clearly heard to say, 'Here, let me help you sign it.' And she is burbling incoherently.

"We have a further tape recording of Condorcet as he

hands to you the two abortion drugs, mifepristone and miso-prostol. We hear him read out the names of the drugs from the labels, and he says 'Here you are, the abortion pills you ordered, illegal as hell. I got them from a nurse and they cost me two hundred euros and I need the cash back.' Your voice, Maître Poincevin, is then heard saying, 'Well done, here's your cash and another fifty for your bonus.' "

A silence filled the room, until J-J pushed his way to the front, with Josette and Messager close behind, shouting, "Poincevin, Dominic d'Ensingen, I must ask you both to come with me to the police station."

At this point, a ruler cracked hard against the big table and Rebecca Weil stood there, the thin sheet of metal quivering in her hand, its tinny echo reverberating in the silence.

"One moment, Monsieur le Commissaire. This is my office, and I am not finished. I do not object to your arrest, but I insist on making a critical point of law. It has been said here that the will signed by Monique Duhamel on October twenty-first and subsequently ratified by the national registration agency is no longer valid." Rebecca stared imperiously around the room.

"That claim is untrue. The will of October twenty-first remains valid, because on the day before her death, in this very building, on December eleventh, Monique Duhamel, knowing that her unborn baby was dead, signed an official codicil to that will, adding some details and clarifying some points. That codicil stressed that her will of October twenty-first was still in force and she added only that she was now leaving nothing, absolutely nothing, to her husband, Dominic d'Ensingen. The original agreement signed on the eve of their wedding, that there would be a complete separation of goods between her and her husband, Dominic, was still in force. He would inherit nothing, not the penthouse apartment, nor any fraction of the family notary business, nor any furniture or possessions he could not prove to have brought into the marriage. Other than that every bit of her October twenty-first will was to remain in force, and that codicil and renewal of the original will was ratified by the Fichier Central on Friday and I have here the official confirmation."

She turned to Laura and the other women of Monique's team. "*Mesdames,* the company Monique built now belongs to you, and the thirty percent that remained hers is being divided among you, the gardeners and the housekeepers who contributed to the company's success, according to the codicil of her will. This is a fitting memorial and tribute to a very fine woman."

Bruno had Poincevin immobilized, bent over a chair as he put the cuffs on the lawyer's wrists. J-J and Josette had already handcuffed Dominic and were marching him out the door.

"Allow me, please," said Condorcet, and pulled Poincevin upright by his collar, and then released him into Bruno's custody. Bruno straightened his jacket and began to march him to the door, when Laura whispered to Bruno, "See you tonight."

Epilogue

Bruno remembered the trouble he'd had barely two weeks ago when trying to find the small château tucked discreetly into the hills between Les Eyzies and St. Denis. This time there were signposts of giant Santa Claus figures holding electric lanterns and pointing the way. And once over the rim that led into the hollow, he saw so many lights blazing in Ghislaine's old family home that the whole hillside seemed to glow.

"I remember being here for the christening of the second child, a little girl who must have been Ghislaine, four or five years younger than her brother," said the baron, sitting in the passenger seat of Bruno's Land Rover. Balzac had his nose between the two front seats to be sure of missing nothing of this unexpected adventure. They were on their way to the *conciergerie*'s legendary Christmas party, to which half of St. Denis appeared to have been invited. "I think our mothers were somehow distantly related. I'll be interested to hear what Ghislaine says."

Behind Bruno's vehicle came Fabiola and Gilles in her Renault, with Pamela and her stable boy, Félix, in the back seat. Behind them came Jack Crimson's old Jaguar with his daughter and Colette from the *mairie*. The mayor and Jacqueline were being driven by Xavier and Mirabelle in their Renault. Xavier was still deputy mayor, at least nominally, and Bruno would have given a week's pay to have listened in on the conversation in that car. The only friend not present was Florence, who had gone north with her children to spend Christmas with her parents in Lorraine, where she had been born and raised.

Bruno had sacrificed one of his last remaining bottles of his homemade *vin de noix* as a Christmas gift for Ghislaine, and another for Becca Weil, whose management of the dramatic scenes at the reading of the will had won his sincere admiration. And from that moment, things had moved very quickly indeed.

Poincevin and Dominic were under arrest for conspiring to procure an illegal abortion along with conspiracy to ratify a fraudulent will, and Dominic's foster aunt had been suspended from the college of *notaires* and was expected to face criminal charges. Maître Weil had filed a formal demand for Monique's will and recent codicil to be ratified by the courts, and Laura and her fellow directors of the *conciergerie* were waiting for a judicial decision before moving the base from Sarlat. Although the lease on the Sarlat offices had three years to run, Laura and her partners were firm in their decision that they should move. There was, however, little agreement about the new location. Laura and her supporters wanted Bergerac, with its own airport; others wanted Périgueux, and two members of the team wanted Brive, with its airport and fast train to Paris, but that was no longer strictly the Périgord, where almost all the properties were based.

Bruno had been kept both informed of and involved in these various changes by Laura, and there were moments when he felt that these precious early days when he could never get enough of her embraces were being overwhelmed by the problems of the *conciergerie*. Laura's phone began ringing before eight in the morning, and the conference calls with her colleagues went on late into the evenings. This had come as a surprise to Bruno. Pamela's work at the stables had never been a fraction so demanding of her time. Laura's discussions with her colleagues never seemed to reach a clear conclusion as the partners tried to adjust to the end of Monique's unquestioned leadership of the business. Laura's assumption that as the senior partner she would automatically accede to the prime role had proved to be mistaken, or at least premature.

These internal wranglings were in addition to endless queries and demands for favors or advice or action from the various customers of the concierge service. Which church offered the best Christmas concert, or the most child-friendly religious celebration? Which restaurants might be open on Christmas Day and which *traiteur* might be relied on to deliver the finest Christmas lunch or dinner? Where might a Father Christmas costume be rented at the last minute? Why was there so little gas left in the tank and how might it most swiftly be replenished? Why had the customer not been warned that the car insurance was about to expire?

Usually the various automatic emails which contained all of the requested information that went to each client had been mislaid or ignored. But the company was expected to resolve such petty inconveniences. Bruno had been startled to learn just how much the customers depended on Laura and her colleagues to do their shopping, their planning, their paying of bills and even their thinking. It seemed like a laborious way to make a living, but Laura and her fellow concierges each had iPads with detailed schedules for each of their clients, their particular needs and preferences. And Bruno had been awed by the endless reserves of patience that Laura could deploy. It was not a job he could have done with a smile.

Just like Bruno, nearly every day she rose early and took her dog for a brisk walk or run. She was usually at work by eight and ready to work all day, while breaking off to meet planes, ferry clients, book restaurants and wine tastings, all the time making sure that the housekeepers had detailed instructions about the clients and their guests. It had made for a strange start to their love affair, although they had managed to spend most nights together either at Bruno's place or at the house that she owned in Sarlat.

Laura had assured Bruno that the pressure would ease once Christmas and the New Year holiday were over and she could then start looking for new offices and probably a home near Bergerac airport. How would that work? he wondered. At Sarlat, she was just thirty minutes away. At Bergerac, it would be closer to an hour, and his job kept him fixed to the Vézère Valley. Such petty logistical concerns could be forgotten in the early days of their affair, but at the back of his mind Bruno knew they would come to matter soon enough.

He led the small convoy of vehicles around to the rear of the château to park by the big barn and then shepherded the mayor and Xavier and their partners and his other friends to the main entrance. Its front door was now guarded by plastic snowmen, and the strains of "Père Noël Arrive Ce Soir" rang out across the garden.

Clad in a floor-length evening gown of gold brocade topped with a red Santa Claus cap with a white bobble, Ghislaine embraced each guest in turn as Bruno introduced each new arrival, not forgetting to suggest that the baron might be a long-lost relative on his mother's side.

And then Laura seemed to fly down the stairs and into his arms, George Sand leaping down after her, long ears taking a swing at each bound, with joyous barks of greeting for Balzac.

After a long career working in international journalism
and for think tanks, Martin Walker now gardens, cooks,
explores vineyards, writes, travels, and has never been bus-
ier. He divides his time between Washington, D.C., and
the Dordogne.

A NOTE ON THE TYPE

This book was set in Adobe Garamond. Designed for the Adobe Corporation by Robert Slimbach, the fonts are based on types first cut by Claude Garamond (ca. 1480–1561). Garamond was a pupil of Geoffroy Tory and is believed to have followed the Venetian models, although he introduced a number of important differences, and it is to him that we owe the letters we now know as "old style." He gave to his letters a certain elegance and feeling of movement that won their creator an immediate reputation and the patronage of Francis I of France.

Typeset by Scribe
Philadelphia, Pennsylvania